DRAGONSLAYING

IS FOR

DREAMERS

DAVE MARKS

NATIONAL WRITING INSTITUTE

Manufactured in the United States of America

ISBN 1888344-26-1

For information on discounts for classroom sets or for institutional use, write National Writing Institute, 624 W. University #248, Denton, TX 76201 - 1889

1

There Are Two Kinds of Falling

Axel stood on the sharp end of the narrow boulder and could feel the toes of his boots hanging over the edge. His head was tilted slightly upward, and his damp, light colored hair stuck to the sides of his face. His eyes were tightly closed and he rocked slowly forward and back over the long and very steep slope below him. Large stones projected from the first grass covering the ground as it fell quickly to the river, heavy and full with the spring runoff. Far to the east lay the rounded humps of the Blue Mountains, their tops in pale sunlight, leaving dark their shrouded valleys, misty and sullen in the early evening. To his left, the few small houses of Greenwater lay scattered along the western bank of the river as if they had been cast there by some long-ago flooding.

From where he stood he could see the road as it passed his village and then forked: one route bending north and following the river into the still snow-covered peaks, just visible above fog and low clouds, the other running east over a narrow bridge, then becoming lost in the dark and heavy forest.

Behind him, to the south and west, the shadowed, flat land ran smooth and level into the dim and distant mist. He looked toward the houses and through tears he couldn't stop watched smoke from their chimneys as it rose slowly in thin lines then flattened into a faint haze that followed the river.

On the far bank, hidden by trees, was the very small, wooden building the townspeople used for their temple. In the darkness of the limbs that hung over the older depressions was the lighter color of the fresh dirt where they had covered his father that afternoon. He squeezed his eyes tightly, forcing the tears to run, and could see again the wound the hole made in the ground at the side of the temple and recognized the plowsmell of fresh soil.

When he breathed deeply, he caught the scent of spring in the fine mist that fell from the few low clouds, but there was a force that pulled him down. He was drawn by the desperate ache of his wanting to be with his father—wherever that was—to follow him and be near him again. For he had imagined the last two days what it would be like living alone with his mother and doubted that he could do it. Arms hanging straight at his sides, his thin fingers curled and flexed.

Before his father had fallen sick and grown thin and weak with pain, they had worked their small farm together. Though he had the role of strong son to play when they had been waiting for the end in the last months of the sickness, he had been both a young man and a lost child.

There was a strong pulling from the rocks below. He pushed with his toes to straighten his body, but there was no stone for leverage. As he felt himself starting to tip forward, he reached back with both hands to balance and felt rough cloth. He grabbed a handful and pulled himself upright.

Molly's voice was soft against his ear, "Axel, why are you up here like this?" Axel opened his eyes and carefully turned to face his friend. When she pulled him away from the edge, she saw the tears and reached up with the fingers of one hand and wiped them away, first one cheek then the other.

Axel hadn't cried for years, and he wouldn't allow himself to at the funeral, but now he couldn't stop. It was as if there were a hole in his chest, filled to bursting, and the only way he could get out the air was by sobbing. Molly held him as his body shuddered. The gulps finally quieted, and he began to breathe as if he had been running; then that too eased and he laughed as he wiped his face with his hands. "You must think I'm a fool, crying like some baby."

Molly's voice was low and soft, not like he had ever heard it before, "No, I understand, Axel. It's all right." She held him, her face against his chest.

Her fine hair against his lips and the warmth of her through their clothes felt good. He saw in his mind the delicate features of her light-skinned face framed by dark curls. They had not touched like this before, and it was a new feeling for both of them. He put his hands on her shoulders and said to the top of her head, "I'm all right now, Molly. Thanks for understanding."

She leaned back and looked up into Axel's face and said softly, "I've been worried about you ever since your father got sick. When I saw you up here, standing on the edge of that stone and looking down, I didn't know what you were thinking. Are you sure you're going to be all right?"

"I am now, Molly."

She held his shirt in both of her hands and shook him lightly and said, "Because I really worry about what happens to you. You know that, don't you?"

Axel had never had a conversation like this with anyone before. No one had ever asked him how he felt or if he would be all right. It was strange, but good. He smiled at her and said, "Sure, I'll be fine from now on, I promise."

Taking her hand, he helped her down the first step off the big rock. They held hands as they followed the path down the steep hillside, sometimes sliding, sometimes jumping from stone to stone. The wet grass was slippery, and once they saved each other from falling.

When they reached level ground and were on the winding, narrow track to the village, Axel released Molly's hand. He didn't want to, but there was no excuse for holding it. She glanced quickly up at his face, then watched again where she was walking in the mud-rutted and wet dirt and said, "What will your mother do now, Axel?"

Axel had asked himself this question many times in the last weeks of his father's dying. He really didn't know what would happen to them and said, "I don't know. What can she do?"

"You won't move away will you? I couldn't stand. . .I mean, you wouldn't. . ." She wiped her still-wet palm on the rough material of her cloak.

"We have nowhere to go. I can work the farm as good as my father did, or almost as good."

She stopped walking and held him back with her hand on his arm, "You'll stay in Greenwater then?"

"I wouldn't want to leave. . .people I've known all my life." This time he looked quickly at her then back at the road.

Molly stopped again, and he had to turn toward her. She looked into his narrow face as she said, "I know how you feel about your father, Axel. When my mother died, I really missed her. I still do, but it was real bad for a while. People need each other, don't you think so?" Axel looked into her eyes for a moment and nodded.

They started walking again, and Axel felt that their relationship had somehow changed. They were the same people, but things were not like they had been before his father died.

When Axel's father had first been really sick and there was so much pain and he could hear him moaning in his bed, even when he was outside doing the chores, it had been like he was still a child. Molly had been there, and it was the way it always had been, but now she looked different to him. More grown up. More like a woman. Not like his mother was a woman, but not like Molly was still a girl, either. He reached down and took her hand again and they walked that way, hand in hand, back to Greenwater.

Sometimes Molly would step to one side so that their arms were stretched out straight and then pull Axel to her so that their shoulders would bump lightly. They both would laugh and walk together again. It was nearly dark by the time they reached the inn where Molly lived with her father.

They felt very private in the darkness of the porch when they stopped before she went in to help her father clean the tavern. Axel leaned back against the railing. "Thank you for coming up the hill to get me, Molly. You know, I almost fell before. . .when I reached back and you. . .I couldn't stop."

Molly stepped closer and touched his arm. "I'm glad I was there. It's good to know you're needed. . .or wanted."

Axel suddenly felt warm. It couldn't be the night for it had grown cooler since the sun had set. He was now short of breath. It's almost like I've been running, he thought. He started to tell her that she was needed, and the words wouldn't come. His chest felt tight and he wondered if he were going to cry again. Molly could tell he was having a problem saying what he wanted to, and she helped him. "We're special friends now, aren't we, Axel?"

"I'd like that, Molly. You're the only friend I've got. I mean. . .there's nobody else. Even if there was, I would— you—"

"I know what you mean, Axel. I feel the same way about you." She reached out and took his left hand in both of hers and held it. This time their touching hands felt natural to him.

"I better get back to my mother," he said. "She'll wonder where I went."

She stepped away from him and said, "Will you be back tonight?"

Axel shrugged, "I should be. When my father got really sick and couldn't walk at all anymore and spent all day in bed, moaning, she starting drinking ale. She never used to drink at all, but now she starts in the afternoon. I guess it's because she feels so bad. So, I think she'll want her jug of ale. Probably she should have it tonight, too."

Molly squeezed his hand. Her dark eyes shone in the yellow light coming from the tavern doorway. "I'm sorry about your father, Axel. I know how much you loved him."

Axel could feel the tears start again. Releasing her hand, he turned and stepped quickly off the porch and headed home, making his way around and over the puddles standing in the road.

2

The Mother of All Mothers

When Axel reached home that evening, his mother did want her ale, and she was waiting for him at the doorway of their small house. He could see her leaning against the door frame. Her skinny body was outlined through the thin material of her dress, the one she had worn that afternoon, and the lamplight behind her created a shining crown of her hair, but Axel knew that it was wild and stringy. When he turned from the path that ran past the farm toward their house, she started talking to him as soon as she could see who was coming.

With her hands on her hips, Axel's mother looked up at him and said, "Where have you been? I've been waiting for you. Now that your father's not here, you think you don't have to do a thing. Well, let me tell you something, Axel, I can't do it all alone. You had no call to go off for hours and leave me all by myself." She was blocking the doorway, and Axel knew he wouldn't get in the house until she had said what she wanted to.

"I'm sorry, Mother. I—"

With her fingers interlaced, she held her hands in front of her chest, rubbing the palms together. "Don't give me any excuses. I know you been with that girl from the tavern. Just 'cause your father's dead, you think you can do anything you want. Well, you can't. I been alone here all afternoon with nobody to talk to or anything. When your father was well there was someone around once in a while. The least you could do is get me a drink now that I need it so bad." She reached out and pushed her fingers against Axel's shoulder. "This hasn't been the best day of my life, you know. It's not every day that a new widow buries her man. Now you think about that instead of that girl."

She handed him a coin she had in the pocket of her dress and said, "Here, take this and get your mother a jug." Axel made two trips to the tavern that night. He felt awful about his mother starting to drink. Bobson, Molly's father and the rest of the people in the village thought the ale had been for his father. Now they would know it wasn't.

When he stepped into the dimly lit tavern, he could smell the old ale and smoke from the fireplace and lanterns hung on the walls. The room was small and dark, and the low, beamed ceiling was blackened from the years of smoke. There were two rough tables near the center of the room and a plank bar along the right wall. The three men sitting at the table stopped talking and turned to see who had entered. He could just make out their faces, and they looked as if they were surprised. Now they must think that the ale's for me, he thought. *Well, that's all right, I don't mind. Better me than my mother, and it doesn't make any difference to me because Molly knows.*

Bobson was sitting at the table drinking with the

farmers. "Axel, what are you doing here? I'd think you'd be with your mother tonight." The others waited to see what he would say.

"I'd like a jug of ale."

Bobson said in an impatient voice, "Well, what you want, boy?"

Axel spoke much louder, "A jug of dark ale." He looked for Molly, but she wasn't cleaning up yet.

Bobson took Axel's jug and filled it from a barrel. When he put it on the bar and had taken the coin, he said, "Sorry about your father, Axel. That was a bad way to go. Lots of pain. We all got to go, but not like that. What ya gonna do now he's gone?"

Axel could hear the men behind him listening for what he would say. One of the farmers had tried to buy his father's land last year, and he was sure he would try again now. When he turned to leave, his name was spoken softly. He looked back and the fat farmer with a heavy beard and very black eyes was holding up his hand and crooking his finger at him. He had a large farm just west of the village. Axel had never met the man, but he knew of him through his son, Cedric.

When Axel had walked to the table and was looking down at the men, the fat man looked into his eyes for long enough to make Axel feel uncomfortable and then said, "Last fall I talked to yer father and we agreed about his farm. He told me he'd sell it ta me this spring."

Axel didn't know what to say or what to do. Looking at the man, he waited for him to continue.

The man smiled and said, "It's spring."

"Yes."

"Yes, what?"

Axel didn't know if the man was telling the truth or not. If his father had agreed to sell the farm, he hadn't told him, and he didn't know what his mother would want to do. If what he said was true, then he and his mother might have to honor that promise. They might have to sell, and then what would they do? If his father had been planning on selling, what did he have in mind doing next? They were farmers. They would just have to buy more land somewhere else. The farm wasn't very big and they wouldn't get much for it. Sure not enough to buy a bigger place. While Axel was thinking this, the men watched him. "My father never said anything to me about selling to you. I don't know anything about it."

The fat man turned half away now and said, "Ya think about it. We agreed, yer father and me. Ask yer mother if it's not so. And ya should do that before you drink all that ale." The other men laughed. Axel nodded and left the tavern. It was raining harder, and the wind lashed strings of water into his face as he walked toward home.

He was sure that he and his mother would have to make some decisions now. *If she wants to sell the farm, what will I do? I don't want to leave Greenwater and Molly. I can't do that. But, if mother sells, we'll have to move. There's nothing for us to do here. I'd have to go with her and take care of her, and I don't know how to do anything but farm. We'd have to work for someone else on their farm.*

Greenwater's so small there isn't anyone here we could work for except that rich, fat man. I don't want to spend the rest of my life working on someone else's farm. I'd never get to see Molly and I'd spend all my time with Mother.

Maybe the fat man's lying. We might not have to sell. We could stay in Greenwater and I could work the farm. It's not so big I couldn't do it. It could be just the way it's always been except that my father won't be here. Maybe some day me and Molly could— He couldn't get past the beginnings of that thought.

He thought that his mother might be right and he was just a kid and didn't know anything. Maybe he had no right to start thinking like he was a man. He was the same kid today as he'd been yesterday. He'd ask his mother what she thought, and then they'd do whatever she said was the right thing for them.

When he got home his mother was sitting at the table. She pushed the smoking lantern to one side as she looked up at him, then motioned toward the chair across from her. "Sit down, Axel. We got to get some things talked out."

She filled her cup from the jug, and after drinking most of it in one long draught and making a face, she wiped her mouth with her thumb. Leaning forward, she said, "You're going to have to do your father's work now. This farm's so small that it was just big enough to let us live. You'll have to do all the things he did."

She leaned back in her chair and continued in a softer voice. "When he was your age, he had it really hard. There were dragons then and he had to watch for them all the time he was working his father's farm. But there's none around here now, and you got it real easy. So, you think about doing what's right for your mother or we have to sell this farm and you can work for someone else. We'd have to move where there was someone for you to work for." Resting her chin on both of her hands, she looked at him with her head cocked to one side. "You're too old to start an apprenticeship. Besides, you wouldn't make enough to support us. That's your job now you know. That's what your father would have wanted.

"I made an agreement with Walter to farm here this spring. He'll give us half of all he makes for the use of the land. But, that won't be enough for us to live on. You'll have to come up with something. Next year you'll have to do the farming by yourself." She drank the rest of the ale in her cup. Axel was sitting with his head down, looking at the worn and scarred table top. "Well?"

"Do I have to decide now? Tonight?"

"I figured you'd want to put it off. You think you're going to take up with that tavern owner's girl, don't you? You think you'll just forget about your responsibilities, eh? Just go off somewhere and let your old mother starve?"

Axel's mother started crying. She put her head down on the table and Axel could see her shoulders shake. He got up and put his arm around her and patted her shoulder. This was a new experience for Axel and he didn't know what to say. How could he comfort his mother when he didn't know if she was crying for his father or for herself? He guessed it didn't make much difference which it was; she felt bad and he felt sorry for her. "It may be all right, Mother."

"Axel, I feel so bad." His mother sat and cried and Axel watched her through the yellow light and smoke from the lantern. She looked up at her son and wiping her face with the back of her hands said, "It's not been easy for me this last year, you know. What with your father sick and in so much pain. There's been no one I could talk to about anything. It seemed like I was all alone with the world coming down on top of me." She tried to smile at her son, failed, and poured out the rest of the ale into her mug and looked up at him. "Run and get me a bit of ale like a good boy, before Bobson closes."

Axel picked up the jug then paused and said to the top of his mother's head, "Have you had enough for today? Maybe you should go to bed now. You're not used to drinking hardly anything at all, and you've had lots of ale today."

She looked up at her son and said softly, "I know, Axel, but this hurts so much, and the only thing that helps is if I drink a bit now and then. I don't really like the taste of it, and I'll probably quit in a day or so. . .but, for now I really need to stop thinking about your father being dead and how much he hurt the last few months.

Axel took the jug back through the rain to the tavern.

3

How Dreams Get Born

*T*he trail ahead was covered with light green grasses showing through the dark brown of fallen pine needles. When the white warhorse shook its head quickly, its mane followed the movements a fraction of a second later, like small whips. A lance, with its oak shaft and its shining, two-foot point upon which the sunlight danced, bobbed slightly up and down in front of and to the side of the great white head.

Dark green leaves of giant oak and fine pine needles filtered the sun, which threw gold circles and bars of light on the trail, while dark shadows covered the face of the mountainside. Rocks and boulders, fallen from the high cliffs, were scattered to the right and left of the path. The larger pieces had dark green and gray moss covering their shaded sides, and the dampness that hung over the forest floor was rich with the smell of mushroom and mold.

The young man, clad in shining plate armor and a bright red cloak, held his lance steady as he swayed slightly in the saddle. He glanced occasionally up to the *dark mouth of the cave at the top of the cliff, hundreds of feet above him.*

The horse pawed the narrow stone ledge below, as the young warrior entered the cave's mouth. Once inside, he drew his sword before walking deeper into the mountain. At a dimly lit corner he came upon the dragon. It glared through evil, dark red eyes and shifted its massive weight on its scaled front feet. Wisps of smoke trailed from its nostrils.

Raising his sword above his head, the warrior charged, swinging the blade. The dragon inhaled deeply and blew long blasts of flame. Tongues of fire raced forward, but the young man bounded nimbly out of the way. The cave was filling with smoke, but the beast kept its eyes on him as it swung its large head on the end of its snake-like neck. The man flashed his sword towards the dragon's neck and created a red mouth and a shrill screaming erupted, which turned into a familiar sound calling his name. "Axel. . .Axel!" Above him the spring sun had drifted down the blue sky into late afternoon, and his mother was rushing up the small hill through last year's broken weed stalks.

"Axel," she yelled, her face bright red. "You little fool. What do you think you're doing up here sleeping all day when you know you should be bringing down the wood?" Her dark eyes, close-set on either side of her flat nose, glared at him. Her thin arms quivering, she lifted up her hands in which she held two wooden buckets. "See these? Now you get down to the spring and fill them up and haul them back to the house, and then you bring down the rest of the wood."

Axel looked up, shading his eyes from the sun, and said, "I just sat down, Mother. I've already brought down three loads of wood."

"Don't back-talk me, you. . .you. . . Now do as I say." She turned and started down the hill. He could hear her talking on the way down, her voice getting fainter until he could no longer make out the words, but he knew she was talking because he could see the back of her head moving and her arms waving, and he knew her very well. He had heard her talking all day every day for the past sixteen years.

Axel stretched, breathing deeply the smells of spring on the hill top, as he watched his mother walk back down through the woods to their wooden, one-story house that leaned away from the winds that blew through the valley. After picking up the buckets, he looked over at the few low buildings below him. The smithy and the tavern where Molly lived were at the far end of the village, and he could just see them. Looking at where she lived, worked, and slept quickened his heartbeat. He and Molly had met every afternoon since the day she had saved him from falling. When he wasn't with her, he was thinking about what she had said the last time they had been together, or he was remembering what she looked like and how she moved.

They met every evening just before the sky started to darken in the east over the low mountains. They would walk toward each other in the stillness of the shadows, and Axel could see Molly smiling at him as she drew near. Her face would glow as she stepped out of the patches of shade cast by the old oaks that lined the roadway and entered the soft and slanting sunlight. He would hold out his hands,

17

and Molly would skip, laughing, and grasp his hands and swing around and pull him along in the direction she wanted to walk that evening.

They talked of everything and of nothing special. Axel found that he could say things that before he hadn't thought about at all. He would talk about his parents and the farm and what he wanted to do with his life, and Molly told him that what he said was interesting and that he was wise. And he believed her.

Molly talked about the inn and her father and what she would like to do for the rest of her life. Axel was very interested in how she felt about everything, and he told her this. She believed him and told him so.

One evening Axel told Molly about wanting to farm the rest of his life. How he felt about planting and watching things grow that would feed a family. He even told her something that he had never told anyone before. He explained about his feelings when he had to kill chickens. How he felt guilty for killing them. Molly was very interested in this. She had never heard of anyone who felt that way about chickens. This made Axel seem gentle and not like the other boys she knew from the village. She liked him all the more for it.

In the clear air, he could hear the rhythmic clang of the blacksmith pounding out a horseshoe or some tool. He turned his back on his home and the village and walked the short distance to the spring where they got their water. It boiled up from between large stones and created a small pool. The overflow ran in a thin stream that fell to the river, called Greenwater River, because of its slightly greenish tint. That same colored water gave the village its name.

As he scooped the first bucket full, he saw small, speckled fish dart along the bottom and turn, and wavering in the slow current, come to rest in the cold water. After filling the second bucket he began the walk back towards his house, water sloshing over the rims. He turned at the wheat field he and his mother owned and followed the well-worn path. The sky was light blue, and his eyes studied the few small, white clouds floating slowly above the distant, blue-gray hills.

When he was in their vegetable and herb garden, he could hear the clucking of the chickens in their yard and his mother talking in the house. There might not be anyone in the house with her, because for almost the last year she had been talking even when she was alone. He studied their house as he walked toward it and thought to himself, *There's got to be something better for me than this.*

Stepping through the rough doorway, he set the two buckets down on the dirt floor. The odor of cooking food was strong, and he saw that a kettle of stew was heating in the fireplace. His mother sat at the lopsided table, a battered bowl half full of stew in front of her.

She tossed her head toward the fireplace, "You might as well get yourself some stew and sit down and eat." He got a bowl from the shelf, scooped out stew and went back to the shelf for a spoon and sat. Axel's mother watched him move about the small, dark room. "You haven't done half the stuff I told you to. We need the garden dug up and that's hardly enough water. You know you have to wash clothes today, and you—"

Well, thought Axel, as his mother ran on, she's really

upset and I can understand that, but she can cook good stew. He put a spoonful of the hot food into his mouth.

". . .why, when your father was alive, all the work got done. I hardly ever got to talk to him he was so busy, but now you got to do it, but you don't." She picked up a small piece of wood that Axel had been carving into a squirrel and tossed in into the fire. "You spend all your time thinking about that girl and carving little pieces of wood, and all they're good for is starting fires."

When they heard the banging on the door, she quickly stood up, patted her hair, straightened her dress and went to the door. Opening it, she said in a young girl's voice, "Why, Good Farmer John. How are you today?"

In little more than a croak, the thin and bent man said, "Okay." Holding his hat in his hand and banging it against his leg, he sent billows of dust into the sunlight of the open doorway with each slap.

She leaned against the door frame and said, "Would you like some stew? You don't look like you been eating well at all lately," and she used both hands to tuck a strand of hair into place. "One thing I always say is that a man's gotta eat if he's gonna do a good day's work. I was just saying to Axel the other day that when his father was alive he always ate good." She stood still for a moment looking at the floor. "Hard to think that was just five weeks ago." She laughed too loudly. "We don't have much, but we eat good here. Don't you think that's important? I know what a good man wants, I can tell you." She reached up and straightened her collar. The farmer shuffled his feet and looked at the table. "Here, sit down and have some stew with Axel. He never moves much, but he's always hungry.

You're hungry, too. I know you are."

"I s'pose."

"Axel, get the good man a bowl of stew." She pulled out a chair for her guest, and she sat in the larger chair at the end of the table. Axel dished out the stew, put a spoon in it and put it on the table in front of Good Farmer John. Dripping stew off his spoon each time he brought it to his mouth, the farmer ignored streams of grease that ran down his whiskered chin, splattering on the table.

"So, what brings you over?" she asked.

"I just," said the farmer, sputtering droplets of stew in a shower that fell on the table as he spoke, "wanted to know if I could use yer axe for a bit cause mine broke its blade on a stone." He continued to spoon in food.

"Now, you want to borrow our axe? Well, I see no problem with that, since the boy never uses it anyway. Axel, go get the kind man the old axe." She turned back to her bowl and said, "I don't know what we'll do now that my husband's gone. There's so much work and the boy can't do it all. What do you think I should do, Good Farmer John?"

As Axel was shutting the back door, he could hear his mother saying that she had just finished bringing down three loads of wood, so they wouldn't need both axes for at least two days.

The door of the chicken coop was missing a hinge at the bottom, and Axel had to lift it to swing it outward. Upon entering, his nose was assaulted by the smell of ammonia and feather dust, and he saw the setting sun shafting through the cracks in the rough siding create light bars in the dimness.

The old axe leaned in the corner. His father used it for years, and seeing it again made him think of when his father had been alive. How different his life had become since the sickness. He could remember how his father and he had exchanged looks when his mother had yelled at them. They had had a special bond that didn't include anyone else, knowledge about their lives that they shared. When she would start in, there was always something to be done, and Axel knew his father would include him in his plans, just to help him get away too. As he grasped the weathered handle, he could almost feel his father's hand on his shoulder and hear him say, "Axel, you gonna help me with the fence. . .or the wood. . .or fixing the roof?" Then there would be that special look that said, "Let's get out of here."

But now that Axel's father was gone, his mother centered her attention on him. He knew she told people lies about how he treated her. It was clear when she had told new ones because of the way people in the village looked at him. Like when he was sent to the tavern for ale. He could see people watch him walking with the jug, and he knew they thought the ale was for him. Lately his mother was always talking about not knowing how they were going to get along, and here he was drinking up what little they had. Such a thankless boy. And he couldn't tell anyone the truth. They probably wouldn't believe him anyway.

He left the shed and walked back to the house. As he opened the door, he heard his mother saying, ". . .and that boy never minds me. All he does all day is dream about the tavern keeper's girl, Molly, and I'm so tired because I'm always fetching wood or water, and cooking and doing this or that in the garden. And, I'm too good to that boy, so kind to him.

"What he really needs is a good man to set him right. He could be a real good worker with the right kind of handling. A good man, needing help around a place, could sure find that he would be a good one to have working for him. He needs a strong hand is what he needs. I try to make a home for him, and it's not easy now that I don't have a man anymore. It used to be hard enough looking after the two of them, but at least then some things got done without me doing it all, but now, sometimes I don't know what I'll do." She leaned forward to look into the man's face, reached out and touched his arm, and continued. "You must know how I feel, having lost your wife last year. You know how lonely it can get, and how hard it is going on alone." She turned at the sound of the door. "Ah, here's Axel now with the axe. Thank you, Dear."

"Yes, Mother." After leaning the axe against the wall, Axel sat and began eating.

The farmer wiped his face on his sleeve, rose, and picked up the axe. Axel's mother stood and said, "I would offer to have Axel help you with the wood cutting you got to do, but I need him to help me here with this small place. We don't have much land but it's enough. . .now, if it were added to another place, like yours—if they were added together—that would make a nice farm, don't you think?" She looked up at Good Farmer John, but he was already headed for the door, the axe in his hand.

Axel's mother hurried to open it for him and said, "If you git hungry again or just want to visit, you come back."

"All right," the farmer said, as he walked down the path to the cart track.

When the man was out on the path, Axel's mother turned to her son and in a very reasonable voice said, "Axel, why can't you be more like Good Farmer John? You're just so slow." She sat again at the table and said, "You know, Axel, I never used to drink at all but now I need to forget about your father and all the pain he had. It's the only way I can make it at all. This will be better soon, I promise you. But for now I want you to go the tavern and get me a jug. I got to plan for our future. There's lots of things to think about.

"Can I finish my stew first?"

She shook her head and said, "It'll be here when you get back. All I do for you, the least you could do is get me something to drink when I need it so bad. I get tired you know. When your father was alive he took care of lots of the things I have to do now. You just don't know what it's like doing without him. When you grow up, if you ever do, you'll understand a lot more. Hurry now. I told the blacksmith you'd haul charcoal for him first thing in the morning when the chores were done, so we can have some money. If I can get you out of bed at all."

"I'll need to pay."

She threw a copper coin on the table, and it wobbled to a stop next to his bowl, and she said, "Here."

Axel left the house excited, for he was going to have a chance to see Molly. In the few short weeks since the funeral and their walk home, he had discovered he was in love with her. He liked to think about what it would be like if she felt the same way about him.

The week before, while Axel had been walking back from the blacksmith's shop, he had seen Molly's father sitting on the bench in front of the inn. At that time, if he had thought about it, he would never have had the courage to stop and say what he did, but the man had been sitting there so relaxed that he didn't think about what he might say. Bobson was a short, fat man with a ring of white hair just above his ears that stuck out in a wild crown. Axel had stepped onto the porch of the inn and cleared his throat. Bobson's eyes opened and he said, "Hello, Axel. Here for your ale?"

Axel said, "No, I want to marry Molly." *I can't believe I just said that.* He had meant to talk to Bobson, but he had no plans to say this. He was frozen. The noises of the town and the wind that usually followed the river were still. Axel waited.

Bobson looked up at him and said, "Well?"

Axel's voice was a squeak, "Well, what?"

"Light or dark?"

He didn't hear me. Now that I've asked him once, maybe I can do it again and loud enough for him to hear. He tensed his muscles and said it again, but much louder, "Bobson, I want to marry Molly."

The tavern owner, after a moment of sitting very still, looked up and down the street before he laughed and said very slowly, "And how would a boy like you take care of my girl?" Axel wished he could squeeze down through one of the cracks in the boards of the porch. "I guess you think you'd take over my tavern and do it that way? Is that what you've on your mind? Is it?" Axel couldn't speak, but he shook his head. "I talked to your mother at the temple last week about what kind of a boy you are, and I sure don't want the likes of you for a son. No thanks, boy. Just forget that idea."

When Axel turned to go, Bobson reached out and held him back by grasping his sleeve between his thumb and fingers and said, "Besides, Cedric's father and I've talked. Nothing set yet, but he talked about investing in the inn. It needs work and he has the money, and there's nothing better than keeping it in the family. So, just forget all about those silly ideas." That had been the most embarrassing thing that had ever happened to Axel, and he felt his eyes sting as he hurried toward home.

On this spring evening, the sun was setting as he made his way toward the inn, his shadow a thin, long mimic that extended to the right of him. He turned onto the well-worn track, which ran through the small village. Past the smithy, which was now closed, though he could see embers glowing in the forge, he walked towards the tavern and inn. A board, with a black cat and a red jug painted on it, hung from a post that leaned out from the side of the building. As he swung open the door, he heard laughter.

Three men, seated at one of the tables, stopped their talking and laughing and turned to look when Axel entered. He crossed to the bar, and the three leaned together and whispered loudly, then laughed. Axel wondered if they were laughing about some new story his mother had told about him.

Bobson was standing behind the bar, sweat running into his fringe of grey hair, his bald head shiny. His leaning against the bar heavily indented his paunch. His body shook when he laughed as he talked with the three men, although Axel didn't think he could have heard much of what they were saying. Sometimes Bobson couldn't hear what was said to him even if the person talking was right in front of him.

He watched their lips, Axel noticed, when people spoke to him. Maybe he had read the lips of the whispering men. Axel put the jug on the bar and said, "A jug of dark, please."

Bobson frowned and said, "Axel. What'll it be tonight, light or dark?"

"Dark, please."

"Speak up, boy. I got things to do here besides wait on you."

Axel spoke much louder, "A jug of dark, please."

"I guess you expected to see Molly serving tonight?"

"No, I know you don't want her working in the tavern."

"You know why too, don't ya?"

Axel looked over his shoulder toward the back room as he said, "I think so."

One of the men laughed and called out, "You looking for Molly, Axel? Ain't Bobson good enough for ya?"

Another said, "I saw Cedric around here, somewhere." They all laughed again.

Bobson put his arms on the bar and said, "Molly's at work in the back. You'll have to get your jug without her seeing you tonight, Axel." He then leaned over the bar and shouted to the three men. "This boy wants to take over my bar. He thinks I'll let him take both my Molly and my inn. I had to set him straight last week."

The three drinkers laughed and one called out, "That'd

be a good way to get free ale, Axel." Another said something softly, and the three laughed again.

Axel could feel his face becoming hot. "I'd like a jug of dark," he shouted to Bobson.

"Why didn't you say so? And you don't have to yell, you know," Bobson shouted back, and he took Axel's jug. He held it under the spigot of a large barrel set against the wall. While the jug was filling, Axel moved so he could look again into the back room.

One of the men said, "What ya looking for, Axel?" and they laughed. Axel turned back to the bar just as Bobson set the jug down. He paid for the ale, and as he turned to go, he heard a man say, "Save some for when you get home, then you won't have to come back so soon." He turned and looked at Molly's father, who hadn't heard the man. Just as Axel started to close the door, he looked at Bobson again and saw him looking at the three men and shaking his head from side to side.

It was dark as Axel walked toward his home. He watched the moon keeping pace with him as it slid along behind the trees. He remembered the time his father had said to him that when he was old enough he should think about moving away from Greenwater. He said he didn't want to lose him and that he could use his help on their small farm, but he wanted him to have a better life than he had. At the time, Axel didn't think that was such a good idea, but it sure sounded good to him now.

He would have to take Molly with him. And Cedric was a problem now, too. How could Molly's father do that to her? Axel knew that she didn't think much of Cedric. But his family did have a lot of land. And Axel had no money. If they went away together, they both would starve. What he needed was a way to make money in a hurry. The problem was that there was almost nothing he could do that anyone would pay for. He'd sold three carvings to some people who were traveling through their village in the winter, but they hadn't bought enough for him to think he and Molly could live off of his woodcarving, no matter where they lived. He wouldn't miss his mother too much. Oh, he loved her, but she sure was hard to live with. Talk. . .talk. . .talk. And all the time finding fault with everything he did. *Now, if me and Molly could get some money, but that's not about to happen. I do know of men who split up their farms and gave the pieces to their sons, but it can't be done for me. There's no way for me to make enough to live on, unless. . .unless I could get some money by. . .I don't know, by killing a dragon or something.*

That thought stopped Axel in the middle of the path. *Kill a dragon.* He had heard that towns used to pay a bounty for a dead dragon. *Of course, it's dangerous work, and there aren't many left. Most of them have already been killed. I'd be lucky to find even one, but if I could kill two or three, I'd make enough money so Molly's father wouldn't need to marry her off to Cedric, and he might let her marry me. And then we could buy a farm somewhere else. And raise a family. Have kids. Babies.* The moonlight shafted through the trees and covered his face.

"Axel, what's the matter with you? Get in here with my ale. You'll never amount to a thing. All you do all the time is dream." His mother had been waiting for him and came out to the path and took the jug from his hand. "It was such a simple thing for you to get me a bit of a drink, and it took you half the night to do it. Sometimes I don't know how I'm going to stand it. I can't never get you to do right. Now, if your father was here, he could help, but I got to do it all alone. You better get to sleep. Remember, you got to haul charcoal first thing in the morning."

He looked down at his mother and said, "Molly said that her father had promised Cedric's father that—"

"Can't you think of anything else except that girl? We have important things to think about here."

"I think that Molly having to marry someone she doesn't love or even like is impor—"

His mother cut him off, "Axel, you do as I say. I'm your mother, and I know what's important. Now, you think about making some money working for someone this year." His mother closed the door and Axel was alone again in front of their small house. It was the same path and the same moon, and the dream that had evaporated when his mother opened the door lived again in the pale moonlight shining through the mist rising from the river.

I'm going to do it. I don't know how, but if some men can make a fortune, I should be able to. I can put what I'll need in a bag and pack some food. Cheese and bread, that's all I'll need. My extra shirt and a blanket. The nights are getting warmer. If I stay here, I'll never make enough money to be able to get what I need to be a dragonslayer. He said the word again, out loud, and it sounded good to him, "*dragonslayer.*"

Let's see, I'll need a sword and armor and a lance and a horse and. . .I don't know how I'll get all that, but I know if I stay here I'll never get any of it. Somehow I'll be able to do it. I have to for Molly. He turned and looked toward the tavern, then opened the door.

Axel wasn't surprised to see his mother still at the table. Most of the ale was gone and she looked to be asleep, her head on her arms. He felt sorry for her and at the same time guilty that he wanted to get away, then remembered the little house that he wouldn't be able to see from his and Molly's farm. He set about gathering what he would need to start his search for money.

By the time Axel returned to the inn, the lights had been put out. He opened the gate in the fence at the side of the building and walked along the edge of the garden Bobson made Molly tend. At the back of the tavern there was a pile of ale barrels and some fence posts he had to be careful stepping over. Molly's room was on the near corner. A scream of some small animal came from the field behind the building. An owl with dinner, he thought.

Molly must not have been asleep, for she opened the shutters as soon as he tapped on their wooden framework. Her face flooded with moonlight and she had her arms crossed in front of her light nightdress. She said, "Axel, what are you doing here?" The things Axel had thought to say had sounded so good when he had gone over them in his mind as he was gathering his things together at home. He opened his mouth but nothing came out. "I—"

Molly laughed. A light sound. A beautiful song to Axel. "What is it, Silly?"

He managed to get out, "I'll come back."

"No. It's late. You shouldn't be here now. What if my father wakes up?"

The moon had slid behind a cloud but now broke free

again and covered her face in gold and light shadows. He reached up and touched her cheek with his fingertips and said quietly, "I mean after I have some money, I'll come back then."

Molly spoke much too loudly. "Where are you going?"

"Shhhh." He put his fingers over her lips. He was in love but he had never touched her lips before. He had no idea that they would be so soft.

She kissed his fingers. Her voice was much lower now, "What are you talking about, Axel?"

"I'm going to get enough money so we can get married."

Molly leaned back and said, "Well. Nobody told me anything about this. My father's talking about me marrying Cedric late this summer. Besides, who said I would marry you?"

Axel realized her father hadn't told her that he had asked to marry her. She didn't know anything about it. He felt like a fool. *Now what?* Her hands were on the sill. He put his hands on hers. "I asked your father if I could marry you. He said no. Didn't he tell you?"

"No. Oh, Axel, why didn't *you* tell me? Did he tell you about Cedric? I don't even like him, and I can't stand the thought of him touching me." She turned her hands over and held his tightly.

"He said I couldn't support you. He's right. I can't. But, Molly, I will. I mean, I'll be able to when I get back."

She leaned forward and asked intently, "Where are you going, what are you talking about and what's going on?"

He moved closer. Their faces now were only inches apart. He whispered and she leaned closer to hear him. "I have to leave until I can make enough money so your father will let us get married. I'll never get enough if I stay here. Nobody but Cedric's family has any money in this village. I won't be gone long."

Her eyes, reflecting the moon, were close to his. "Where will you go? I don't want you to leave. Stay, Axel." She tilted her head slightly and closed her eyes.

Axel thought she looked beautiful like this, in the moonlight. He put his hands on each side of her face, his long and slender fingers just touching her cheeks. "I love you, Molly. I'll be back as soon as I can. I promise."

Molly leaned further. Their noses were almost touching now. "Don't go."

"I have to."

Their lips touched, lightly.

The world tilted for Axel. He had never felt like this. He had kissed Molly. They were in love. They would be married. She loved him. She had to. She had kissed him. It was going to be wonderful. Now he knew that he could do whatever he had to.

He realized he had told her that he loved her. Where did the courage to say that come from? And they had kissed. He could kill a dragon right now.

She still had her eyes closed. He leaned a bit and kissed her again. "Goodbye, Molly. I'll be back as soon as I can, I promise."

Molly leaned further and the sleeve of her night dress caught on the edge of the shutter. She pulled at it without looking and a bit of lace tore free. She pulled it from the splinter of wood and held it out to Axel and said, "Take this and there'll always be a part of me with you wherever you go."

Axel took the piece of cloth as he backed away from the window, but he stepped on the pile of fence posts and fell into the stack of barrels, which started rolling off of each other onto the ground. Yelping, he grabbed at the closest one which fell on his foot. This time he yelled.

When he turned back to Molly's window, he saw that the light was on in the tavern. Her father was up. He grabbed his bag and ran. On the way through the rows where vegetables would be planted, he yelled towards Molly's window, "I'll be back."

4

All Losers Have Stories to Tell

After the first day of walking, Axel spent the night wrapped in his blanket, cold and damp, shivering under the upthrust roots of a fallen tree. His love of this adventure had been cooled a good bit by a light rain in the night.

A fine mist came through the dirt still clinging to the maze of roots above him. It fell in muddy clots, one of which hit his nose, causing him to jerk awake and open one eye. His quick movement alarmed a small squirrel which had made a home in the fallen tree. It burred at him and watched his awakening with its unblinking, black eyes shining in the dim light. A fine start, Axel thought. *Here I am, one of the last great dragon hunters, being driven off from my first home away from home by a squirrel. If I leave here, it'll think it chased me away.* He opened his other eye.

The squirrel was scolding him from a small tree which leaned over the deadfall. *If I stay, I may be able to take over its home. At least I know I can beat this beast.* He shut his eyes again, hugged himself and shivered. The squirrel changed position and continued to complain. *If I get up and leave, it will have driven me off. What a start to my new life.* He had opened his eyes to a very wet, gray morning. Dark clouds hung low over the countryside, and he could just make out the rain-black trunks of the nearby trees through the mist and shadows of the deep woods that lined both sides of the roadway.

Axel's first day of walking had taken him further away from home than he had ever been before. The only thing he knew for sure from all that he had heard about dragons was that they liked to live near water, so he had started traveling east. He knew that the ocean lay in this direction.

Greenwater had never been bothered by a dragon, nor could he remember from stories he had heard from his childhood that anyone in his village had ever seen one. Oh, the people he knew talked as if they knew all about them, but not from first-hand experience. He had thought, W*ith this much lack of knowledge, I might as well go east as in any other direction. At least somewhere in this direction I'll find water, and the king lives near the ocean. That would be something to see, the king's castle.* He had thought that out last night when he had run as far as the edge of his village where the road forked. He had walked all of that first night and the next day. By evening of his first day ever away from home, he was so tired, the slight hollow beneath the upthrust roots had looked comfortable to him.

He broke off a piece of the dry cheese he had packed and ate it while he rolled up his damp blanket. As he tied his long, blonde hair back with a piece of twine, he looked up into the branches and called out, "You beat me this time, beast, but down this road somewhere your big cousin is waiting for me, and I'll put up a better fight then."

Late that evening, after walking all day on the path that wound through the hills to the east, Axel saw, off to his right, partly hidden by the trunks of massive trees, the dimly lit window of a small house. A track he could just make out led off the road between high bushes that were sprouting their new leaf growth. He squatted by the side of the road and watched the house for a long time, waiting to see movement. What he saw were pictures of hot food and a pile of dry straw.

He had just started down the path when a large, dark dog charged toward him, barking loudly. One defeat by a small animal this week is enough for this warrior, he thought. He didn't even look at the dog. He ignored it and kept walking toward the house. The dog, getting no reaction to its attack, skidded to a stop and cocked its head to one side. Axel walked on. The dog followed close behind, sniffing. "That's better," Axel said under his breath.

"Hello," he called loudly when he was near the house. "Hello the house."

There was no response, and Axel thought that the people were gone, but a very old woman in a dark, homespun dress stepped out of the open door. She watched Axel walk toward her, and when he was close, she called out, "Dog," and the shaggy animal ran to her side, turned and growled again. Axel, stopping a few feet from the doorway, said, "I'm traveling east and need a place to sleep tonight. Can I use your barn?"

The woman was one of the oldest people Axel had ever seen. Her arms were as thin as the handle of a hoe and her cheeks were sunken and dark with shadow. In the dim light that came from the doorway, he could see that the knuckles of her twisted fingers were swollen and knobby when she reached down and rubbed the dog's head with the back of her right hand.

She looked at Axel for what he thought was a long time, then said in a soft, hoarse voice, "Come in, boy."

The dog backed away from him when he entered the small, dim house. It had just one room. There was a fireplace on one wall, and a small fire was sending puffs of smoke into the room. Against the opposite wall were two cots, and in the center of the square room were a table and two stools. This is much like my house, he thought.

A voice at his back startled him, and he turned to face a heavy-bodied man, much younger than the old woman, standing in the doorway. "I heard ta dog. Who are ya?"

Axel's voice was higher than he wanted it to be, "I'm Axel, and I need a place to spend the night. I can cut wood or something to pay."

"Where ya from?"

"Greenwater."

"Where ya goin'?"

"East."

"Why?"

"Why am I going east?"

"Why ya goin' east?"

"I'm headed for water."

The man turned to the old woman and said, "Mother, get ta boy a drink." Stepping into the house, the man pointed to a corner near the fire. "Ya can sleep there."

Axel dropped his pack in the corner then turned to the

man and said, "What do you want me to do?" The old
woman was holding a cup out to him. The water was cold
and welcome.

The man moved closer to Axel. "Now, where ya
goin'?"

"What?"

"Ya gotcha water."

"Thanks."

"Well?"

"Can I cut wood or do something for spending the
night?"

"No."

"Nothing?"

"No."

"I'm willing— "

"No. Now, where ya goin'?"

"I don't know what you mean."

"I done mean nothin'."

"But. . .you said—" Axel turned to the man's mother.
She smiled at Axel and said, "Ya want more water?"

"No, that was fine, though."

This was the strangest conversation Axel had ever had.
Everyone in the house was talking about something
different. Like there had been three different conversations
going on all at the same time.

The woman stirred in a pot swung over the low fire in
the grate of the fireplace. He was given a plate of the grey-
brown food and told to sit at the small table. The meat
might have been rabbit, but he wasn't sure. It had been re-
heated so many times, it was like mush. Lifting a spoonful
of the mess caused strings of food to drip back onto his

plate. The piece of bread she placed in front of him was heavy and too hard to break into pieces. He had to chew off chunks small enough to eat.

The man sat at the table and watched Axel eat. His small, dark eyes, partly hidden behind his swollen cheeks, followed every move Axel made. He watched the spoon go from the plate to Axel's mouth. When Axel chewed a piece of bread off the larger piece, the black eyes watched the crumbs fall. The old woman lit a candle and put it on the table between them and then sat on the bed and watched them both.

With his large hands lying flat on the table, the man sat strangely still. "Why ya goin' east?"

"I'm looking for dragons."

"Ya lookin' for dragons." The man's voice was highly pitched and full of eagerness. Like a child's voice, Axel thought.

The old woman pulled a wooden box over to the table and sat on it and leaned forward and rested her arms on the edge of the table. "Did ya say ya was looking for dragons, boy, did I hear right? Did I?"

"Yes, that's why I'm headed east. I hear they live near water, and the ocean's that way."

Her voice now took on some of her son's eagerness. "Some used ta, that's a fact. They used ta live east a here." She cocked her head to the east. "But they don't all like that much water. Not all." The man's eyes now watched her thin lips move with as much interest as he had shown watching Axel eat. "Some live in swamps an' some in dry places, where there's no water. Why ya looking for dragons? What ya want a them? That's a question. You looking for their treasure? What they keep in the cave?" The thin, twisted fingers now played with each other on the rubbed-smooth top of the table.

Axel looked into her dark eyes and asked, "Do they keep treasure?"

The man leaned forward and looked at his mother, "Tell about ta treasure."

She turned to her boy and touched one of his large hands with her fingertips, then looked back at Axel. "Is that what yer about, looking fer gold? Dragon gold? Do I got it right? Ya looking for gold?"

"Yah, gold and other things," and the man swung his large, round head toward Axel. "Tell em, Mother."

Axel asked, "Do you know about dragons?"

The old woman squinted her eyes and looked into the far corner of the room. "When I were a girl there was dragons. That were a long time ago. . .when I were younger. But I remember it clear. Sometimes it don't seem like that long ago, but I know it was. I know that to be a fact."

The old voice had lost some of its hoarseness when she spoke again. She leaned into the light of the candle. "When I were little, I remember there was dragons. There was some then. I never seen 'em, but I knew some who did. I heard talk. I even knew a girl what were carried off by one. Valerie, her name were. Lived down the track from us. . .in the same village. The men all went ta try and bring her back. They took what they had ta try and kill it. Some had axes, some pitchforks, some just clubs. They went ta kill it. The men did. . .some a 'em."

She stopped talking, but her lips kept moving as if she

were still forming words in her mind, and the hairs on herchin moved up and down with the silent speech. When her lips quit moving, Axel was sure she was living again in that long-ago time. He didn't want to interrupt her memories, but he was sure she knew many things that he could learn.

After silently watching her for a moment, he asked, "Did they find it?"

Her eyes darted to Axel's face, and her lips again began to form words. Axel leaned forward trying to hear.

The son also leaned toward her and said, "Tell about ta gold."

She glanced at her son and continued, "They never found that'n, but ther was others—other dragons. I remember that. Dragons keep treasure, ya know, where they live. They keep it with 'em. Some went ta look fer it. Most never come back. Never saw 'em again. . .Gone. Story was they died." She was silent for a long moment, then said, "Them as weren't kilt an found gold went somewhere else ta spend it. Went away." She paused again. "Dragons like shiny things. Little things that shine and give off bits of light." Her eyes squinted almost shut when she smiled at Axel. He could hear the man breathing and shifting his weight from one side to another. Axel had never heard that about dragons before.

"Valerie's mother went one night ta where they said that dragon lived. In a swamp, it were, where it lived. She didn't tell where she were going. Kept it ta herself, she did. Valerie's father got up inna morning and she were gone. They found her three days later. She never talked none again. Never said 'nother word, she did. Some say she tried ta talk the dragon outa keeping her daughter, but she never told. Never 'nother word.

Her voice grew lower, and Axel and her son leaned even closer to hear. "There were an old woman lived in the village who said if anyone looked in the eyes of a dragon he could never talk again. She tol' people that. That's what happened. She found the dragon and tried ta sweet talk it. It stole her voice. So she couldn't talk. Not ever again."

"Sweet talk?" Axel asked. It was fully dark outside now, and the three of them sat in the circle of the yellow, flickering light.

"Sometimes dragons can be sweet talked inta giving up ther treasure. Mostly they just kill ya, but it works some-times. Sometimes it works. . . fer some. Her father sold that farm an' took all that money and looked. Took off walkin' ta find that dragon. Most think he found it 'cause he never come back. We thought he tried to bribe it, and it killed em and took all he had."

The man's voice had a whine to it when he said, "Mother, ta gold."

The old woman smiled at Axel and began to talk in a singsong voice, like she had said the words many times. "Dragons all keep treasure, ya know, keep it with em. Mostly they like bright things. Things that shine. It's not they want gold." She lifted her eyebrows at Axel, "What'd a dragon buy? It's just pretty. The men used ta talk about finding a dragon's cave and taking ta treasure when it was off feedin'—gone off ta get food." One of her dark eyes winked at Axel. "There'd be old pots and buttons an spoons an stuff. In that cave. What they'd find, tha men." The old woman put her head back and laughed. Axel could see she still had three teeth behind her thin and wrinkled lips.

The man banged his fist down on the table and shouted, "No. They keep gold. Ya said so. Ya told me they keep real treasure. Ya said they sleep on piles a gold coins like pillows. Now ya tell about that."

Axel spoke into the silence the man's outburst caused, "I need money so I can start a farm."

The man squeaked out, "See. He's gonna look fer gold."

"Lem, the only ones what keeps gold are the black ones. I told ya that, an they're all gone now. There's no more black ones. . .dragons." She looked back at Axel, "There must be ways ta get money 'sides looking fer dragon gold. Ya don't look all that strong. Ya built like my boy here, I could understand, but yer just a skinny thing. You ain't even had yer growth yet. Not a lot a meat on ya. Not too big."

Axel wasn't insulted by this. He knew he was thin, but he was strong. "Dragons may not have gold, but there's a reward for dead dragons. Some towns pay if you kill one. That's where I plan on getting the money from."

Nodding his head wisely, the man said, "That'd give ya two monies. The gold an that reward. That's a good plan." He smiled at his mother. "See?"

She put her thin knuckles on the table and lifted herself from the box. "Ya can sleep there by that fire. In that corner. By yer pack. It's better'n outside. In here it is. Lem, ya put out that candle."

In the morning Axel offered to work for the food and the place by the fire, but the man again said, "No." The three of them ate eggs mixed with a ground grain and Axel started the third day of his adventure. He now knew a lot more about dragons than he had learned in all of his previous sixteen years.

5

Pre-Game Analysis

He had no route in mind, but Axel was headed in what he had heard was the direction of the king's castle on the ocean. He wasn't sure how far away it was, or what he would do when he got there. The road he was traveling on was muddy in the low spots where the water collected and was cut in many places by snow melt from the mountains. But, it was better than walking cross-country. He felt good about the things he had learned and was rested from sleeping warm by the fire. Axel knew he was lucky to have been able to cover as much ground as he had.

The people in Axel's village had no great need to travel, so there was much in the kingdom that they had no knowledge of. Most of the things they needed they could produce right there. Some things had to be brought in, but traders did that. His father had been to the nearby towns and liked to talk about it, but it hadn't been often. Axel was now further away from his village than most of the people there had ever been.

Near the end of the third day, Axel had to turn off the road to keep heading east. The road bent north at this point, and he still felt it was more likely he would find some place that had dragon trouble near the coast. He turned into the Blue Mountains. They weren't rough or sharp because of being old; they had been eroded into great rounded mounds. As the sun dropped, mist rose from their sides, and it looked as if there were fires on the heavily forested slopes. The valleys, as they passed into shadow, took on a blueness and they seemed to deepen. Behind him, the skyline had its trees thrown into sharp relief against the sky's lighter blue and the setting sun. The branches, in silhouette, even with their new growth, looked spidery and bare.

There was the smell of wood smoke and food cooking. He stopped walking and stood still. . .listening and sniffing the damp air. Someone had a camp near here, or it could even be a small farm. Not many tried it, but he had heard of a few people who lived in the mountains. People who wanted to be alone, didn't like living in the towns and the farms that clung to their edges. They wouldn't want visitors and would be suspicious if they saw him near their buildings.

With all of the mist in the mountains, he knew he wouldn't be able to see the smoke from their fire, but it had to be from the valley to his right because the wind was blowing from that direction. He turned slightly left and thought that he would soon have to find a place to spend the night himself. Axel worked his way uphill through large trees and followed the ridge to a wall of rock. There was a thin stream of water running from a crevice in the stone, and beside it there was a small level shelf sheltered by an overhang. Soon he had a fire and was heating water in a small iron pot he had suspended from a notched limb propped over the flame. When the water was boiling, he dropped in some of his dried beans and the last of his ham. He still had some of the dark bread and cheese he had taken from home.

After cutting pine branches to sleep on and laying out his blanket, he ate. He had just finished the last of the beans when he heard men's voices. There was nowhere to hide. His camp was up against the stone wall, and the men were approaching from below. They must be headed for here, he thought. There was nothing he could do but wait for them. In a few minutes he saw someone climbing toward him through the trees, then two more. They were three rough looking men with packs, so they must be traveling, he thought. They either saw the smoke of his fire or smelled it because they stopped and stood still. He could see them sniffing and looking around. One of them spotted him or saw the smoke and pointed uphill toward him. Spreading out, they came toward his camp.

Axel knew enough not to appear frightened. He called out, "Up here. Join me at the fire." The men stood still and looked his way for a long time. Axel realized they too were wary of strangers in the mountains. He stood so that they could see he was alone.

They talked together for a moment then came on. The men were bearded and very dirty, and all three were thin and their clothes were rough and patched. Relieved that Axel was no threat, they settled down around the fire and prepared their own meal.

They were from the coast. A small town called Highcliff. Their talk was mostly grunts and mumbles, but

Axel did learn something that was exciting. They had been driven off their farms by a dragon and were wandering in search of work of some kind. The tallest of the three looked closely at Axel and asked, "So what's yer name an what ya doin' in these mountains, boy?"

"My name is Axel, and I'm going to be a dragon fighter."

All three men stopped eating, and Axel saw them glance at each other. One tried to hide it with a cough, but Axel was sure he had laughed. He covered the laugh with a question. "Did ya say ya wanted ta be a dragon fighter?"

Another spoke up, "Thas' wha' he said, Len, a dragon fighter." The third man nodded his head and started eating again.

The one called Len looked at Axel with his very dark eyes partly hidden under the edges of thin eyebrows over his heavy forehead. "Wha' ya know about dragons, boy?"

This was certainly a strange reaction, Axel thought. "I don't know very much at all, but I want to learn all I can."

The man who had said nothing yet leaned his slender back against the wall of stone. "I'll tell ya all ya need ta know." He waited, looking at Axel. When Axel nodded, he continued. "Them beasts are nothin' ta mess with." His voice got hard. "I seen tha one took my Dory, big fella. Dark green, scales all over. They wasn't nothin' I could do. He jus' grabbed her, screamed one time and took off." His voice had caught on the last words and he drove the knife he had been eating with into the ground. "What ya need ta know?"

Axel looked from the knife into the man's eyes and said, "Anything you can tell me will help." He spread his hands. "Start anywhere. How do dragonkillers kill them?"

"Mostly they don't. Mostly they die theirself."

"Do they keep treasure? Do they have piles of gold in their caves?"

The other two men looked up now. The first man continued, "I heard they do. 'Course, I don't know. One thing they do keep—" He paused.

"What's that?"

The man looked at the others, then back at Axel, and said softly, "Bones."

"Bones? What would they want with bones?"

"It's what's left—" The man's voice broke again. Axel could see his eyes shine in the light from the fire.

"Oh, you mean—"

"Ya. An they talk. To people if they wanna."

Axel didn't know if he should believe the man or not. He certainly has had more experience than I have, he thought. "What else? How are they killed?"

Looking off into the darkness, the man said, "If ya soak in their blood, ya s'posed ta get right strong. I don't know if that's the truth or not. It's what I hear. Ya can believe it if ya wanna."

"How are they killed?"

"Knights can do it. They got armor and lances. I'd like to see one a them get run through just once." The other two nodded.

The taller of the three, the one called Robert, spoke up, "That's what happened up ta Highcliff. That one killed three knights what come to try em. Then he 'bout drove everybody away. All the farmers, at least. Some stayed." He waited a moment, then said, "They'll leave too."

The only other thing that Axel learned that night that sounded like it might help him was that there was a man who claimed he was a wizard who lived in this part of the mountains. An old man who was supposed to know about dragons and many other things. His name was Sidney, but the three men couldn't tell much about him. Just where he lived. A valley or two to the east. They were headed that way but hadn't been to his valley yet, just heard about him. Len said, "I wouldn't go over there where no wizard was if it was just me alone. Ya can't trust 'em. They trick ya."

One of the other men said, "Ah, he just claims to be one. He's probably just talkin."

"But, you think he might know about dragons?" Axel asked.

The man leaning against the wall pulled his knife out of the ground and wiped the blade on his pants. "Ya keep asking about 'em and pretty soon ya think ya know enough to try one. Then ya gonna learn more than ya want ta."

In the morning Axel started walking with his face to the weak sun. His plan was to search for the valley where Sidney had a small farm. If anyone could tell him about dragons, a man who might be a wizard sure should be able to. The three men had started off much earlier. They seemed to be in some hurry. Just before they walked back down the side of the mountain, they had pointed in the direction of the valley where the man lived. Axel wasn't sure just how he would find this Sidney, but he was going to try. The going was rough because he couldn't keep to the valleys; he had to cross ridges that were sharp with broken boulders and ragged cliffs. As he walked, he thought of the questions he should ask.

Axel had never met a wizard before. A man, who the villagers had called a wizard, had come to their village one time, but his mother had made him stay in the house. The men in the village had talked about him for a long time. Each week Axel heard new stories about what the man had done. Before they found something else to talk about, they had him making gold out of some rusty iron in the back of the blacksmith shop. Axel was sure some of it was just talk, but still, wizards were supposed to know a lot. He was sure it would be worth the side trip to the valley where Sidney lived.

If he were able to learn something others didn't know, he might be able to fight a dragon and live through it. For the first time Axel felt he might be getting somewhere.

6

A Wizard At His Game

The next afternoon Axel crested a hill and saw, stretched below him, a long and narrow valley. Its rounded floor was lush and green with long, heavy grass. A small creek ran from the hills on the right to a round lake near the center, which sparkled with points of sunlight. On the far side of the valley squatted a one-story, log house with a shed in back. A slight movement in the edge of the far tree line caught his attention. Axel shielded his eyes from the sun and examined the valley. Three dark figures faded into the shadows of the trees and then were gone. He felt it wise to be careful, so he waited before he entered the valley.

Angling down the hill, he crossed through a field of short, yellow flowers that had just blossomed. Near the lake, the noise of his steps made a group of ducklings paddle frantically into deeper water. When he was near the house, he could see it was surrounded by beaten and bare ground and had a well in front and an outhouse behind.

As he rounded the corner of the house, he saw, standing next to the front door and chewing on the wooden latch, the most sorry looking donkey he had ever seen. It was sway-backed and its floppy ears looked so fly-chewed Axel could feel how much they hurt. When he stepped onto the bare ground in front of the house, he could hear a conversation through the partly open door. The donkey brayed, and a thin-fingered hand crept around the door jam and slapped the fly-covered nose, then withdrew. Axel was about to knock on the frame of the door but stopped next to the sad looking animal when he heard a name that sounded like his.

"Tho, Axthel, I will agree to help you if you can pay me or work off my fee." Strange, thought Axel, that there should be another person here with a name so much like mine. The voice went on, "How much money do you have? . . . That'th not near enough. You'll have to do better than that. Whoopth, here I go again. Hello, Axthel, I've been ethpecting you for the latht three minuteth." Axel didn't want to interrupt, but he was beginning to feel foolish standing next to the donkey, which had begun to lip his neck and slobber down the back of his shirt. He knocked.

The man who came to the doorway was dressed in a roughly woven, dark tunic with light colored stains extending down the front from below the shoulders. He was thin enough to not have eaten for at least the last month. The pale gray eyes he looked at Axel with were almost luminous. He is about my mother's age, Axel thought, but his face has no wrinkles. The man shifted his eyes to the side after he had focused on Axel, almost as if the object of his interest was too slippery to hold his attention.

"Axthel, my boy, welcome. We've jutht been having the nithetht coverthathion, and I've agreed to help you if you will work off my fee."

"Hello. My name is Axthel. . .er. . .Axel."

"Of courth it ith. Come in again."

"But I just got here. I've come to see Sidney. Do you know where he lives?"

"I know. I'm Thidney."

"No, I'm looking for Sidney. I was told he lived in a valley near here."

"That'th me, Thidney."

"Thidney?"

"No, Thidney."

"That's what I said, 'Thidney.'"

"We've been all through thith about three minuteth ago. We thouldn't go through it all again. Come in and finith the drink you thtarted." Sidney retreated into the dark interior, and Axel could see that he had the same white stains down his back. Axel had to lean over to follow through the low doorway.

"Here, finith your drink," Sidney said, giving Axel a full cup of water.

"Thank you. Are you really Sidney and are you a wizard?"

Sidney looked into Axel's face for a long moment, then his eyes slid away. "Yeth, thath me all right, and you've come to have me teach you about dragonth, right?"

"I don't understand how you can know that."

"I know thtuff."

"You know what?"

"Thtuff—You know, thtuff."

"You mean stuff?"

"That'th what I thaid."

Axel was confused, but then he had reason to be. He said, "Maybe I'm not hearing you as good as I should be. Did you call it *thtuff*?"

"Yeth, I don't have any choith. I lotht my etheth when I had a printing go bad thome time back."

"What did you loose?"

"My etheth."

"Etheth?"

"No, etheth. You know, like in Thidney."

"You mean you can't say your esses?"

The old man lifted one shoulder, then let it drop and said, "It doethn't bother me near ath much ath it doeth otherth."

Axel put his cup on the table and looked around the small room. There was a cot in one corner with a chicken clucking on it as if it had just laid an egg. Every other flat surface was covered with books and papers, some lying in piles and some rolled in cylinders.

"That's too bad about your esses, but that's not what I asked you about. I was wondering about how you knew who I was and what I'd come to see you about."

Sidney's eyes slid back onto Axel's face. "That ith the other thing that happened at the thame time I lotht the etheth. I don't thtay in time like I thould. I thomethimeth jump a little." He moved one hand in a short wave. "Never more than for a thort bit." Sidney held his thin hands in front of him and gestured with first his right and then his left one. "Thomtimeth I jump into the patht, and thomtieth into the future. It wath confuthing at firtht, but now I'm

56

uthed to it and it'th not tho much bother anymore." His eyes slid to the right.

Axel moved to his left to see if he could step into line with the man's eyes. "Who were you talking to when I first came to the door? I heard you say a name something like mine."

Sidney smiled. "That wath you. We had met in your future by the time you got here. I uthually can tell when the jumpth thart, but I jutht theem to thlip back into real time gradually."

"That must be confusing. Is there a cure?"

"Not until I can get a carver to cut me a new eth."

"Oh, why's that? What's a carver got to do with it?"

Sidney pushed on the chicken, and at first it resisted, then, with much loss of dignity, it fluttered to the floor. Sidney said, "Oh Thilvia, you can jutht lay another one." Looking at Axel, almost as if he were making sure he was being seen doing it, he picked up an egg and held it in his hand for a moment as if warming it, blew onto his closed fingers, then slid it under the blanket. As he sat on the edge of the bed, he waved his hand toward the only chair in the room. "Thit down, boy." Axel dropped his pack on the floor and was grateful to be able to sit. He hadn't realized how tired he was. When he moved, the chicken, with much squawking, fluttered to Sidney's shoulder. So that's what the stains are, Axel thought. Sidney held his hands out to the side and said, "My donkey ate my eth. It'th that thimple."

"Do you mean the one outside? How could that dumb beast do that?"

Leaning forward, Sidney said, "Thee, when I have a

complicated thpell, I print it out tho I won't make any mithtaketh. I wath doing the printing outhide in front where I could thee good, and the donkey ate the eth."

"You mean the letter ess? I saw him chewing on the door latch when I walked up. He must like to chew on things. Are the letters made of wood?"

"You got it now, boy. Tha'th ethactly what happened. He ate the eth. I wath right in the middle of the thpell, and I couldn't thtop. No telling what might happen. Tho I kept right on, but I had to print the retht of the thpell out without any etheth in it. I think that'th what happened to meth up my time too."

"Can't you make another eth—er—ess?"

"Not with thethe handth." He held his slender fingers in front of Axel's face. Axel could see that the knuckles were swollen and the fingers twisted and stiff. Sidney leaned back against the wall and said, "What do you want to know about dragonth for?"

"I have to become a dragonslayer."

Sidney looked at the boy for a long moment. Axel was surprised that the man's eyes did not slide away but continued to drill into his own. Then the wizard said very slowly, "Why?"

Axel found now that he couldn't move his eyes away from the wizard's, and the words seemed to just run out of his mouth faster than they ever had before. "I have this problem at home. My mother doesn't want me to get married because she thinks that then I would leave her, and she wants me to stay and help her with the small farm we have." The words were spilling out in a stream now. He didn't even have to think about what he was going to say.

For the first time he was putting into words things he had only thought about. He told Sidney all about his problems with his mother, Bobson and money. "All I can do is carve wood. But I have to try something to get money, and this is the only thing I could think of where I might have a chance of getting rich in a hurry."

The wizard nodded his head and continued to look into Axel's eyes.

"So, I asked people I met who I could find who could teach me about fighting dragons. I know it's dangerous work and most of the people who try are killed, but I hear the rewards are large. I figure if I can learn enough about dragons, maybe I won't get killed. I plan to quit when I've enough to get married. I don't want to do it all my life. But I just have to marry Molly."

Sidney smiled and said, "Why?"

"'Cause I love her." Axel surprised himself. He had never said the words to anyone but Molly. It just seemed to jump out of his mouth. In a way it was a relief to have said it out loud. He now felt committed. He had a goal. He felt very grown up. A man with a future. On a mission. And he would succeed. He felt for the first time since he had left home that he just might be able to do what he had set out to do. If he could only get this strange man to teach him what he needed to know. Almost all the men who chose to fight dragons were killed. In fact, he hadn't heard of one who hadn't died or been so badly wounded that he wasn't good for anything ever again. "What would you charge me to teach me about killing dragons?"

Sidney leaned back against the wall and appeared to be deeply in thought. He ran the back of one crooked hand across his mouth, looked up at Axel for a long time and said, "Nobody hath ever athked me to do that before. Exthept for you, of courth."

"You know about dragons, don't you?"

Sidney rose from the bed, crossed the small room and poured himself a cup of water. He drank and then turned to Axel and said, "Oh yeth. It'th jutht I've never had the call to teach anyone about that. I don't have a prithe thet." His eyes slid away now, first to Sylvia, who had flown to the floor when the wizard had stood up and was now pecking at Axel's boot. Then his eyes slid to Axel's pack, which was lying next to the table where he had dropped it. "How much money do you think that kind of very valuable information ith worth?"

"I have very little. I'm sure not enough."

"How much do you have?" The man's eyes now stayed on Axel's face.

"I have a little bit, but I'll need all of it and much more to pay for my armor. I thought I might be able to work for you and pay your fee that way." Some of the confidence he had felt earlier was gone now.

"I don't really need help around here, my boy. There'th not too much to do. When I work for thomeone I uthually get paid in gold." He pulled back the blanket on the bed, picked up an egg and began to peel it, dropping the pieces of shell on the floor. When it was peeled, he began to eat it. Sylvia scolded him, and Axel didn't know what to think. *It couldn't be the same egg, could it? Hard boiled?*

When Sidney finished the egg, Axel stood and picked up his pack. "Thank you for the drink. I don't have any gold. If I can get some somehow, I'll come back. Can you tell me how much I'll need?"

Sidney stood and looked about the room as if he were searching for a book of prices or a rate chart. "You underthand I've never rethearched thith before. Let'th thee, I'd have to read at leatht eight. . ." he glanced at Axel, "no, nine bookth. I have motht of them here. Then I'd have to think on the problem a good bit. Take me a long time to do that. How much would you have to know?"

"Everything."

"Everything?"

"If I'm going to kill dragons and not get killed or anything, I'll need to know more than all the other dragon-fighters knew." Axel sat on the bed. He felt and heard what sounded to him like an egg breaking. He put his hand under the blanket, and when he pulled it out, it was covered with raw egg. As he wiped his hand on his cloak, he watched Sidney carefully.

Sidney didn't appear to notice as he drew out the words, "I thee," and crossed the room to a shelf against the far wall and pulled down a large book. It too had the white stains on its cover. He blew on it and small, white feathers fluttered to the floor in a shower of dust. Sidney leaned over the table for a moment and when he straightened up he had a small burning stick in his hand. He lit the lamp with it, but the light must not have been bright enough to read by. He wiped the cover with his sleeve and stood in the doorway. Axel followed the old man to the light. "Old book. No call to uthe it in a long time. Very rare. Dragonth are mothtly gone now." He was mumbling so low that Axel was able to pick out just a few of his words.

"Dragonth. . .yeth, here we are. . .Oh, well. . .Yeth." He coughed and said, "It would be very exthpenthive." He looked up at Axel. "How much did you thay you have now?"

Axel said, "I'm sure not enough. I'll just have to do without your help, I guess." This was a real setback, and Axel felt disappointment, but there didn't seem to be anything he could do about it. He just didn't have the money to get the education he needed. He picked up his pack and turned toward the door.

Sidney shut the book, and as he put it away said over his shoulder, "Now wait. We don't want to be too hathty here. Your thtory intretheth me." He looked at Axel from under his thick eyebrows. "Why don't you thtay the night. We can talk about thith again in the morning. You can thleep there in the corner." The wizard pointed to a corner of the cluttered room. "Whoopth, here I go again." Sidney looked toward the door as he spoke. "If you could do that for me, Axthel, I would teach you all you want to know."

When Axel looked where the man was looking, he could see that there was no one there. What had the wizard said? ". . .I would teach you all you want to know." Axel thought the wizard must think he's in the future, because he hadn't said that before. *Now, all I have to do is figure out what I said or did to make him say that, and maybe he'll teach me. But, what could it be?*

Sidney picked up a long box from a low shelf next to the one window and said, "Look at thethe, Axthel. It would have to fit the retht of the thet." Axel started across the room to look, but the wizard quickly placed the box back on the shelf. He turned and faced Axel. "That wath a quick one. Now, where were we? I wath only gone for a thort time then, wathn't I?"

Axel didn't know what to think of all this. He explained, "I was just leaving when you went into the future—or something. I can see how that could be a problem. I wish I could help you with it. What would it take to make an ess?"

"That'th not an eathy thing to do. It would have to be carved out of a thpethial wood. And, it would have to be done jutht tho. It would take a great deal of thkill. I'll have to wait until I can find thomeone who ith a really good woodcarver and hire him to make me a new eth. Onthe I have that, I can print the thpell all over again and maybe undo thith meth I'm in."

Axel could see the future too now. He knew what the man had meant about what had happened when he said the time shifted. He just had to be careful now what he said to this man. He wouldn't want to make the carving sound too easy. He would do to this man what the man had done to him.

He was learning to deal with the outside world the way adults do. He was full of confidence again. Maybe they could trade, if he put it just right. He scuffed at the floor with his boot. "I can carve wood."

"I'm thure you can, my boy, but thith ith very prethithe work. Not jutht anyone can cut thith very hard wood."

Axel dropped the pitch of his voice. He wanted to sound confident. "I'm really a good woodcarver. I've done it for years." He looked back at the wizard to gauge the effects of his words.

"Yeth, but thith ith thpethial wood. I got it from a man

that was working on a thailing thip. It'th very rare wood."
Sidney waited till Axel was looking then turned toward the
door as he spoke. "If you could do that for me, Axthel, I
would teach you all you want to know." He picked up a
long box from a low shelf next to the window. "Look at
thethe, Axthel. It would have to fit the retht of the thet."
He opened the box and tilted it toward the light. There
were neatly arranged rows of stamps. Near the beginning
of the last row there was an empty space. Axel picked out
one of the stamps and examined it closely.

The wood was indeed very hard. It was wood like Axel
had never seen before, dark, heavy and closely grained. He
had picked up the letter *M*. It was intricate and beautifully
carved. He looked at the man who had been studying him
intently and said, "I will have to look at this in good light."
Axel went outside where he could see well and stood by the
door. The donkey came over to him and tried to take the
block out of his hand. He pushed the animal off with one
hand and held the letter up to the light with the other.
Sidney followed Axel out and watched him anxiously.

"What do you think, Axthel, can you do it?"

Axel spoke slowly, "Carving. . .yes, here. . .and
here." He ran his finger over the letter very professionally.
He rubbed the side of his face for a moment and thinking
hard and speaking slowly said, "It could be done, but it
would be very difficult, and so it would be very
expensive." He looked at Sidney. "How much do you think
it would be worth to have this carved for you?"

It may be that the man remembered the earlier
conversation he had had with Axel and how it had gone. At
any rate, he smiled and said, "I think we're going to get

along jutht fine, my boy. I'm thure we can come to thome arrangement that will benefit uth both. Come back inthide and we'll dithcuth it."

Sidney picked up Sylvia and held her much as he would a cat. He stroked her feathers and cooed. "Do you really think you can carve me an eth? Would it be ath good ath the otherth? If you could, my boy, we could trade thervitheth."

"Trade what?"

"Thervitheth. . .thervitheth. . .ah. . .thkillth. Yeth thath it, thkillth."

"Oh, thervitheth. Of course. We can trade. I'll cut you a new ess, and you teach me all about dragons. That will be great." Axel stopped talking because he didn't want to sound too eager. He sat at the table and rested his head on his hand. "But. . .it may take me a long time to carve the letter. And, it may be worth much more than some information that I could get about anywhere." He turned and looked up at Sidney.

Looking hard at Axel, Sidney said in a low voice, "Don't overdo a good thell job, boy. We can work together, jutht don't puth too hard." He smiled, and Sylvia, with much fussing, fluttered to his shoulder.

So the bargain was struck, but the man insisted on one condition before he would agree to teach Axel what he needed to know. He swore Axel to secrecy. Axel was never to tell a living soul what he was about to learn. This Axel was glad to do. In fact, it increased his desire to learn, for secrets are always more fun to know than just general information anybody can learn.

Axel and the old man worked together every day for

almost two weeks. While Axel carved the very hard wood, Sidney studied and read to him. Sometimes the old man just talked about dragonfighters he had known in the old days. Indeed, there were some legendary heroes. He told about Frederick who had slain six dragons before he was burned to death by one. There was Ralphson who died the first time he met a dragon. He had tried to capture it with a net. The dragon had stomped him to death. Axel learned the sad story of Simple Ronnie. He had tried to best a dragon by giving it massive doses of a purgative. It was believed that Simple Ronnie had drowned.

Because it was so dim in the house, they had pulled the table out into the yard. They tied the donkey to a broken wagon wheel so they could work without being chewed on. The weather was warming, and it was very pleasant reading and carving in the early summer sunshine. Axel took much longer carving the letter than he had to and thought that Sidney was taking longer to teach him about dragons than was necessary.

Most of what the old man taught Axel about dragons was of no value. But, there were some things he learned that surprised him. Dragons communicated with each other. If one learned something about a new dragon fighter who was a danger to dragons, it would pass it on to the others.

All of the information was very interesting, but there was one fact that fascinated Axel more than the rest. That was the dragons' ability to breathe fire. He learned that dragons had a number of stomachs, much like cows do. One of them was used to store decomposing matter. As this organic material broke down, it produced a gas that was very flammable. Sidney explained that this gas was produced by a mess of vegetable matter in the beast's third stomach. Of course Sidney called this matter a "Meth of matter." Dragons had a substance in their mouths which ignited the "meth" gas when they belched. What an amazing animal. Axel was fascinated with this idea, and he was sure that, if he thought about it long enough, he could put this information to use.

One morning when the carving was almost done, Axel asked Sidney to explain exactly how dragons breathe fire.

Sidney said, "I've got a whole book jutht about that thomewhere here." He began shifting books and papers about the room. Under some boxes of old cloaks and charts, he pulled out a very large and old, leather-covered book, "Yeth, here it ith. I knew it wath here. Letth thee, thixth." He walked out into the yard with Axel close behind him. "It thayth here, 'Dragonth which live at high altitude are particularly dangerouth becauthe of their ability to breathe fire. The lower preathure at height giveth them more forthe for their gatheth. A dragon living at a mountain top might be able to thoot a tongue of flame thirty thtepth or more. Woe be to any dragonthlayer who would come within thword range of thuch a beatht.' And, here'th another part about the gath." Sidney looked up from the book and said, "Now, Axel, thith ith the only copy of thith book in the world. It was written by a friend of mine. No one but him and me know of thith book, and I've not read thith to anyone elthe. My friend ith dead now, tho you are the only other perthon to know of thethe facth. Remember you thwore." He looked closely at Axel. Axel felt very privileged and nodded.

Axel spent the morning learning about the fire breathing

ability and mechanisms of dragons. He learned that just before a dragon shot fire out it had to suck in a great gut-full of air. Much of the air it took in went to that stomach which produced the gas. This was so that when it squeezed its body there would be a lot of gas and air mixed and the resulting belch would have force. Axel spent the next two days thinking about this and trying to figure out a way it could be put to use. There was an answer here somewhere, he thought, but it was just beyond his reach.

The answer came to him on the second night after he had learned about the fire mechanism. He and Sidney had been sitting at the table. Sidney had been reading to him by the light of the lamp. When it was time for them to go to bed, Axel watched as Sidney blew out the flame. He first leaned toward it and took in a lungfull of air. Then he put his hand on the far side of the flame and blew hard toward his hand. This image stayed with Axel for a long time that night and kept him from sleeping. Just before he drifted off, he saw himself at the entrance to a dragon's lair. The dragon was just about to blast him with flame. It was sucking in a great whoosh of air, and he held up a lamp to the dragon's mouth. The flame was sucked down into the dragon's "meth" stomach.

Axel sat up in bed, fully awake. *If the gas burns. . .and the flame is pulled into the dragon. . .there would be a mixture of air and gas in the dragon. Do dragons burn? What would happen? How would I get close enough to the dragon to hold a lamp up to its mouth? That would be really dumb, holding a lamp up to a dragon. One swipe with its front claws and—*Axel jumped out of his bedroll and lit the lamp with one of Sidney's firesticks.

The old wizard had showed him the fireboard and firesticks that he had been working on the first night Axel had stayed with him. Sidney had dipped one end of short sticks in a yellowish powder he had mixed with glue so that it would hold to the sticks. One of these he would put in a hole he had cut in a small board. Near it he had fastened a piece of steel. When he scraped against the steel with a piece of flint, the sparks given off caught the mixture on the stick on fire. He then could pick out the stick and put the fire to whatever he wanted. Axel was very impressed. It made fire starting quite easy. Sidney called it his fireboard.

Sidney sounded cross when he said, "Axthel, what are you doing? Ith it morning already?"

"Come over here and watch what I'm doing, Sidney." Axel turned up the lamp and waited for Sidney to get out of bed. Sidney shuffled over to the table and leaned on the edge of it with his hands.

"What'th the problem, boy?"

Axel pushed the lamp over in front of Sidney. "Blow it out."

"It'th thill dark out. Are you ready to go back to bed now?"

"No, I think I know how I can kill a dragon. Now blow it out like you did when we first went to bed."

Sidney leaned over the table close to the lamp and sucked in air.

Axel held up his hands. "Stop."

Sidney held the air in his lungs and looked at Axel. Axel was smiling. Sidney started to turn red in the face. Axel continued to look from the lamp to Sindey's face, nodding as he did so. When the air exploded out of Sidney's mouth, it

69

blew out the lamp. The room was suddenly black. Axel reached out and found Sidney's thin shoulders. Holding the older man, he danced him around the room, knocking over the one chair and bumping into the table. Sylvia woke and squalled into the darkness. Axel was shouting, "I found it! I can kill dragons. I know how to do it. Sidney, light the lamp. Let me tell you what I figured out."

"Where'th the fireboard?"

Axel felt around and found it on the table. Remembering that there were a number of the firesticks in a cracked dish next to it, he soon had the lamp relit. Sylvia squawked and scolded them. "Your book explained that dragons have to take in a great breath of air before they breathe fire, right? Well, if I can get them to breathe in some fire when they take in the air, they'll burn up inside."

Sidney picked up the chair and slumped down. He looked very tired, with his thin fringe of hair mussed and his long night dress twisted from the dance around the room. With a sigh he said quietly, "How will you talk a dragon into doing that?"

Axel was shifting from one foot to the other. He said, "That's what we have to figure out. There must be some way to do it. We have to find out what dragons do when they're scared or threatened. Maybe one of your books'll help us."

"Good idea, Axel. Let'th look in the morning." Sidney stood and headed for the bed.

"We could, but this is what I've been searching for. I couldn't go back to bed now. Could you?"

"Yeth." Sidney turned and faced Axel, and his head dropped onto his thin chest.

"No. Sidney, we have to look now. I can't wait for

morning."

"I think I would rather lithp than go through much more of thith."

"This will be the last of it. If you help me now, I'll know enough to be able to leave and start to hunt for dragons. I'm done with your letter anyway. I could leave in the morning."

"I'll hate to thee you go, but I really need my thleep now. Being a wizard ith hard work."

They spent the rest of the dark hours before dawn pouring over Sidney's books. Axel learned that dragons liked to bluff rather than fight. Oh, they could fight all right. There were accounts of great battles where dragons had killed scores of men. But, if they could bluff their way out of a fight they would. It was typical of a dragon to stomp its feet, thrash its tail, belch fire and generally act mean before it charged and fought.

This was what Axel needed to know. It would be during this bluffing stage that he would have to figure out how to get the dragon to breathe fire in instead of out. There had to be a way to do it.

When the sun lit the oiled paper tacked over the one small window, Axel took the ess out of his pack and gave it to Sidney. Sidney carried it into the morning sunlight and examined it carefully. It was beautifully carved. There was no way to see that it was any different than the rest of the letters. When Winthton tried to get at it, Sidney held him away with one hand. "Winthton, you ate one eth, you can't eat thith one, too."

Axel laughed. "Now you'll be able to call him Winston. He'll like that."

Shaking his head, Sidney said, "He wouldn't know who

I wath talking to. He ate the eth the firtht day I got him. The only name he knowth ith Winthton. If I thaid it with an eth he wouldn't recognithe it."

Axel laughed again and said, "Winthton's a good name." The donkey rubbed up against Axel's back and lipped his ear. "I'll be sorry to leave you, Winthton," he said, as he rubbed the long ears.

Sidney was still examining the letter, but he looked up at Axel. "You really like that donkey?"

"Oh, yes. We're good friends now."

"I'll tell you what I'll do. If thith eth workth, you can have him."

Winthton drooled down Axel's shirt front. "I'll need a mount. Don't you need him?"

"No. I took him inthtead of a fee. I helped a farmer out of a problem with thome wartth he had on hith feet, and he paid me with that beatht. He'th been nothing but trouble thinth. I'll be well rid of him. Now, help me pull the table out into the light tho I can print out a new thpell and get rid of thith lithp. Then you tie Winthton to the wagon wheel tho he doethn't eat another letter."

Axel helped set up what Sidney would need then tied up the donkey. Sidney went into the shack and returned in a long cloak and a pointed hat. There were faded markings on both and white stains down the front and back of the cloak. "Do you have to dress like that to cast a spell?"

Sidney laughed, "No, but it'th much more fun thith way. Bethideth, people exthpect it of me. After all, I am a withard."

Axel had not seen him so excited. Sidney sure was having a good time. He set out his papers, printing blocks, a sponge and a small bottle of ink and rolled up his sleeves. Axel watched as he mumbled under his breath printing his new spell. When Sidney had covered a sheet of the paper with small letters, he stood and waved his arms over his head, turned around three times, and picked up the paper and read quickly. Axel was amazed when the old man shouted toward the sky "Ess." When Axel clapped his hands, Sidney glanced at him and held up a hand to stop the interruption. Holding his tall hat to his head, Sidney performed a short dance step, then took off his hat and slapped it to the ground. "There, that ought to do it. Now, my boy, hear me." He looked into Axel's face. "Ess. . .ess. . .ess. That's super special essing. I've never said so good esses before. Thank you, my boy, thank you. You've performed a real service. What a relief this is." Sidney held his hands in front of him, the fingers pointing toward each other, and made the motions and sounds of two snake heads hissing at each other.

Axel picked up the pointed hat. It was crushed and very dusty, and he brushed it off against his leg. "I can leave now to find a dragon. You have your esses back and I know what I need to know to start making money. We had a good bargain."

Sidney reached out and took Axel's hand in both of his. "Yes, we did. I think you did more for me than I did for you, but that's the way it's supposed to be when you deal with a wizard." He turned and began to pick up his printing things and asked, "Is there anything else you need to know? Or is there anything you need I can help you with? Say, why not take a fireboard with you? It might come in handy." Sidney put his equipment back on the table and turned to go into the shack.

Axel followed him saying, "That's a good idea. I might need to light a fire in a hurry. Do you know where I can get some cheap armor?"

Sidney turned in the doorway and shook his head and said, "There's no such thing as cheap armor. It's all very expensive." He pointed at Axel and said, "Wait a bit," and he put the fingers of his right hand to his temple and pushed. Axel could see the old fingers bend with the pressure. He stood that way for a moment then said, "I've got an old, rusty sword in the house. You can have that if you want it. It wouldn't cut anything, but take it if you can use it." Sidney entered the shack and Axel stepped through the doorway and bumped into Sidney as he was stepping back out with the sword in his hand and Sylvia on his shoulder.

Axel tried to take the blade from its scabbard but it was held fast with rust. "I can't pull the blade free. It's stuck."

"If you think that's hard, you should try pulling one from a stone sometime." Axel stopped working with the sword and frowned. Sidney didn't notice that, but he did take hold of the scabbard and motioned for Axel to pull on the handle, and with much effort by the two men, the blade screeched free.

Sylvia answered.

Axel ran his hand along the rusty edge and said, "A little oil will take care of that."

"A little oil and a hot pan will do nicely. I should have cooked that bird a long time ago."

"I meant for the sword," Axel said, running his finger along the flat part of the blade. Flecks of rust fell to the ground.

Sidney shook his head and said, "This doesn't solve the

problem of how to get the dragon to breathe in fire."

"Have you thought about it at all?" Axel asked as he looked up from the sword.

Sidney scuffed the hard ground with his soft slippers, turned as a dog might before lying down and sat on the ground. Then he motioned for Axel to join him. Squinting into the afternoon sunlight, he said, "We have to look at this as a problem."

Axel mimicked the movements of the old man, then sat down next to him, "How about a long stick?"

Sidney was thinking hard and there was a short pause before he spoke, "Too close. Dragons are fast. You're going to have to be a good ways away to be safe."

"Could I throw burning sticks at it? I can throw real good."

"Too uncertain. What if you missed? No, you have to have distance and accuracy. You have to get fire to the dragon's mouth when it's breathing in. That means it will have to be bluffing at the time. But, you won't want to be close enough to get burnt, or to get stomped if it decides to charge." Sidney shook his head slowly from side to side as he looked off across the lake to the mountains with the mist rising from their blue slopes being burned off by the morning sun. "Now if you had an arrow, you could shoot it into its mouth. . .if you had a bow to shoot it with.

Axel jerked to an upright sitting position, "That's it. I'll get a bow and shoot an arrow with a rag tied to it." He was talking very fast now. "I can dip the rag in oil and light it, and when the dragon takes a deep breath, I can shoot the arrow into its mouth." Axel jumped up, "I knew we could come up with the answer."

Sidney worked himself to his feet by leaning against the side of the house. When he was upright, he rubbed his bald head and, looking thoughtful, said slowly, "Yes, it just might work." He now looked at Axel with a frown and continued, "Mind, it's never been tried before. We're breaking new ground here. When there were still lots of dragons around, I never heard of it being done." Now Sidney looked and sounded excited. "A whole new approach to dragon killing." He put his hand on Axel's shoulder and looked into his face. "If this works, my boy, you could become famous and very, very rich. . .and if it doesn't, you could become. . .dead."

Axel hadn't thought about that part of it before. He didn't like the sound of that, but he had to try. Molly would be counting on him. It could work. "It will work, Sidney. I know it will. All I need is to get a bow from somewhere."

The old man watched some ducks landing on the lake, then said softly, "I've got some arrows in the house and I used to make bows."

Axel heard this and moved around so he could face Sidney. "Can you do that?"

"Oh, yes. I used to when I was younger. Shouldn't be hard to do. I've got the right kind of wood in the shed. We could have a rough one that would work for you by morning. That's if I could still work with these hands." He held up his twisted fingers.

Axel looked at Sidney's hands then held up his hands next to Sidney's and looked the old man in the eyes. After looking from his hands to Axel's, Sidney shut his eyes for a moment and said, "Sure, you can do the work, Axel." He turned to the east and looked again at the mountains that ringed the valley. "You know, there are other ways to get what you want; you don't have to fight a dragon." He watched for any reaction to that on Axel's face. When there was none, he continued. "That's just one of the ways. Why don't we talk about what else you could do?"

Axel drew lines in the dirt with the toe of his boot and said, "I've been over and over this in my mind. There may be different ways to get there for others, but this is the only way for me. This is a dream I've had for a long time now."

The old man looked at Axel sharply, then he took a walking stick that had been leaning against the shack and also started making marks in the dirt. He was silent for a short time, then looked into Axel's eyes, nodded, and said quietly, "Well, it might work if you can find a dragon. The last ones I know about are east of here, a good week or so away. On the coast. I heard something about there being only three or four left." Then his eyes slid away from Axel's face and he said quietly, "You might be lucky and not find one." When there was no reply, he continued, "They can be very dangerous. You sure you want to do this?"

"I sure do," Axel answered.

Sidney turned and looked into Axel's eyes and said very clearly, "You could stay here if you want to,"and he lifted one hand, then let it drop. "I could teach you how to be a wizard."

Axel shook his head and said, "I'd really like to stay here with you, Sidney, but I've got things that I've got to do."

"I know you do, my boy. It was just a thought; I. . .get lonesome sometimes."

"I'm sorry. But I can't. I'd. . .like to," Axel shrugged, "stay, but—"

"I understand, Axel. You have to go."

Axel waited for a long moment, then was surprised that his voice was high and squeaky when he said, "I want you to help me make the bow. Then I'll have all the equipment I'll need. I'll have a sword, a bow and a mount."

Sidney sighed, and there was a moment of silence. He turned to look at Winthton and said, "I meant to tell you about that. You won't be able to ride Winthton. If anyone gets on him he lies down and rolls over on his back. You can have him to carry your stuff, but you won't be able to ride him yourself. Sorry."

Axel shrugged his shoulders, looked at Winthton and laughed, "That's all right. Let's start on the bow now."

In two days Axel was ready to begin the next step on his way to becoming a dragonslayer. Now for the hard part. He had to find dragons.

7

There's Lots To Learn From Failure

After a week of walking, Axel came to a well-traveled path that followed a wide river, full with spring snowmelt. The water was dark brown from the dirt that was being washed downstream, and there were swirls of gray foam and limbs and even whole trees being swept quickly along by the current. He spent the next day leading Winthton north along the riverbank on a path that was obviously used more for foot traffic than for carts and wagons.

The bushes had their leaves out in full now, and the trees had begun their early growth. It was a glorious day and Axel was full of confidence. He stopped when the sun was overhead and had a piece of cheese and some hard, black bread Sidney had baked for him. Sitting on the bank of the river, he ate while Winthton moved along the gentle slope feeding on the lush, new grass. At this point, the banks of the river were low, and Axel could hear the water rushing quickly over and past the stones, mud and tree roots. There was a chuckling and laughter to the moving water and Axel thought of Molly. Her long, dark hair shone in the sunlight of his mind, and he could look into her brown eyes and see small green flecks of light, and he knew that she was waiting for him and that he would return rich and maybe famous and he would marry her, and they would invite Cedric to the wedding, and they would have. . .he heard horse's hooves on the pathway coming from the direction he had been traveling.

Not all travelers on the roads were the kind he wanted to meet. He had heard stories of robbery and even murder for very small prizes. He had almost no money, but he did have Winthton and the old sword. It wasn't much, but he sure didn't want to lose them. He turned over on his stomach and inched up to the crest of the bank by the path.

The pathway swung near the river at this point, but he couldn't see anyone coming. He could hear the creak of leather and the clink of metal on metal. After sliding behind some low bushes where he wouldn't be seen easily, he thought of Winthton. He turned and saw his friend down by the river's bank. He too had heard the approaching horse and was looking up toward the path. Axel could tell that the traveler would not see either Winthton or himself unless he were to leave the path and come toward the river.

Then, through the thick branches of the bush, Axel could see the lower half of the horse that was approaching. Judging by the size of the legs of the beast, it was huge. When the horse and rider got to the point in the path where Axel was sure that the river could be seen, he heard a grunt and the horse stopped and then snorted. It wants water, Axel thought. They'll turn and come down to the river.

Axel reached for the comfort of his sword's handle when the horse turned off the path and started down the slope. He knew the rider would see Winthton as soon as he came past the bushes that lined the pathway. Only the lower half of the horse was visible, but when it passed his bush he stood and could see the rider as well.

The horse was the largest Axel had ever seen, a beautiful beast. But, the man slumped on its back looked as if he might fall off at any moment. In fact, he started to tip toward Axel as the horse stopped. Axel slid his half-drawn sword back into its scabbard and rushed to the side of the huge, black horse and caught the man as he fell.

The weight was too much for Axel, for the man was still partly dressed in armor. They fell together, but he had saved the man from a bad fall. The man moaned but said nothing. His eyes were open, but he was dazed and barely conscious. When Axel stretched him out on the ground, he could look at him closely. The man had no beard, but strong features and dark blue eyes. His eyebrows and light brown hair were nearly gone, burnt to a dark stubble. His chain mail was torn and twisted, and there was dark, dried blood on his hands and along one arm and the side of his face. Axel could see a large gash in the man's left shoulder, the blood dried and caked in the wound.

This man's armor had been of very good quality, and it fit him well. The horse had a breastpiece and a fine war saddle with a new mace hanging from a thong on the saddle. The man's scabbard was empty, and there was no helmet, either on the man or tied to the horse.

He's been in some fierce battle, Axel thought. There's been much fighting and a fire to have burnt his hair like that. Hurrying to his pack, he took his extra shirt and slid to the edge of the river and soaked it in water. He unbuckled the man's armor and cleaned his wounds.

The man said nothing but watched Axel move about helping him. When Axel had done what he could for the man's cut and beaten body, he sat back on his heels and looked into the man's eyes.

"Water." The voice was no more than a hoarse whisper. Axel held his water bag and the man's head while he drank and coughed, then drank again. The man revived somewhat after drinking. He was able to prop himself against a tree and even eat some of Axel's bread and cheese.

Axel led the horse away from the edge of the water and loosened its saddle. It grazed nearby, ignoring Winthton. It feels itself too grand, thought Axel. He next helped the man out of the rest of his armor, and when he was again leaning against the tree, Axel asked him, "Where was the battle?"

The man's voice was still hoarse but much stronger now. "On the side of a mountain." There was a slight smile on his face. "I lost."

What bravery, thought Axel. To fight and to be beaten so badly and still be able to smile. This man was in a really big battle. He must have left the fight with lots of dead and wounded opponents.

Axel saw himself on such a horse, fitted out with armor as this man must have started with. *In front of him is the long, curving line of the enemy. The sun glints off their weapons, and their banners snap and dance in the wind. Suddenly, there is a stillness in the air as before a storm. He sits tall upon his horse, and then with his knees, urges it slowly forward. He can hear his men behind him murmur in admiration. He can even hear their thoughts, "He's going out alone to do battle with the best they have. What a leader."*

There is a stirring in the line before him—a nervousness in their ranks when they realize who approaches them. He can hear them whispering, "It's Axel. Axel's coming. Who can we put up against Axel?"

"What are you planning to do with that old sword?" *He sings the shining blade out and holds it in front of his face. The line of enemy warriors shifts back.* Axel felt a hand on his arm. *He takes his eyes off the milling line in front of him and looks down.* The man lying against the tree had hold of him. "What are you carrying that old sword for?" the man asked again.

At first Axel didn't understand what the man meant. But when he touched the hilt, he knew and said, "I may need it when I meet a dragon."

The man's eyes left the sword, and he looked into Axel's face for a long moment. "Oh, I see. You plan on meeting a dragon?"

"That's why I'm on this road. That's what I plan on doing to make enough money to marry Molly." Axel found that it was easy talking to this wounded warrior. The man said very little while Axel told him of his dreams and plans. Of course, he couldn't tell him about Sidney; he had sworn to that secrecy. But, he did tell him about living with his mother and what she was like. He explained about the problem he had with Molly's father and Cedric and his decision to go into the dragon slaying business so that Molly's father would see him as someone who would be worthy of his daughter.

When Axel ran down and there didn't seem to be anything left to say, he felt embarrassed that he had talked so much about himself to this brave man.

The warrior pushed himself higher against the tree. Axel could see by the changes in his face that it hurt to move. When the man was settled, he looked at Axel and said, "Would you like some advice, boy?"

This was indeed an exciting question for Axel, for this

man had obviously been well trained and fitted out to do battle. He certainly was experienced, and Axel was sure he could learn a good deal from him. In his excitement, "Yes," was all Axel could get out.

The man looked first at Axel's face, then his eyes traveled down to the rusty sword at his side. He turned and looked toward the river where Winthton was still grazing and slowly shook his head. "Go back home."

Axel felt as if he had been slapped. Is that all this man could tell him? He didn't seem to understand how important this was. "I can't go back now. I haven't even tried yet. Anyway, I think I know enough to be successful."

"Go back home and work in the bar with your Molly." The man put his fingers in his mouth and blew. The sharp whistle brought his horse to stand beside him. He pulled himself upright by holding onto the stirrup. When he was erect and tightening the saddle, he turned and looked down at Axel. "Do like I tell you."

Axel couldn't let this man go without learning something about fighting. He had never talked to a warrior before. There must be a world of things he could learn that would be very valuable. "Can't you tell me about fighting?"

"Not the kind you have in mind. I'm not so good at that," the man said.

"How do you know you wouldn't be good at killing dragons? Have you ever tried?"

The man was quiet for a moment, then turned and looked at Axel, "That's what I was doing all day yesterday." He dragged himself into the saddle, and with much pain on his face, sat upright. "I can tell you this much, you won't stand a chance. Dragons are smart and mean. And very tough. They been killing livestock around Tightly since winter.

You'll just get killed. Go back home while you still can." He looked at Winthton, then turned back to Axel again. "And take that with you."

Axel took hold of the reins near the bit and led the man's horse up to the path, asking questions the whole time. "How did you come to fight the dragon?. . .Where did you find it?. . .How did you plan to get the reward?. . .Did you kill it?. . .Wound it?. . .Did it burn you? Please tell me."

"Go back home, boy. Tightly's dragon lives near the top of that mountain," he said, pointing north toward the tall, snow-covered peak. "Even if you could climb to its lair, you would be killed. I only made it to the first ledge, what with the weight of all this armor. Even without any, you couldn't make it. It's too hard a climb." The tall man rode out of the clearing and on to the trail. Axel watched him until the brush at the sides of the trail hid him from view. He stood there thinking about what the man had said as he listened to the sounds of the man's equipment and horse fade to silence.

He went down to the tree and got his sack, put his fingers in his mouth and blew. Saliva ran between his fingers. Glancing at Winthton, he wiped his hand on his shirt. His friend continued to graze. Putting the sack down, he walked to where his donkey was and pulled him back to the path. He tied his sack onto Winthton's back and taking the reins, started off again, full of hope, for now he knew there were still dragons, and there was one nearby. The village had been willing to pay to have it killed. The warrior hadn't been able to do it. The village still must want to get rid of it. And he was just the one to do it. He knew how.

8

The Practice And The Prize

T he road had led gradually uphill for the last three days, still close by the river; they could see it far below on their right. Steep banks hemmed it in on both sides, and the trees and bushes had hidden the water from view for most of the morning. The sun was at their backs, and a slight breeze kept them cool.

It was no longer necessary for Axel to lead Winthton. He had laid the lead rope over Winthton's back, and the donkey followed him willingly. As they walked along, Axel practiced with the old sword. He had started talking to Winthton and was sure that the donkey could understand him, even that he would answer if he could.

"Now, Winthton, it probably won't ever be necessary for me to use this sword at all, but I have to have it with me, and I have to look as if I know how to use it. We can't let anyone know how we plan on killing the dragons. If anyone finds out how we kill dragons, then they could do it too, and we can't have that. If this works like I think it will, we'll be the only ones who can kill dragons and get away without being killed or wounded. So, you have to be careful that you don't give us away."

He slid the sword from its scabbard. He had polished and oiled it, but it still gave off flakes of rust. He was afraid to scrape off too much rust. "Now watch this, I'm getting pretty good at pulling it out." He turned and walked backwards in front of Winthton. Sliding his sword away, then quickly pulling it out, he held it in front of the donkey's nose. Winthton yawned. "Yah, but you know it's just for show. No one else will know I don't kill dragons with it. They have to think I cut and hack them to death. Or—whatever warriors do."

The practice with the sword Axel viewed as a kind of play acting. He accepted it as a show, but the work with his bow he took very seriously. He spent at least two hours a day practicing. He could hit his target almost every time from twenty paces.

He had constructed a dragon's head from a bag of rags. This he would hang from a limb so that the target was as high as he could reach. Dragons leaned forward and down when they prepared to take in air just before they shot out flame. It had something to do with straightening their long throats so they could take in air quickly. No matter how big the dragon would be, when it was taking in air, it would never have its head higher than Axel could reach.

At first he wrapped rags around the heads of his arrows so that they wouldn't go so far or wouldn't stick in the trees, but, for the last practice session, he had taken the rags off because he was hitting the bag regularly. It was satisfying to see the arrows bury themselves in the target.

The first time he hit the bag with an arrow with the point on it, his mind raced with excitement: *The flame goes down the dragon's throat, the ugly beast roars and there's a look of shock and pain as it begins to burn inside. It had been standing on its hind feet with its tail thrashing behind it. It had been leaning down sucking in air. I hold my aim until just the right moment, then release the arrow. The point sinks into the roof of the open mouth. The burning rags, soaked in oil and tied around the shaft then lit just before firing, continue to burn as the dragon takes in more air. The flame disappears down the green throat and the scales covering the belly of the beast begin to glow. The dragon's eyes get big, and it screams in pain. It lies down on its side and smolders. To hide how I killed it, I slide the sword from its scabbard and plunge it into the still beating heart. I'll have the bloody sword as evidence.*

Winthton was lipping his ear. "You've got to stop that, Winthton. It doesn't look right for a great dragon fighter to have a donkey lipping his ear. I don't mind so much when we're alone, but when we're with other people you've got to be careful. People have to take us seriously if they're going to pay us." Winthton shifted to the other ear. "Now, cut that out, I think we're near Tightly."

And they were. The small town, a much bigger place than Axel had ever been in, was below them in a sheltered valley close to the river. On the far side of town, the foothills led to a towering mountain. *Strange that this mountain is so high and all the others are rounded off, really just huge hills. But something happened here so that this one isn't like the others.* The peak was still snow covered, and the runoff sparkled in the afternoon sun as it rushed in small streams down from the heights to flow into the river. Snow was blowing from the peak and looked to Axel like a large piece of white cloth that had been caught on the pointed top and was sailing in the high winds.

Axel stopped in the roadway to look at the town and the mountain beyond and thought that there is where he would begin to make his fortune. Somewhere in the town there was a man who would pay him to go up on that mountain, and it was up there where he would fight his first dragon.

Axel had never been on a mountain like this one before; he had had no call to. And because of this, the high, snow-covered peak before him didn't look too hard to climb. Of course, he was still a long way away, and he couldn't see what it was like yet, but he imagined that it would be steep and might tire him out, but it couldn't be too bad.

He wondered if the dragon was up there watching the town and his approach, waiting for him. *Can it see me? Of course not. I'm too far away. But, once I start the climb, the dragon will know I'm coming and be waiting for me.* He had seen some of the trouble this dragon had caused the farms that he passed. There weren't too many, but he had seen some farms that had been abandoned. The houses intact but with their doors standing open, as if the owners had no intention of returning. "I'm not sure you'll be able to go all the way up with me, Winthton. It may be too steep for you. You may have to wait for me at the bottom of the cliffs." He turned to get his friend's reaction to this news and saw that Winthton was eating spring flowers at the side of the roadway. Axel started down toward the town and said, "Come on, Winthton, our first kill awaits us."

Axel had never seen a two-story building before, and this town had a number of them. This was the most exciting place he had ever imagined. There was so much going on, he found that he was turning in circles trying to see all ways at once. The shops along the one street looked like stalls. They had shutters that opened upward and downward, top and bottom.

The upper shutter opened up and was supported by two posts that converted it into an awning. The lower shutter dropped to rest on two short legs and acted as a display counter. There were more things for sale than he had ever thought even existed. He thought that just to be here was worth the long walk.

He passed a tailor's shop and saw a short, thin man inside, sewing. When the tailor saw Axel stop, he must have recognized him as a stranger, for he hurried out and seized him by the arm. "That's an old outfit, and I know you to be a young man interested in style. I can tell by the intelligent look on your face. Come and let me show you some new material that just came in. You'll like it." He pulled Axel's arm toward the shop.

Digging his boots in the ground, Axel refused to be moved. "I have no money to buy clothes. I do have a question—"

"Some other time then, boy." The tailor turned quickly and re-entered his shop.

There were hatmakers, shoemakers, candlestick makers, oil merchants, many farmers selling vegetables, a bakery, and wine and ale sellers. It looked to Axel as if he had walked into a fair. The street was full of people buying and just looking. The shopkeepers were in and out of their stalls talking to people and trying to get them to come to their counters. It was the busiest place Axel had ever seen.

The temple was built of field stones, and set into the stonework on the front were runes that he had not seen before. The building was two stories and had a pointed steeple on top of that which seemed to reach up forever into the blue and white sky. When he stood in front of the building and looked up, he had the feeling that the building was leaning over him, then falling toward him. Stepping quickly back into the middle of the street, he bumped into Winthton. When he looked again, he was surprised to see the temple still standing.

People were moving in all directions in the street, but they ignored him and were hurrying with their own business. He had to find someone to talk to about killing the dragon and how to find out about the reward. He couldn't just walk up to a stranger and say, "Where do I get paid to kill a dragon?" He knew that Tightly had been having dragon trouble and that one lived on the mountain on the far side of town and that the town was ready to pay to have it killed. The wounded fighter had told him that much. So, there had to be someone here who would know who he could make the arrangement with.

He was turning around in the center of the street looking for some place to start asking questions when a priest walked out from the side of the temple. Axel had seen priests at home when they had come through his village, so he knew from the long, dark cloak the man wore that that was what he was. He took Winthton's rope and led him to the man. "Could I ask you a question?"

The priest was walking bent forward, as if he were looking for something on the ground. His long robe had some of the same runes woven into the cloth that Axel had seen on the temple. The hood was thrown back and sat on his shoulders, revealing a full head of very white hair that was so roughly cut that it looked as if he had trimmed it with an axe. The skin on his face was a mass of wrinkles that made Axel think of a ball of tightly wrapped yarn. He placed his hands together in front of him, almost in a praying fashion, and his voice sounded wet, as if he were under water, "Yes, my son. What is it you wish to know? Are you lost?"

"No, I need to find the man who can tell me how I can be paid for killing your dragon."

The priest looked over at Winthton, at Axel's homemade bow on Winthton's back, at Axel's sword and then into Axel's eyes.

Almost in a singing way, the priest said, "The temple does not have a dragon. The dragon is an agent of Evil. I know not of a dragon. I am a man of the gods." He turned to go.

Axel touched the rough material of the man's sleeve. "Please, I meant nothing like that. I'm a dragonslayer. I only wish to learn where I might be paid for killing the dragon—the one which has been eating the livestock near this town."

The old man turned, and reaching out, held Axel's arm. "You killed the dragon?" he hissed with surprise.

"No, I plan on doing that."

The priest took a thong from around his neck and ran its knotted length through his fingers. Fastened to it, cut from a dark wood, was a shape that Axel couldn't make out. Stepping closer to him, the priest looked into his face. The old man's eyes were red-rimmed and the lower lids hung away from the cloudy eyeballs. Axel could smell the man's breath, rank and thin against his face. "My son, have nothing to do with Evil. Have nothing to do with Evil's dragon. Have nothing to do with those who do." A fine rain of spittle fell on Axel's face, and when he didn't respond, the priest leaned closer until their noses were almost touching. "Touch not the Evil. Touch not those who touch the Evil. Touch not those who touch those who touch the Evil."

Axel started to back away, "But I—"

The priest held him with his eyes and the crooked fingers of one hand. "Talk not of the Evil. Listen not to those who would talk to you of the Evil. Seek not those who would tell you of those who have talked to the Evil. Give me the gold."

Axel wasn't sure he had heard the old man correctly. "Gold?"

"Yes, son. They will offer you gold to do their evil work. Turn your back on them. Give the gold to me."

"Who—Who will give me gold?"

The priest turned and looked to the far end of the street, then whispered wetly into Axel's face, "The blacksmith's son. He will give you gold to kill the Evil's helper. Save yourself. Give the gold to me."

Reaching behind him for Winthton, Axel backed away. When he could feel the donkey's rough hide under his hand, he turned and hurried down the street in the direction the old man had looked.

When he was well away, he turned and looked back at the priest, who had lifted his hood and was walking slowly toward the front of the temple. Just then he turned to face Axel. The lined face was hidden in shadow, but Axel could see the pale, cloudy eyes shining in the darkness of the hood. Axel hurried to the edge of town.

On his right, set back from the street, was the blacksmith shop. A sign, hanging crookedly, was painted with a picture of a sword. Axel tied Winthton's rope to the rail that ran along one side of the shop's front. The large doors opening to the street were thrown back so Axel could see the forge and massive, iron anvil.

The blacksmith's furnace was table-high, with a back and

a hood. To one side there was a large pile of charcoal. A wood and leather bellows was attached to the side of the forge. Along the other wall hung pieces of armor: breast plates, shields, spear points, axes and two bows. The bows were beautiful. Long graceful things, carved from light-colored wood and highly polished. "You want a bow?"

Axel whirled around. Standing just behind him was a large-chested man. He had no shirt on and his front was covered with a dark mat of curly hair. He was smiling, showing a missing front tooth. The rest were dirty and crooked. "No, I. . .yes, they're beautiful. I would like one, yes, but I have no money now. After I kill the dragon I'll buy that one," he pointed, "the one on the right I think."

The laugh started deep in the large man's chest. It rumbled like summer thunder and burst from his mouth in waves. He kept his eyes on Axel, but he threw back his head and was thoroughly enjoying himself. Axel started to back out of the shop. Just as he turned toward Winthton, he heard another voice from the back of the dim building.

The laughter had brought from the back of the shop a much older man who frowned as he came into the light. "What is it, Hammer?" Then he saw Axel. "What have you done to set off my idiot son?" The large man was now bending over holding his stomach. This second man was much older, though Axel could see that his chest and arms were much larger than they should be for the size of his hips and legs. He was talking as he made his way around the furnace. "Hammer gets like this. Pay no attention to him. What do you want, boy?"

Axel found it difficult to talk with the blacksmith laughing so loudly, but he tried to explain. "I have come to kill the dragon. I was told you have a reward for this. Have

I come to the right place?" Hammer was now laughing so hard that he had to sit down and was holding one hand against his side and was supporting himself with the other one.

The old man looked at Hammer and nodded his head, "No wonder. Our bad luck makes this your lucky day. There's only four dragons left that anyone knows about and we got one. Follow me." He turned and walked toward the street. Axel followed and they stood near where Winthton was tied. The old man looked Winthton over very carefully, almost as if he couldn't believe what he was seeing, then he turned and examined Axel in much the same way.

He was shaking his head from side to side as he turned and pointed to the high peak of the mountain. The eastern side was now dark in late afternoon shadow. "Up there is where its cave is. Hammer will show you in the morning. The town has collected money to pay anyone who can kill it. Just yesterday a fine warrior almost died trying. Too far to see much, but we watched what we could see of the fight from here. There was some smoke that drifted away from the first ledge, and we saw the warrior get thrown off the edge and fall. Didn't kill him, but should have. You're welcome to try. Anyone is. All you have to do is bring back fresh dragon teeth to prove you killed it. We have a saying here, 'It's our dragon but your teeth.'" He laughed, but much softer than had his son.

Looking where the man had pointed, Axel could not make out any of the small features of the cliff's face, but could see a path of sorts that twisted up the lower slopes. The part of the mountain that he could see from the town was faced with flat slabs set at many different angles. It looked as if someone had sliced large pieces off with a dull knife. The one western-most slab, in contrast with the other dark vertical walls, glowed in the late sun. It looked a much harder climb from here than it had from the other side of town. He understood now what the wounded warrior had meant about the tough climb. "How much is the reward?"

The old blacksmith looked at Axel for a moment, then said, "We've set the amount. Come with me." He turned and led Axel to the back of the shop where there were piles of straw. Reaching under a chicken, he pulled out a large brown egg. He held it between his fingers in the light coming from the front of the shop and said, "We will balance gold coins against an egg. The coins will equal the weight of the egg. You must prove to us that you have killed the dragon to collect. The town elders have made this arrangement. I've been selected as the one to pay the reward when the dragon's dead. The priest is keeping the gold."

As they walked to the front of the shop, Axel stopped and examined the bows. He took them both down and strung them, tried them for strength and asked, "How much do you want for the lighter colored bow? The longer one?"

The man looked out toward Winthton then turned again to Axel, "One denier."

Hammer came over to where they were standing. He was still chuckling, the laughs bursting from him in sudden spurts. His voice was surprisingly high-pitched, almost a girl's voice. "You gonna kill the dragon?" He started laughing again.

Axel turned to face the older man, "Can I start early in the morning? I would like to begin before it's light."

"You can sleep in the back on the straw if you want."

Hammer laughed again, "With the chickens, eh, Dragon fighter?"

The old blacksmith pushed away his son's comment, and said, "Pay no attention to Hammer tonight. In the morning, listen to what he tells you. You can eat with us if you want. We'll call you early because it could be your last sunrise." Then he too laughed.

The next morning, before even the first of the roosters had awakened, Hammer woke Axel by pushing against him with his booted foot. "Come, Dragonslayer, your warhorse is packed and waiting." Axel looked up from the straw he had spent the night on. The man stood over him holding a lantern to one side. Its yellow glow created a deep shadow on one half of the large man's face, and his slight movements made the black shadows behind him dance on the wall. Axel rose, and after luke-warm porridge and a piece of bread, they started the long walk into the darkness at the base of the mountain.

When they reached the last fold in the mountain's skirt, Hammer stopped and pointed the way. "Follow this ridge until you get to there." He waved his hand in the direction of a narrow ledge that lay between huge boulders then hung on the face of the first tall cliff as it climbed sharply upward. "You won't be able to use your warhorse. Want me to take him back?"

Axel looked upward. "No. Winthton will wait here till I come down again."

"I'll just have to come back and get him tomorrow then. . . What did you just call him?"

"Winthton."

Hammer chuckled and said as he turned to go, "Sounds like a good name for a warhorse." The large man's laughter echoed off the cliffs as he made his way back down between the boulders.

Axel rested on the grass by the narrow, upward path until Hammer was out of sight. He didn't want to have anyone seehim tie rags to the tips of his arrows. When he had wrapped and tied the rags, he took his pack with a stoppered flask of lamp oil and the fireboard, slipped the bow over his shoulder, and tied the cloth quiver of arrows Sidney had given him to his belt and started out. "Wait for me, Winthton. I should be back before dark."

9

When First Meeting A Dragon. . .

T he mountainside was a series of ledges and cliffs—like stairs made by giants. On the third ledge was the dark, shaded entrance of the dragon's lair. His head tilted sharply back, Axel counted the ledges as he looked for an easy way up. There was none. The vertical slabs were not entirely smooth, as there were breaks in their stone faces, but none that he could see that would make the climb easy or even safe. Looking at where he would have to go, he wished that he had had a chance to talk longer with the wounded man about his climb. There was nothing he could do about that now. There was no way he was going to get the dragon to come down to him. He had to go to it. He slung his bow over his back as he walked up the path to the first riser of the stepped precipice.

He clenched his hands into fists a number of times, turned back to Winthton for a final look, then faced the rock. It was dirty gray with seams of lighter stone running through it. In a few places, ribbons of water came from cracks and trickled down its surface. Reaching up to squeeze his fingers into a small crack, Axel put his foot on a fallen boulder. He pulled himself upward and found a new place in the stone face for his left foot. He looked for a new handhold and saw one that looked big enough for his fingers. In this fashion, Axel clawed his way up the mountain. The rock cliff was cool, moist in places, dry in others, and occasionally in the shaded areas, there were patches of lichen.

Soon his back was warmed by the midday sun, and a triangle of sweat formed between the shoulder blades of his tunic. Drops of perspiration rolled down his forehead, getting into his eyes, making them sting and blurring his vision. He had to blink rapidly to clear them.

Once he stopped, hanging halfway up the first riser on the great steps, and looked down. Hundreds of feet below he saw the small shape of Winthton grazing in a patch of light colored grass. Nearby, a stream rushed quickly, turning from clear and sparkling to white and foamy at rapids and small waterfalls. Far in the distance he could see, in a blue haze, the rounded tops of the mountains where he had stayed with Sidney.

Taking a deep breath, he continued upward and heard faintly a distant humming. The cliff he was climbing was leaning out over him, and his hands now had to search the stone for holds, for he couldn't see above him without leaning out, and he couldn't do that. Sometimes he could see projections where he could place a foot, but by the time he reached that spot, he would have to feel with his boots for the purchase he had seen. After shifting his weight to that foot and pushing himself upward on that leg, he then had to reach one of his hands above his head and feel for the next projection or small ledge with his fingers. After an hour's climbing, he reached the first ledge. One hand grasped the edge, then the other, and he clambered onto the long, winding shelf. There was a small shady crevice, and he leaned back against the stone wall, his chest heaving with each labored breath. He leaned his head back and ran his arm across his forehead. Scratches and cuts covered his hands, and his nails were broken and torn. His mouth was dry and he was glad that he had a chance to rest and drink. He reached into the pouch hanging from his belt for his leather water flask but couldn't feel it. He groped, then looked in. It was not there. It's still tied to Winthton, he thought.

Axel cradled his face in his hands for a moment and then leaned back once again. Soon he stood and walked back out into the sunlight and ran his fingers through his blond hair as he looked off into the valley, at the wooded areas and small farm plots. He was surprised at how small the town's houses looked from where he was. A hawk, rounding the cliff, was as startled as Axel by their meeting. A high, thin cry, and the bird cut sharply away. Axel watched it sail with the wind rushing up the mountainside.

He faced the next cliff and reached for his first handhold. As he climbed, he began to sweat again. The humming was growing steadily louder. Thirty feet up from the first step, the only handhold he could find was at the extreme end of his reach. He probed with his right foot for purchase. Nothing. He slid his hand, one finger at a time, to the left and replaced his left foot with his right. Now he felt with his left foot. A long narrow slab of rock jutted out from the wall—enough for the toe of his boot. He shifted his weight to the left. The slab tilted. Scrambling with his right foot, he searched for his previous foothold. The slab broke loose and his left foot came free of the face of the cliff. He heard the piece clatter down, bouncing off the rocks below. Now, hanging by his hands, Axel felt frantically with both feet for a foothold.

To his left, at knee level, there was a slight projection—not good, but all there was. He swung to the right to gain momentum, then flung his left leg up and caught the small dimple of stone with his foot. When he moved his weight over to where his boot had purchase and searched upward for a new handhold, he realized his hands were wet and slipping on the lichen-covered stone. His body was slung hammock-like between his hand-hold and the one projection he had found with his left foot.

In front of Axel's face was a vertical crack. He could see into it for ten inches or so. It looked to him as if there might be a break in the stone about five inches in on the left side of the large crack. If he let go with his right hand and jammed it into the crack to find out if it would give him a place to hold to, he would have no way to regain his position. He had to do something soon. His hands were slipping, and his leg was beginning to cramp. When he let go with his right hand, all his weight would be shifted to his left foot and his left hand. He had just a moment to find a hold with his right hand; he couldn't stay this way for longer than seconds. Letting go with his cramping right hand, he rammed it hard into the crack, felt along the face of the rough stone and found the split he had counted on. He bent his fingers around it and could relax his numb left hand. It was enough to hold him.

The crack in the face of the cliff got wider the higher it went. Axel was able to climb the crack, hand over hand. When he was high enough so that he could put a boot into the crack and carry some of his weight on his left leg, the climb eased somewhat. Bracing himself against the interior of the split, he swung his right foot to the crack and wedged it in. His whole body was shaking with the strain of the last few minutes. He could relax.

Now that Axel was able to put both feet into the crack and wedge them in, it was much easier to push himself upward. Soon he lifted himself onto the next ledge. He rested in the shade of an overhang. When he was able to breathe easily, he became aware that he had been breathing in a foul odor. It reminded him of the time he had come upon a dog that had died and had been lying rotting in the sun.

Once he felt ready, he began the climb to the final ledge. The higher he went, the worse the odor became and the louder the humming. Near the cliff's top he could see clouds of swirling black dots. The smell now was so bad that he tried to breathe through the cloth of his shirt, but it didn't help.

He continued the climb breathing through his mouth. A bit higher and the humming turned to buzzing, and its volume steadily increased. Thirty feet below the ledge, he could tell that the dots were large black and green flies, and at ten feet below, he was in the midst of a cloud of them. He now had to breathe with his teeth clenched together to keep them out of his mouth.

Gagging at the smell, he pulled himself up to the shelf but stopped when he could see over the edge. Directly in front of him was the dark entrance to a cave. The flies were massed around the opening, and the air vibrated with their buzzing. Turning his head to the right, he saw, in a patch of sunlight, the huge dragon. Its head was facing him—the largest animal Axel had ever seen. Its eyes were shut. Warming itself in the sun, he thought—but the sweat on his shirt felt cold.

Its dark green scales glinted in the sunlight, and its short ears lay flat against its skull. Just above two long, yellow teeth, one on each side in the front of its mouth, were its two nostrils—black and hairy ovals. They were set high on the end of its long head, and they flared with each breath as it slept.

Never has there been a more evil creature. There aren't many men alive who have been this close to one of these. Even asleep it looks powerful and dangerous . Its huge leathery wings, which were folded close to its body, were supported by massive muscles at its shoulders and chest. *It needs large wings to lift that weight.* One front foot was outstretched, and the claws were extended from the pad much as a cat might unsheathe its nails. It shifted its weight in its sleep, and Axel could see the huge muscles of its haunches bunch and flex. He heard its claws cut into the stone of the ledge as it tensed before relaxing again. When it settled back, blowing a long sigh, small puffs of smoke drifted upwards from its nostrils, and its black tongue slid between its thin, closed lips to test the air. Two feet of forked, snake-like flesh, twisted, shiny and wet, then slid back.

There was nothing Axel wanted more than to back down the cliff. He had had no idea what it would be like to face one of these beasts this closely. In his imaginings, dragons were bad, but not like this. This was a horror. The flies, the stink, and the size of the thing. He asked himself, *Do I need money this badly?. . .Is it worth it?. . .Will I end up in the cave, covered with flies, ripening for this beast? Would there be a way for anyone to survive an attack by this thing?—Even with my knowledge of the way dragons use fire, it has to be impossible.* He could see himself thrown off the ledge, burned and screaming, all the way down to where Winthton was.

Yes. It's worth it. I'm committed. I've told Molly I was

going to kill dragons, and if I don't try with this one, I'll never have courage enough to face another, or maybe anything else—ever again.

Watching the dragon to make sure that its eyes were still closed, he very slowly hoisted himself onto the ledge. Creeping around the beast, and being careful where he put each foot, he moved so that he stood in front of the cave. Batting the flies away from his face, he watched the dragon sleep. He didn't really want to, but he knew he had to wake it up. But how? He glanced around the shelf. *If I could find a stick I could hit it and wake it up. No, that wouldn't work because I wouldn't be able to nock the arrow and light it in time, and I'd be too close to the dragon. If I throw the stick. . .but there aren't any sticks up here.*

There were bones in front of the mouth of the cave. Some had been there long enough to be white and clean looking. Some still had clumps and shards of meat clinging to them and were covered with flies and crawling with white maggots.

He reached back and took a cloth-wrapped arrow from his quiver, poured oil over it and lit it. After he had unslung the bow and nocked the arrow, he held them both in his left hand. Dark smoke rose from the arrow and it smelled, but it was much better than the smell from the cave. He picked up one of the cleaner bones. It looked to be a leg bone from a large animal like a cow or horse. His plan was to throw it at the dragon. It would wake up, see him and take in air, preparing to fight with fire.

He wondered where the best place would be to hit a dragon to wake it up. *What a spot to be in. Here I am hundreds of feet in the air on the side of this mountain trying to wake up a dragon and wondering where to tap it. I don't want to make this dragon mad. Maybe we could talk it over and come to some solution good for both of us. There's got to be something better than this.*

Axel threw the bone. It arched through the sun, twisting in its flight, and hit the beast on the side of the head then clattered to the stone shelf. The dragon slept. Axel felt relief, and he thought that that wasn't so bad. *If the dragon wants to sleep and I want to go home, there's no problem. I can just go home and tell Molly I tried to wake up a dragon and it wanted to sleep so we won't be able to get married after all.*

Axel reached into his shirt and found the scrap of cloth Molly had given him. Rubbing it lightly between his fingers, he surprised himself by saying, "No," right out loud. Axel put the scrap of cloth back and picked up another bone and threw it as hard as he could at the dark green head. It hit the dragon near the end of its nose and rolled to the edge of the shelf. The dragon didn't move.

Axel watched the sleeping beast through a veil of flies droning in the sunlight until one of the scaly lids slowly opened, and a giant yellow eye stared at him. The vertical, black slit of its pupil contracted sharply in the bright sunlight. The lid lowered again; a moment passed, then abruptly both eyes came fully open. It stopped breathing. Axel could see its muscles ripple as it tensed itself. He pulled back the bowstring as the beast raised its narrow head on its long neck. With a strange grace for so big an animal, it stood on its four feet. Axel's muscles locked with fear.

This thing was more terrible than he had ever imagined it might be. It never took its eyes off Axel's face but slowly moved to the cliff's edge, opened and then flapped its wings once and waited for Axel to move. He couldn't. Slowly the dragon lifted its body and stood on its hind legs, baring its chest. Axel realized that it was trying to get him to attack. But, it had also blocked his escape down the cliff. *I wonder if it did that on purpose so I couldn't get away.*

Now it lowered itself and stamped its front feet, one at a time, on the stone of the ledge. The sound echoed from the interior of the cave and sent out dark clouds of flies. Axel stood still and stared at its eyes. He didn't dare move. He didn't want it to charge him. He remembered Sidney had told him that they bluff first. That was what it must be doing. Bluffing.

The beast began to thrash its tail, like an angry cat might. Axel could feel the muscles in his neck ache from the strain of looking so sharply upward, and his arm was beginning to shake from holding the bow pulled fully back.

The rag was burning out, pieces of it had been falling from the end of the arrow. In a moment it would go out, then if the dragon took in air, he would have no way to kill it. He would become its next meal. Cooked. The last of the oil burned. The fire died. The blackened end of the arrow smoked. The dragon lowered its head.

Axel dropped the arrow when he turned and ran into the darkness of the cave. For the first dozen or so yards, he could avoid the bones and rotted meat, but the cave abruptly turned to the left, and the light was cut off. He could feel his boots step on things that felt soft and some that were hard and rattled away when he kicked them.

Axel knew he had reached the back of the cave when he ran into it. He bounced against the rough stone and heard the oil flask break as he fell. He turned on his back and looked toward the dark corner that led to the opening. He expected that the beast would follow him into the cave, and if it had, it would be on him now. He could see the light reflecting off the stone at the turn in the wall, but there was no movement. It was still out there waiting for him. But if he had no oil, he would die up here for sure. With shaking hands he took another wrapped arrow and hurriedly wiped it around in the bottom of his pack. The smell of oil was just strong enough to detect in the overpowering stench of the cave, but there was enough caught in the creases of his pack for him to dampen the cloth on the arrow. He now had one chance. Axel put the flint between his teeth, held the fireboard in his left hand, placed a firestick in the hole, nocked the arrow and felt his way toward the front of the cave.

Lucky for me it didn't follow me in here. If it had, I wouldn't have a chance. It doesn't need to come after me, though. There's no other way out. It can just wait out there for as long as it wants to. I'd have to come out to it, sooner or later.

When he got to the turn in the cave, he could see the silhouette of the beast at the entrance. Axel didn't know how well dragons could see in the dark, but, because it was standing in the bright light, it might not be able to see him at all. What do I do now? he wondered.

Sidney had told him that most experts thought that dragons were cowards. If this were true, he might be able to use it. If the beast couldn't see him, and didn't know where he was, he might be able to scare it. *Good thinking, Axel. The dragon weighs maybe twenty times what you do, it's at the entrance to its own cave, you're trapped inside, it can kill you easily and you only have an idea of how to kill it, and you think of scaring it?*

Axel knew he had to do something. He couldn't stay in the cave. He released the tension on the bow and felt around until his hand found a bone on the floor. It was one of the newer ones. He could feel the wetness of rotting meat. He crept closer to the entrance. *The beast could be facing me or looking out over the valley. There's no way to be sure. All I can see is its black outline against the brightness of the sky.*

He tossed the bone past the black rounded shape and over the edge of the cliff. The dragon turned its body as the bone sailed over. The dragon had seen it, but Axel still couldn't make out the head. He found another bone and threw it. The dragon watched it fall, then turned toward the cave; Axel could see the head but it disappeared again in the blackness of the silhouette. Axel felt along the floor and found a large piece of meat. It was slimy and covered with flies which rose in clouds around him when he picked it up. He could feel the maggots crawling on his hand, and he yelled in horror as he threw it past the dragon. It twisted in the sunlight as it cleared the edge and fell out of sight.

The dragon looked down at the falling meat, slowly turned toward its cave and roared in a long bellow of anger. Axel could tell it was facing him now for the sound filled the cave and the pressure of it hurt his ears.

He sure had the beast's attention, but he knew it had to be enraged to use its fire. Axel felt for more things to throw, and his hand hit metal. With his fingers running over it, he could tell it was a shield. *Some knight died up here trying to kill this thing* . Careful not to make noise and give his position away, he picked up the round shield and spun it toward the entrance. It sailed out of the opening, spinning in the sunlight. The dragon turned and watched it all the way to the rocks below. *That's better.*

Axel had learned that dragons like to collect things, and that might have been a prize. His hand found a helmet. When he thrust his hand into the face opening, his fingers fit into what felt like the eye holes of the skull that had been trapped in the metal shell. He took a short run and flung the helmet out of the entrance. This time Axel could see the dragon's head as it turned and watched the helmet fall to the ledges below. That must have infuriated the beast. It stomped its feet, screamed in rage and lowered its head.

Do it now. He put the fireboard on the stone floor of the cave and struck the steel with the flint. The firestick caught and he pushed it onto the rag tied to the arrow. The oil flamed. Over the sound of the flies, he could hear the wet whistle as the beast drew air into its meth stomach.

Axel pulled back on the bow. *But, where's the head?* The beast was still in silhouette, and he could see only its body outline. Its tail was lying in the sunlight and was lashing back and forth on the ledge, scattering bones, but he couldn't see the head. *It must be lower than its back. Sidney had said they need to lower their heads to draw in air.* It was doing that now, for he could still hear air being sucked in, but it wouldn't be doing it much longer. In a moment it would have enough air in its stomach to fill the inside of the cave with flame.

I have to see the head. I have one shot. I'm out of oil, and this is the only chance I'm going to get. He ran to the far side of the cave. With this new angle he could just make out the beast's open mouth against the light at the entrance. He aimed and shot in one movement. The arrow created a sparkling bright line as it streaked through the cave's darkness. He had shot just as the beast was taking in the last of its air. Its jaws closed on the arrow. Axel could hear the snap of the shaft as its teeth crushed down.

Axel was thinking that he had fired too late when he was

blown off his feet and hurled against the wall at the bend in the cave.

He wasn't sure how long he had been out, but he felt it must have been for quite some time, because there was no sign of the dragon when he was able to stand and look toward the light at the mouth of the cave. The sun was still hitting the ledge, and if the beast were there, it would be easy to see. A number of thoughts ran through his mind. *Does it think I'm dead and did it go off somewhere?. . .Did it get scared of the fire I shot at it?. . .Is it waiting for me just around the corner of the opening?. . .Did I die?*

He no longer had the bow, and he couldn't see well enough to look for it, but he was lying on the fireboard. Moving carefully and making no noise, Axel crept to the mouth of the cave. There were more pieces of meat and bones lying around than he remembered. *I must have been out for a long time. The dragon has flown out and killed another animal and scattered these pieces here from its feeding. If I'm quick, I may be able to get out while it's gone.* He hurried to the sunlight.

On the ledge in front of the cave Axel saw pieces of what had to be a dragon, for they were covered with large scales. Either this one or another one. He had never heard that they kill and eat each other.

There were scales, claws, large pieces of flesh, teeth and bones scattered over the entire shelf. He stepped into the sunlight. There were gouts of blood and large pieces of flesh all around the entrance and even some on the face of the cliff that went up past the opening. When he looked down at himself, he saw that he too was covered with blood and smaller pieces of flesh. It wasn't his; he wasn't cut or wounded as far as he could tell.

It must be that the dragon blew up, he thought . *How could that be? Meth gas and air mixed in its stomach. I shot fire into its mouth as it was breathing in. It sucked the fire down and. . .that's the last I remember.*

He looked down to where he had last seen Winthton. It looked like his friend was looking up at him. *Pieces of dragon must have landed all around him. He must think I'm really something. I blow up dragons.* After picking up two teeth and putting them in his pack, Axel started the long climb down. It took the rest of the day for the new dragonslayer to reach the ground.

10

Even Before There Was Small Print

By the time Axel was able to work his way down to the lowest shelf of the cliff, it was early evening, and heavy shadows covered the ground where he had left Winthton. He had to feel his way down the last hundred feet because it was too dark to see any hand holds or places to put his boots. When he finally stepped off the last stone riser, it was fully dark at the base of the mountain.

He knew Winthton would be close. "Winthton?" There was no response. "Winthton, where are you?" Axel felt his way among the huge stones. "Winthton?"

He thought that his donkey must have gone back to Tightly without him. With his back against one of the boulders, he looked up to the top of the mountain. He could just make out its dark shape against the last light in the sky. At least he didn't have to carry anything except his sword and the small fireboard back down with him. He thought that his bow might have been shattered; at least it was lost and the arrows and oil bottle were gone.

His ear was being lipped. Axel threw his arms around his donkey's neck and yelled, "Winthton. I knew you wouldn't leave. You should have seen it. I killed the dragon. It's up there all over the ledge and cave. When I shot the arrow, I wasn't sure if it would work, but it blew that beast up. Some of it must have come over the edge of the cliff. Did you see any pieces?" Axel couldn't stop hanging on to Winthton's neck or stop telling about the killing. After he had told Winthton most of the story and no longer felt his legs shake, he let go and could hold his hand out in front of him and keep it steady.

"We'll get you a back pack, a new blanket, a feed bag and I'll buy that bow and some new arrows in the blacksmith's shop. How much gold do you think would balance an egg? There ought to be enough to get a new sword, too."

The two friends made their way by moonlight back over the hills to Tightly. The whole way Axel talked about the killing. He told Winthton over and over again about the bow shot, the blow-up, the mess, and what the dragon looked like. He tried to make noises like the dragon had made. He even got down on his hands and knees on the path, and in the moonlight, pretended he was the dragon so that Winthton would understand what the dragon had done.

Winthton didn't act as if he were interested, but that was just the way he was, and it didn't keep Axel from even more detailed descriptions. By the time they reached the road that snaked into town, they could see the buildings were dark, and Axel remembered that the town shut up early. Axel opened the doors to the blacksmith shop, and the faint glow from the forge gave enough light for him to find a lamp. As soon as he had given Winthton water and grain, he threw himself onto a pile of straw and was asleep by the time he shut his eyes. He slept till after dawn the next day.

Axel woke to the sound of voices coming from the light

at the front of the shop. "That dumb beast must have come back by itself in the night."

"Could we sell it?"

"We could, but the priest would want the money. He'd say he was saving it in case the boy comes back."

"Will we have to feed it then?"

"Can't let it starve. We could take the feed bill from what we end up selling it for."

Axel rose from the straw and Hammer saw him first. "Look, the boy come back. He must not a found the cave."

Axel felt very sore and stiff as he walked from the darkness at the back of the shop toward the light and the two men. "The dragon is dead. I killed it yesterday afternoon," he said.

"You killed the dragon?" Hammer asked, his voice rising until it was almost a screech.

Axel stepped into the light and closer to the two men near the doorway. "Yes, it's dead. I let myself in, in the night. I hope you don't mind."

The old blacksmith walked around Axel looking him over carefully. "You don't look so bad," he said. When he grabbed Axel to turn him, he felt the crusted blood on his tunic. "Your hair is burnt, and there's a lot of blood on your clothes. You aren't hurt are you?"

"My ears stopped ringing, so I guess I'm all right."

Hammer followed the old man around Axel. He touched the blood and smelled his finger. "He couldn't a done it. He's just a kid. He's lying. We don't have to pay him. If he got to the cave, he'd be dead now, and he's not dead," and Hammer pushed at Axel with his fingertips.

The old man stepped in front of Axel and looked into his eyes. "Did you bring back any teeth?" Axel could hear the laugh starting in Hammer's stomach. Turning to the pack that he had left near the pile of straw, he took out the two large teeth he had found in the cave. Returning to the light and the two men, he held them out on his palms. There were blood and bits of flesh on them, and they appeared to have been torn out of the dragon with great force.

The blacksmith touched the teeth with a finger, pushing them slightly so they moved on Axel's palm, and said, "Hammer, run and get the priest." Hammer left the shop, backing out, still looking at Axel's clothes and hair.

After Hammer had left, the blacksmith said to Axel, "Boy, if the priest says you killed the dragon, we'll have to pay you. That's a lot of money." He backed away from Axel and looked him up and down. "Are you hungry? We got some food we brought for lunch. You want it?"

Axel was well along with the food when Hammer and the priest walked into the shop. The priest went directly to the blacksmith without paying any attention to Axel, who was sitting on a box eating a piece of bread. "Show me the teeth."

The blacksmith motioned with his head and said, "The boy's got 'em." The old priest turned to Axel and held out his hand.

Axel stuffed the rest of the bread into his mouth and dug into his pack, saying, "I only brought two. I could have taken more, but I wanted to get down before it got too dark." He stood and handed the two bloody teeth to the priest.

They were so large that the priest had to hold them with both hands when he walked out into the light of the doorway to examine them. The larger was almost eight inches long, jagged and sharply pointed. The priest looked at the blacksmith and said, "Dragon's teeth all right. No question about that. The flesh is fresh, and the blood is dried but it looks new. No way he could have taken these from a live dragon." He turned and walked toward Axel until his face was very close. "How'd you get these, boy?" He looked closely into Axel's eyes as he returned the teeth.

"I brought them from the dragon's cave. I took them after I killed it. It sure was big. I didn't think at first I'd be able to kill it." He turned and said to the blacksmith, "I'll buy that bow with some of the gold."

The priest motioned for the blacksmith to follow him, and they walked outside. Stepping close to Axel, Hammer asked, "How'd you kill it? Tell me. Did it shoot fire? Is that how you burnt your hair? Was there bones in the cave?"

While Axel was telling Hammer what the dragon looked like and about the cave, the two old men returned. The blacksmith then took Hammer outside. The priest turned to Axel. "I'll have to keep the teeth, you know. When we pay you, the teeth will belong to the temple. You must not want what does not belong to you. You must not ask for what others have. You must take only what you have earned. Give the teeth to me." He held out his hand. Axel gave the two teeth back to the priest. When the blacksmith returned, he was alone. He looked at the priest, and Axel saw him nod. *He must have sent Hammer for the gold.* The priest stood close enough to Axel for him to again smell the old man's breath. He smiled as he asked, "Did the blacksmith tell you how we would pay you?"

"Yes, he did. He said the reward would be enough gold to balance an egg."

The priest smiled tightly and said, "That's right. We'll use a scale. We'll put an egg on one side and enough gold on the other to balance it. That is the agreement. The good people of this town have trusted me to keep the gold and to see that it is paid as a reward." He leaned even closer and said, "You trust men of the gods, don't you?"

"Oh, yes, I trust you."

"That is wise." He pulled at the thong around his neck. "Do not waste your trust. Do not place your trust falsely. Do not ask for trust you cannot give. I have chosen the egg."

Turning to the back of the shop, Axel said. "There are eggs back in the straw. I felt one this morning when I got up. I can get it now." He started toward the back of the shop.

The priest spoke sharply, "No. I have chosen the egg. We will balance the gold with an egg I choose. That is the way it is done in this town, and it is what the people in this town want."

Axel turned to face the priest and said, "That seems fair to me. I trust you."

"You're a good boy." He put his hand on Axel's shoulder. It didn't feel like his father's hand had felt or even like Sidney's hand. "I like you, son." The thin lips smiled again. "Now remember, if there had been two dragons, I would let you choose the second egg, so you can see I am a fair man. After all, the gold belongs to the town. It is not mine. I am only doing the town's work. . .and the work of the gods, of course."

"Thank you." Axel turned to the blacksmith and asked, "Can I look at the bow now?"

Hammer returned while Axel was examining the bow. He said in a high and excited voice, "I found one. Look here." He held his palm near the priest's face.

After looking in Hammer's hand, the priest said, "You did well, Hammer. Now get the scale and we will balance the gold." He untied a small bag that had been hanging from his waist and bounced it in his hand while they waited for Hammer to return. Axel watched the bag and wondered how much it might weigh.

Carefully, Hammer placed a very small scale on the anvil and stood back, a large smile on his face. "There's the scale. Now we can pay the dragonslayer."

Axel still had the bow in his hand and walked with it to the anvil. There was a small metal bowl on each end of the balance arm. In the center of the shaft was a pointer, and just below that there was the balance mark. The priest placed a very small egg in one dish. The pointer hardly moved at all as that dish settled just slightly lower than the one on the other end of the arm. He opened the bag and took a small, very thin coin and set it in the other dish. The pointer settled back on the mark. He turned to Axel and said, "Does it look balanced to you, boy?"

Axel couldn't believe what was happening. When the blacksmith had told him about the reward, he had been holding a chicken's egg. Axel had been sure that was what they would use to balance against the gold. This looks like a songbird's egg, a thrush maybe, he thought.

The fear he had felt at the mouth of the cave came back to him. Was he being cheated? To give himself time to think, he knelt and examined the scale carefully. The pointer was centered on the mark. He touched the dish that held the egg, and it swung down then rose slowly back again. The pointer settled on the mark. He looked up at the priest and said, "Yes, it's balanced. Is *that* the reward for killing your dragon?"

The priest was tying the bag to his waist. "That's what we agreed on wasn't it, enough gold to balance an egg?" Axel stood and now the priest looked up at him. "That was the trust the townspeople gave me. They gave of their gold to rid themselves of that devil dragon. I held the gold. The blacksmith was selected to pay. You have earned the gold. We are happy for you, son."

The priest reached up and put both his hands on Axel's shoulders and looking into his eyes said, "Spend wisely what you must spend. Spend not that which you do not have at hand. Ask not to buy that for which you have not the price. Take your gold."

Axel turned to the blacksmith and found that he had trouble talking as he asked, "How much do you want for this bow and a quiver of arrows?"

The old man reached out to the scale and took the small coin. "This will be enough for the weapon and the food for you and your donkey."

The priest was looking hard at the blacksmith as Axel left the shop. While he was untying Winthton, Axel looked back into the dark shop and saw the gold piece being passed to the priest. Axel took hold of Winthton's lead and said to him, "Come on, Winthton. We have a longer way to go than I thought we did."

Leading Winthton out of town, Axel played back what had happened and tried to think of what he could have done to make it come out the way he thought it should have. He knew that what had happened wasn't right, but there wasn't anything he could think that he had done wrong or what to do about it now. He had kept his part of the bargain, and the priest did what he had said he would. So he hadn't really been cheated. And a priest wouldn't do that. He wasn't sure what had happened, but he knew that things hadn't turned out the way he expected they would. He didn't feel good about the reward, but he didn't know how to put it into words.

Maybe this is just the way people are, he thought. I'll have to learn to be very careful of what I agree to.

When Axel got to the edge of town where the road forked and where he and Hammer had turned to take the path up to the mountain, he turned and looked back. The blacksmith and Hammer were standing in the road watching him.

"We'll know more about how to deal with people next time, Winthton." He threw the lead rope over Winthton's back and looked again at his new bow.

11

Axel Two, Dragons Zip

For eight days Axel traveled north on his way to Highcliff. If he were to make any money he would have to find the dragon the three men he had met in the mountains had told him about. For the last four days he had met no one who was going his way, toward Highcliff, but the closer he got to the town, the more people he met who were leaving. There were single men riding on farm horses and families with carts and wagons. Some were even walking, pushing hand-carts.

It looks like all of these people have had a really bad time of it. I'm very lucky to still be alive, but when I get to town, I'll have to be a lot more careful about the reward money. I've sure learned not to be so trusting and to think about what people tell me they'll do.

An old woman and a very young boy were sitting at the side of the road, their hand-cart piled high with the few belongings they could take with them. Axel stopped, and leaning down, said to the woman, "Is your cart broken?"

The woman didn't hear him; at least she didn't react in any way to him looking closely into her face and speaking to her. The young boy was sucking his finger but watched Axel closely. Axel knelt next to the boy and said to him, "Is this your grandmother?" There was no response. "Are you all right?" The boy looked at Axel's face and continued to suck his finger. Axel rose and looked toward the town, thinking that there could be help for these poor people that might come along, but the road was empty for as far as he could see. In the other direction, there was a wagon just going out of sight around a bend in the road. He didn't want to leave the old woman and young boy sitting there, but he didn't know how he could help them. He had no money to give them, and he couldn't just give up his efforts to save Molly to help them go the way he had just come. Axel felt bad about it but took Winthton's lead and walked on toward Highcliff. Turning once, he looked back down the road and saw the woman and boy pulling the cart. He felt better about them.

While he was still many miles from town, he began to see abandoned farms. The small houses, with their doors left open and clothing and furniture scattered in the yards, looked as if they had been deserted in a hurry. The fields hadn't been plowed and had gone to weeds, and the barns attached to the backs and sides of the houses were open and empty.

Near the end of that day, Axel realized that it was strangely quiet in the countryside. No dogs ran to bark at him as he passed. There were no children at play. As the shadows of the trees along the roadside grew long and fell darkly across his path, the valleys and hollows he walked through grew dim and damp. When the road turned downward, the air grew cooler, and there were patches of fog that covered the empty fields. Night came quickly in the summer. Axel reached back and took hold of Winthton's lead and walked beside him.

On the long slope up to Highcliff, Axel saw, in the dim distance, a man walking toward him. He could just make out the man's shape against the shadows cast by the large bushes which now lined both sides of the roadway. Axel was in even deeper shadow, for he was much lower than the approaching man, and there were layers of fog that rose as high as his chest. He had just turned to say something to Winthton when he heard the man scream. He quickly looked up and thought he saw the man waving his arms about in the air.

A much larger dark shadow lowered itself down onto the road. Axel couldn't see what was happening, but he was sure the man was in some kind of trouble. He jerked on Winthton's lead and at the same time pulled out his sword. It was then that he heard another cry. This time it didn't sound like the man but was much louder and higher in pitch. A long screech. Axel began to run. When he was close enough to have thrown a stone and hit the spot, he heard a great leathery rustling, and a thumping sound beat against his body. The sky was now a bit lighter than the roadway, and against it, he could see large wings beat the air and the tail thrash against the ground as the dragon rose. The man's body, held by talons, dangled below. Very soon the dragon and its meal were lost in the darkness and fog. When he got to the place of the attack, he found a torn sack with its contents scattered across the road.

Axel entered Highcliff in the dark, but he could tell that it was much smaller than Tightly. It had a temple in its center and a few shops on each side of the street, but there were none of the large buildings that had given Tightly the feeling of a city. Even though it was still early evening, the towns-people had shut up for the night. He could see thin bars of light from some of the houses, but there were no people on the street, and all the windows in town were shuttered or boarded up.

Axel found the livery stable and beat on the door. The sound, echoing off the low buildings across from him, was loud in the deserted street. A soft voice came from behind the tall, wooden door. "What do you want?"

Axel pressed his face close to the rough wood. "Feed for Winthton and a bed for myself."

"Come to the side door."

Axel left Winthton by the front of the building and went down between the stable and the small shack next to it. There was no door. It must be on the other side, he thought, and went back to the front and down the far side. He found the door open and a short man waiting for him, dark against the light within. The man sounded impatient. "What kept—Where is—Come in."

When he stepped into the light, Axel could see the man's features. He was full faced, and his skin was wrinkled and dirty. His hair was coarse and his eyebrows grew with no pattern, large brushes over his eyes. "No good time to be looking for a—Well, you're here now, so I might as— Where's your friend?"

"Still in front."

"Call him back and—"

"He doesn't come when I call. Besides I can't whistle."

"He comes when you—"

"That's just it, he doesn't."

"Winston, you—"

"Winthton."

"What ever you call—He's hungry, and you—"

"Yes, oats if you have it for Winthton. We haven't eaten

125

much for days. Oh, he's had grass and stuff, but he needs his oats."

"Grass and oats?"

"And I'd like a place to sleep as well. I don't have much money. Just a dry corner will do."

The stableman had been peering up at Axel, and all this time he had been tipping his head from one side to the other like a dog which wants to understand something. "We don't get many strangers—not since the trouble—everybody leaving town and take—of course, you and your friend can—go and get—" The short man opened the door and motioned Axel out.

Axel said, "I'll be right back." He heard the door shut firmly behind him as he felt along the dark alley to the front of the building. Winthton was waiting where he had been left. Axel led him between the buildings and tapped on the door. It opened at once. The man must have been waiting for them.

The short man spoke through the doorway. "I wondered where—A donkey—Where's the friend you—"

"This is Winthton. And, you're right. He's a good friend to have. We're dragonfighters."

"Dragonfighters? Come in. Oh, come in. Bring Winthton with you. Come in. Hello Winthton. Welcome. We've been hoping that—I'll get the town elders and we'll—You wait right—I'll be back in—"

Taking a lantern from a hook on the wall, the very happy man slipped out the door and pushed it shut behind him.

Axel led Winthton to a stall and gave him a pail of water and a bag of oats. Very shortly the man returned with four others. The five of them crowded around Axel, eager for news and eager to tell news to him.

"Dragon fighter, these are the—"

"Young man, we need your services."

"We can pay well."

"Lots of dragonfighters have been—"

"We'll give you all the help we can."

Axel was overwhelmed. He held up his hands until they calmed down and waited for him to speak. "I'll help you get rid of the dragon. I saw it kill a man on the road outside of town."

"Who was it?"

"Did you get to see—?"

"Did it carry him off?"

Axel asked if the stableman had any food. All five began to talk again at once, planning on what they could get Axel to eat. Finally, one man left to go to his house and return with food. While they waited, the men told him what the last three years had been like. The dragon had been killing livestock until the farmers could no longer work their farms and make a living. They had all left the area now. The only people still in Highcliff were a few older ones who had no place else to go and some of the townspeople, like the merchants. Life had been very hard for them this last year. They had posted a lookout on top of the temple during the day to give warning if the dragon approached, but there was nothing they could do to protect themselves at night except stay indoors. Last year the dragon had started taking people when the livestock ran out. The man on the road that Axel had seen killed, they were sure, had been Walter, who had lost first his farm, then his children. His wife had died of grief just this last week. The men felt he wanted to die. There wasn't anything else left for him.

When Axel had heard most of the stories at least once, he

asked, "What of the reward?"

"That's all we—"

"Enough gold to last a man a—"

"Almost all the money in town."

Axel learned that it was indeed a great deal of gold. It was being held by the village priest. That didn't sound so good to him. He told the men about his last experience with a priest. They assured him that their priest was honest and would pay him the reward. There was no way that he could be tricked, even if the priest wanted to. The gold was kept on the platform by the altar. The holy stones were kept on one side, and the gold was kept on the other.

Axel frowned, "Holy stones?"

The youngest of the four elders spoke up for the first time. "Yes, we been buying 'em for as long as any of us can remember. It used to be that we bought 'em for good fortune. Lately we've been buying 'em to keep the dragon away from our homes. They've worked for some of us."

"And not worked for—"

"Where do the stones come from?"

"The priest finds them for us."

"And charges you for them?"

"Of course not. He's a good priest."

Axel felt relief and said, "He gives them to you free. That's good of him. I could trust a man who would do that."

The man who seemed to be the leader of the group said, "He wouldn't just give them away. Then they wouldn't be worth anything."

That sounded to Axel more like what he had come to expect. "How much do you have to give for them?"

"There's no price. It's just whatever the priest thinks we could afford to donate to the temple. No set amount. It used to be that only the better families were offered the chance to get them, but lately none of us have any money left. They're pretty easy to come by now."

Axel wasn't so happy now about the arrangement with the priest paying him. This didn't sound so much different than in Tightly. "Where do they come from?"

The tall man spoke, "The priest collects them. He knows which kinds are best. It used to be he collected them down near the sea. Since the dragon's been here, he's been getting them from his garden."

Axel asked many questions that night before he got so sleepy that he had to ask the men if they could continue in the morning. He told them he would kill their dragon in the next day or two.

Axel and Winthton rested. Axel spent most of the next day listening to stories about dragon killings in the area. Because he was so careful when he told about his method of slaying dragons, he had the feeling that they didn't think he had ever killed one. He knew he didn't look like a successful dragonkiller, but that didn't bother him. It seemed to bother the people in the town, though. In the morning, after they were over the excitement of having a dragonkiller promise to kill their dragon for them, they had a good chance to look him over carefully.

They saw a very young man, a boy really. He didn't even shave, or need to. He had long hair that he tied back with a piece of twine. His eyes were clear and a light green. His body was strong looking, but he wasn't built like a fighter. His slender arms and legs were long, not stocky and muscled as they might have expected.

During the course of the day, Axel began to understand the thinking of the people in the town. They didn't tell him outright what they thought, but from the questions they asked him and the answers they gave him to his questions, he began to see a pattern. If the dragon were to kill him, that would mean that it wouldn't have to take someone else who lived here. All in all, the people left in town couldn't lose. If by some chance, he were to kill the dragon—well then, they had the reward already collected and the town could come to life again. Besides, with the dragon gone, some of the farms that had been abandoned were good pieces of land. The people who used to own them were dead now, or gone. Land without owners isn't good for anything. Yes, Axel thought, the good people of this town are truly glad I have come to help.

Late that evening they took him to the temple where he met the priest, and Axel had the feeling that the priest had heard about him and his coming to kill the dragon. He was much different than Axel had expected. This man was large and enjoyed life. He laughed at strange times, almost as if he knew something funny that the rest of the town didn't know about. Axel liked him. The town elders liked the priest, too. He could tell that by the way they looked at the large man and the way they stood close to him when they talked to him.

The priest invited Axel in to look at the reward. Made of large field stones, the temple was cool and dim inside. Axel felt good in the old building, somehow secure. On a platform at the far end of the long, open room, under a large window, there was an altar. The priest urged Axel to follow him, and he led him and the men to the platform. He pointed to a small leather bag on one side of the altar. "On this side we have the temple's holy stones. Special stones selected by the temple and blessed by me to give good fortune and to keep away evil. Like the dragon."

Leaning over, Axel examined the leather bag. "May I see a stone?"

"Of course you can," laughed the priest.

Axel opened the bag. There were a number of smooth stones the size of a child's thumb. He looked up at the priest. "These have been blessed?"

"I did it myself, so I know they are holy."

Axel picked out one of the stones and held it in the palm of his hand. He looked at the group of men and saw they were watching him closely. He rubbed the stone with his thumb for a moment, and then he put it back in the bag and smiled at the priest as he handed the bag to him. "I understand the reward is kept right here in the temple, is that right?"

The priest chuckled, "The safest place in the world." He pointed to the other side of the altar. The men moved that way. "That is where we keep the gold for the reward. Have a look at it if you like. It may soon belong to you." He took Axel's arm and steered him to the other side of the altar. The men crowded around closely.

On that side there was another small bag that looked very much like the first one. Axel knelt and untied the leather cord and looked inside. The men leaned in to look. The bag contained a small pile of gold coins. But a fortune. There would be enough money here to buy the farm and all the stock he would need. He looked up at the priest. "This is the reward for killing the dragon?"

The priest nodded, then laughed again. "All of it, young man. It all goes to the one who can kill the dragon. There have been a number who have tried. They are dead now." He laughed.

"Who oversees the payment?"

The priest spread his hands, "Not me. One of the town elders can do that. We all trust each other here in Highcliff." He looked at the ring of elders for confirmation. Most of them nodded.

"What proof do you need that the dragon is dead?"

There was a moment when no one moved, then the priest smiled. "What do you suggest?"

"I usually bring back teeth."

The priest looked again at the elders. They talked amongst themselves a moment, then the liveryman said, "That will be— We could accept teeth to— Good."

Axel tied the bag up again and stood. He couldn't think of any way there could be a misunderstanding about what was being said and what it meant, but he wanted to be sure. He was facing the priest, who was standing in front of the altar looking out over his temple. He said slowly and clearly, loudly enough for all to hear him, "If I kill the dragon and bring back teeth to you, then you will give me the bag on the left side of the altar?" When the priest smiled and nodded, Axel said, "I will kill your dragon in the morning." As the group turned to leave the temple, the priest gave him such a pat on the back that he almost tripped. He couldn't get his breath for a moment.

In a voice loud enough to fill the room, the priest said, "At noon the gold will be waiting here for you, young man."

As the men turned to leave, the priest took Axel's arm and held him back and speaking softly said, "You will be going into battle in the morning with a dangerous beast. I want you to have a holy stone for protection." He reached over and picked up the holy-stone bag and took from it a small stone which he held out to Axel. When Axel accepted it, the priest closed Axel's fingers over it and held his fist closed over the stone with his hand and said, "We must consider that you might not make it. It is possible that you could be killed. We would have expenses. Contacting your family. Possibly there might be something left that we would have to bury. Not a pretty thought, but men of responsibility have to think of these things."

"What are you saying I should do?"

"We usually like dragonfighters to leave their valuables with us. That way we can be sure they are sent to their families. I could keep anything you might have that you would like us to send on for you. . .if you don't come back."

Axel shook his head, smiled and said, "Thank you, but I've nothing of value. If the dragon kills me, you can have whatever's left, if you promise to take good care of Winthton."

"Who's that?"

"My donkey."

The priest laughed and said, "Of course I will, my boy." He turned and put the bag of stones back by the altar.

Axel watched him and said to himself, *I must not make a mistake this time. Let's see, the town will give me the bag on the left. I was facing the altar when the priest said that, so the bag with the gold must be the one on my left.* He felt he understood now. He felt good about the agreement.

They all left the temple. The priest stood on the steps and watched them walk to the livery. Just before they entered the big double doors, Axel turned and looked back at the temple. The priest was standing there in the long shadows made by the shops on the west side of the dusty street. When he saw Axel turn and look, he waved his hand, and Axel could hear him laugh; the sound was loud in the empty town. Axel told the elders that he wanted an early start in the morning. They left the stable as the sun was setting, and soon after that Axel blew out the lamp and lay in a corner on some clean straw, but he couldn't sleep.

There was something that was bothering him about the agreement for the reward, but he couldn't figure out what it was. Running the situation over and over in his mind, he remembered the words of the payment. He couldn't make a mistake again. Molly was counting on him. He had to be sure. *Let's see, The priest was facing the rows of seats and I was facing the altar. That's right, we were facing each other, and the bag with the gold was on the left. But that means that the priest's left would be my right. Does that mean that the priest will give me the bag on my left or on his left? Which side had the bag of gold? He could hear himself saying, "If I kill the dragon and bring back teeth to you, then you will give me the bag on the left side of the altar?"* In his mind, he could see again the smiling priest nodding his head. That was right, the bag on the left has the gold, but whose left? I have to make sure to protect myself and Molly. I have to get another look at the two bags on the altar.

Axel rose in the dark and felt his way out of the livery. There was faint moonlight between the buildings and along the dark street to the temple, and he was very alert to any sounds or movements. He keep looking toward the cloudy sky and into the black shadows cast by the buildings. A dull, yellow light shown from one of the windows near the back of the temple. He walked up the steps and tried to open the big front door, but it was locked. There was a path through the high weeds on the side of the temple, and Axel followed it until he was under the glowing window. The bottom of the sill was just above his head, too high for him to see in. Large stones lined the path from when the grounds were still being cared for. Piling four of these in a rough pyramid just below the window was enough. By standing on the pile and holding on to the bottom of the window he could lift himself and see inside.

The glass was dirty and the large room was dimly lit by a small lantern hanging on a hook in the back of the altar platform. He could just make out the two bags at the base of the altar, again thinking of right and left sides. A dark shape moved from the side door of the temple. *The priest was locking the doors. That's smart, even if these people trust each other, what with all that gold in the temple.* Stopping in front of the altar, the priest talked to himself and gestured with his hands. Axel watched carefully as the priest knelt and took a few of the small gold coins from the bag on one side of the altar and placed them carefully in the other bag. Then he switched bags. *Now the bag with the gold is on the right side when a person is facing the altar. The other bag on the left has the holy stones in it with a few gold coins on top of them. Strange.* Axel stepped off the pile of large rocks, replaced them along the path and returned to the stable.

It took Axel what felt like hours to get to sleep that night. He was sure that the townspeople were good people, and they sure liked and trusted their priest. But, he couldn't think of any good reason for the priest to exchange the leather bags. The only thing he was sure about was that he had to be very careful so that he didn't lose out again. *Gold is a wonderful thing. It shows what people are really like.*

This town had been named Highcliff because it had been built near the edge of the cliff, high above the ocean. The elders had told him that half-way down the cliff there was a cave that for years had been empty, but now the dragon lived in it. It was not hard to get to. In fact, the children of the village used to play there. There was a path down from the top that was wide enough for easy walking. There was even a shelf in front of the cave. On pleasant winter days the dragon would lie on that shelf, warming in the sun.

Axel didn't think that he would have any trouble with this dragon. He was prepared for the explosion now. When he shot the arrow, he would be in danger and would have to be behind something for protection. The important thing was for him to be there in the morning before the dragon left the cave. He wouldn't want to be surprised by it coming back and landing behind him. If he were on the shelf before the sun came up, he would be able to surprise it when it came out. The cave faced east, so the first light of the sun would shine into the interior. This should be easy. Still, he had to be very careful. Dragons were tricky.

He remembered Sidney telling him that they learn from each other. It didn't seem reasonable that this dragon could have learned about how the other dragon died—that it had blown up, and the dead dragon sure couldn't have told any other dragon what had happened, but this one might have found out somehow.

Axel asked one of the elders to wake him well before dawn, so that he was walking along the top of the cliff while it was still very dark. There was a light wind off the water that smelled of salt and seaweed and still had the feel of winter. The path along the very edge of the cliff was easy to see in the faint light from what was left of the setting moon. Ahead there was a break in the edge of the cliff, and when Axel got there, he could see the path that angled downward toward the sea. After walking down the winding path in the dark to where it grew much wider, he could see against the wall of the cliff a much darker area, and he knew he had come to the mouth of the cave.

Just inside the arch that rose over the entrance was a round boulder, as large as he was tall. Axel quietly stepped behind it and leaned against it, and it moved. That shouldn't be, he thought. Pushing against it, he found that it was strangely light and when he ran his fingers over it, he could feel holes in its porous surface. Axel knelt and waited behind it for first light. He was there for what seemed to him a very long time and grew used to the sound of the waves washing on the beach. The end of his arrow was wrapped in rags and soaked in oil. His new bow was strung, and the arrow was nocked in the bowstring. He was ready for the dragon.

Even though it was early summer, it was cold on the shelf, and Axel shivered from the damp air that ate through his cloak. He was sure he had arrived before the dragon had left the cave. But, he remembered the man on the road and that he had been attacked and carried off when it was dark. Axel kept looking behind him, out over the blackness that covered the sea.

A few stars were still visible and the sky behind him to the east was lighter, and he could see the horizon line: light gray against the black water. He watched for any movement on that line, for if the dragon was out, it would have to fly over the sea before it came to rest on the ledge. It couldn't just dive from the cliff's top to the cave's mouth. It would have to glide in. He hoped this was true. It if wasn't, and he had arrived after the dragon had left this morning, then he could find the beast right on top of him before he could protect himself.

Axel leaned around the boulder and stared into the blackness of the cave and thought that he could see lighter patches and soon even some color. He knew his eyes were playing tricks on him, but he did hear a slight stirring far back in the darkness. It didn't sound loud because of the noise of the waves against the rocks on the beach, but it must have been loud for him to have heard it at all.

The sides of the cave slope inward, like a funnel, Axel thought. Even the floor of the shelf slanted slightly away from the edge toward the black interior. The hole where the dragon slept was little bigger than the boulder, and Axel couldn't see but a short distance down into it.

Axel's body was stiff from the cold and the motionless waiting. He had been kneeling behind the boulder for almost an hour. When he rose to straighten his legs, he was very stiff and was afraid that he wouldn't be able to move quickly if he had to. There was no help for this, and he knelt on his knees again and waited. Soon the sun's edge was a pink rim on the horizon, and the sky was clear and much lighter. When the sun broke the horizon line, the sky suddenly turned a lighter blue, and the sun shone into the interior of the cave. The wind died for a moment and that stink engulfed him. Rolling out of the cave was the fetid, sweet, rank smell of rotted meat that he remembered well. He tried to hold his breath and he gagged. He didn't dare to move now, but he wasn't sure he would be able to make a good bow shot because his eyes were filled with tears. Bile rose into his mouth. Warmed by the sun, the flies rose in black swarms around him.

Axel saw a slight shifting of the dark shadows deep in the back of the cave. He strained his eyes to make out shapes. Then the thin morning sunlight reflected off dark scales, and he knew he was looking at the dragon. Its features weren't clear yet, but it was moving very slowly, cold from the night. Its skin, shining green and black in the dim light, looked damp, like leather clothing worn in the rain. *It's coming to the mouth of the cave to warm itself in the sun.* Axel moved back behind the boulder. He didn't like not being able to see where the dragon was, but he couldn't let it see him before he was ready for it.

Its claws scraped and cut on the stone floor. When it reached the large part of the entrance, just where the sides of the cave began to open up, it opened its wings somewhat. Axel could hear the leather slap as the dragon shook the dampness out of them. It hadn't seen or smelled him yet, and he knew he would have to stay behind the boulder until it got close enough so that he could get a clear shot.

He could hear it breathe now. Long rasping breaths, like a dying old man might make. Was it close enough? He didn't dare lean out to look to make sure. It must have stopped moving toward him, for there was no more noise from it. Axel knew that the decisions he would make in the next few moments would mean the difference between his life and death, between Molly marrying him or marrying Cedric. He was afraid to make his move for fear it was too soon and afraid not to make his move before it was too late. *If I jump out and face the dragon and it's just on the other side of this big stone, and I startle it, it could just reach out and swipe my head off. If I wait any longer, until the dragon comes around the stone and sees me, it will be too close to me for me to shoot and not be blown up with it. It has to be some distance away from me. I have to have some place to hide to protect myself from the blast. It has to be far enough away from me to have time to become mad enough to use its fire. And I have to make my mind up right now.* He slowly leaned out to look, and the dragon was still deep enough in the cave that its upper half was in darkness, and he couldn't see its head well enough to place an arrow in its mouth. Axel was scared. He couldn't make a mistake. He wouldn't be allowed another try. It would be his death.

He checked the arrow, and even though he could smell the oil, he felt of the rag to be sure it hadn't dried out in the wind. *Will I be able to light the firestick? Now is the time to find out. I can't wait any longer. My nerves won't take any more. I'd rather be wrong than wait.*

Axel could hear the dragon moving again on the stone floor as he took the fireboard out of his pack, put a firestick in the hole and struck the flint on the steel. The end of the firestick smoked. . .and went out. With shaking fingers, he fumbled out another and jabbed it into the hole, struck the flint against the steel and the stick flared. Then it too died. *They must be damp.* He could still hear the dragon moving. The smell was much stronger, and he heard the leathery wings further unfold to catch the morning sun. *The beast can't be more than ten paces from me. It must smell me.* The next firestick flared, and when he touched it to the end of the arrow, the oiled rags burst into flame.

He dropped the fireboard, nocked the arrow, pulled back on the bow and stepped out to face the dragon. Startled, the beast reared back when Axel appeared from behind the boulder holding fire before him. It thrashed its tail and pounded its feet against the floor. The cave, acting like a giant drum, amplified the pounding, which washed over Axel in huge waves and made it hard for him to concentrate on his aim.

The dragon rose up on its hind legs. *I hope it's bluffing now. It must be, it's presenting its armored, scaled chest.* Axel could hear Sidney's voice telling him, "Thith ith the time when motht dragonfighterth die. They make a try for the heart. Thith ith the motht heavily protected part of the dragon. Dragonth are thmart. They know they can't be hurt by a blow to the chetht. When the bluff failth, they try for their foe with flame. Firtht they have to lean forward and thtretth their neckth out, open their mouthth wide to take in air and then. . ." Axel had to wait for this beast to do that. *But I'm so close to the dragon, that when it lowers its head to take in air, its head will be right in my face. I have to back up to give both of us room. I hope there's enough shelf left behind me so that I can live through this.*

Edging backward, Axel stepped carefully so as not to trip on any of the bones lying on the stone floor in front of the cave. He had the bow pulled all the way back, and his arms were beginning to shake with the strain. Would he be able to wait out the bluffing of the beast? He had to. He couldn't relax now. If he did and missed his one shot, the dragon would cover him with flame, and he would die here on this ledge. But the dragon wasn't leaning forward to take in air. It was pounding its tail against the wall of the cave now and roaring. Screams of rage squeezed out of the cave around the boulder and rolled over Axel.

Strangely now, the dragon stopped all movement and sound and stood perfectly still, watching Axel. The vertical slits in its eyes reflected light from the rising sun and they glowed against the darkness of the cave's interior. Axel could not hold the bow fully pulled back much longer. Then, slowly, almost as if it didn't want to, the dragon lowered its head. Its tiny pointed ears flattened back against its smooth skull, and it opened its mouth.

Air whistled wetly as it was sucked in. He put the bow string to his cheek and sighted at the widely opened mouth. The long, yellow teeth were covered with slime and dripped with a dark substance that hung in strings that swayed when the beast moved its head. Axel released the string and the arrow struck the dragon in the back of the throat, a perfect shot. As soon as he fired, Axel jumped sideways to get behind the boulder, but he tripped on a large bone and fell against the rough surface. The huge ball began to roll down the slight incline toward the cave and the dragon. The boulder rolled into and filled the mouth of the cave and continued down into the darkness. Axel stood with his back against the wall of the cliff and waited for the explosion.

It seemed a long time coming, but it was just seconds. The flame was sucked into the stomach of the dragon, there it mixed with the gas and air that had brought the flame down, and the mixture ignited.

The cave acted like a large cannon. The boulder that had rolled to where the dragon was standing shot from the mouth of the cave in a high arc. Axel turned and watched it against the lighter color of the morning sky as it sailed out over the waves that sparkled in the sunlight. It landed in the water with a huge splash. Flame and red and black smoke rolled out of the opening just feet from where he stood. He could feel the blast against his back as the rock face of the cliff shook.

While the smoke was being blown clear by the wind from the sea, Axel tried to clear his ears by pounding on the side of his head. They felt plugged up, and there was a ringing sound that was very loud.

When the cave was clear of smoke, Axel searched for teeth. At first he feared they all might have been blown out to sea, but the explosion had covered the dark and narrow interior of the cave with pieces of dragon. He searched in the darkness and selected a few of the smaller teeth and one claw he might need to prove what he had done. He put these in his pack and climbed back up the cliff path to the track that led toward town. When he turned and looked out over the water, he could see that the surface still had rings radiating from where the boulder had splashed down.

He wasn't shaking so hard this time. He had been frightened, but not nearly as badly as during the fight with the first dragon. He almost felt sorry for this dragon. It hadn't known what was coming and he had. He could have been killed, but he felt as if it had been a fair fight. Still, there was something sad about killing, even a dragon, and he didn't really understand why, but he did feel a sadness. Axel looked at the sea for a moment, then went down the overgrown path toward town to collect his reward.

The few people left in town had heard the explosion but didn't know what had happened. They weren't on the street waiting for him when he reached the first buildings, but as soon as they saw him coming, they ran out and followed him to the temple. There were many questions, and he felt proud to be able to tell them that the dragon was indeed dead. He showed them the teeth and the claw. They wanted to know about the loud boom they had heard, but he said he couldn't explain it to them. One of the young men ran on ahead to tell the priest.

The priest was waiting on the steps of the temple for Axel. He called out in a loud voice, "Congratulations, young man. Well done." He laughed loudly. "I didn't think you could do it. You have done us a wonderful service. Come in and collect the gold." The townspeople crowded into the temple after Axel and the priest.

Axel felt that he understood about the priest switching the bags on the altar. He hoped he wasn't wrong, because if he made a mistake now, it would cost him a great deal of money. Before the priest could say anything, he stopped in front of the altar, turned to the crowd behind him and said, "The reward for killing the dragon is a generous one. I know it means that you have sacrificed a great deal and that men have died trying to kill this dragon. It is good that it will never bother anyone again, and it is good it is dead."

Axel waited a moment for the crowd to quiet down and again give him all of its attention. He smiled at the people crowded into the temple then turned and faced the priest and said, "This dragon was the largest dragon I have ever killed." The crowd murmured its wonder. "I feel there was more to my victory today than just my skill. I must have had some help from somewhere." The priest was smiling hugely now. Axel turned back to face the townspeople. He was surprised at how sure of himself he sounded. His voice was pitched low and was very clear. "Last night the priest gave me a holy stone to bring me luck, and that may have played a part in all of this, and so your temple should share in the reward."

The priest was beaming, and he held his palm out facing Axel and said, "That won't be necessary, my boy. You have done enough as it is. You should just take the small bag of coins and be on your way. We all appreciate what you have done for us." He was talking over Axel's head now to the group of people behind him. "But, we don't want to detain you. In fact, we wish you well and hope you will hide the reward money right away so that it cannot be lost."

Axel could hear the group behind him agreeing. He turned back to the townspeople and said, "But I want to do this. I have been thinking about the holy stones. I'm sure that if I were to buy some stones, I would be successful in any future fights with dragons." If Axel was right in his guess about why the priest switched the bags, the priest wouldn't like this suggestion. He wouldn't want anybody digging into the bag that should contain only stones and find it full of gold. And Axel was right.

The priest was shaking his head now and spoke directly to Axel. "I don't think that would be a good idea at all. Just take the bag of gold, put it right away, and leave us with the good memories of what you have done for us." The people agreed with the priest. Some even stepped up and patted Axel on the back and urged him to take all of the reward. Axel raised his voice as he said to the crowd, "If the stones bring you good fortune when you buy them, then why shouldn't I be able to buy some of that good fortune too?"

The people nodded their heads at this and looked at the priest. The large man held up his hands and said, "I will give the dragonslayer all the stones he can carry." He gestured with his hand held toward the side door of the temple. "If you will all come with me, I will even select from my garden ones I know are most holy," and he started moving toward the side door.

Axel heard the people talking about what a generous and good priest they had. Axel stepped to the left of the altar, to the bag that now held just a few coins covering the holy stones. He held it up so the people could see it. "I have earned this gold." The people stopped moving toward the door and turned to face him. "I have also earned the right to spend it as I wish." The men nodded their heads. Axel reached into the bag and took out the few gold coins that he had seen the priest put there the night before. These he handed to the priest and said to him, "Be kind enough to use these few coins to help the people who have been driven off by the dragon." The people cheered. Axel handed the bag to the priest. "I wish to buy a whole bag of stones. I'll trade this bag of gold for one bag of stones," and he handed the bag to the priest. The priest looked shocked for a moment, shifting his eyes from the bag to Axel's face then to the crowd. He quickly raised his arms in a herding manner and attempted to get the people moving toward the door to his garden.

Axel called out to the people as they again started to move, "Good people of Highcliff." They stopped and waited for him to go on. "I won't ask for special treatment from your priest. If ordinary holy stones are good enough for you, then they are good enough for me," and he crossed to the right side of the altar and picked up the bag of gold he had seen the priest put there in the night. He held it up for the crowd to see. Axel carelessly swung the bag by its leather binding and headed through the people toward the front of the temple.

The crowd cheered as Axel walked out of the temple with his small bag. He put it into the center of the sack of rags that he used for a target and tied that to Winthton's back.

Many of the townspeople followed along with him as he rode away from the temple. When they reached the last shop, Axel turned and waved to the priest, who was standing on the steps of the temple watching them walk away. Axel noticed that he had his head cocked to one side and that he held the bag of holy stones by its binding.

12

Home Court

Axel had been told that the king's castle was five or six walking days north, and he and Winthton had been on the road for five days and felt that they must be nearly there. They had been following the high road along the cliffs by the sea. Axel knew that if he kept the sea on his right hand, he would finally get to Willardville and King Willard's castle, Amory. Now that he was sure that he could kill any dragon he met, he was ready to offer his services to the king. If the king was having trouble with dragons, he might be willing to let him help. There was sure to be a reward. He didn't really need much more money to have enough to marry Molly and buy a farm. Thanks to the people of Highcliff and their priest, he felt he was very close to his dream.

The morning sun was shining off the water and bits of light and white foam danced on the tops of the waves. The beach was far below him, but still he could hear the surf pounding on the rocks. The road was a good one, the sky was blue, the morning sun promised a fine, clear day, and he was on the last part of his quest for riches. He wasn't in any great hurry. Oh, he was anxious to get home to Molly, but he knew it would be a number of weeks before he could do that. In the meantime, a few extra hours would make no difference.

Axel had stopped and was resting under a tree, and Winthton was grazing nearby. He was nearly asleep but was startled to alertness by an approaching rider. He couldn't see the man yet, but he knew he was coming quickly for the horse's hooves were pounding on the hard-packed road. When Winthton moved over to stand next to him, Axel reached up to touch the bag of old clothes where he had hidden the gold. They waited by the side of the road for the coming horseman. Soon he crested a small hill in the distance, then was lost again in the next depression. "We're better off out here by the road than we would be if we tried to hide," he said in a half-whisper to Winthton.

Over the top of the nearest hill, the hard-ridden horse and its rider dragged a long cloud of dust behind them. When the horse was near, the man brutally stopped it by yanking hard on the reins and pulling the animal's head to one side. The horse was covered in sweaty dirt and was blowing hard. The young rider, no older than Axel, was also covered with dirt, though from what Axel could see of his clothes, they were very fine. He had a short tunic and long dark leggings. His boots were soft and pointed and his feet were held by rings attached to his saddle by leather ropes. The young man was breathing deeply, and when he looked down at Axel and spoke, he tried to make his voice hard, but it came out high and thin. "Where are you bound, stranger?"

Axel wanted to sound calm, and he spoke slowly, "We're on our way to Willardville."

The young horseman was having trouble controlling his sweating horse, which was clearly excited and eager to run again. "Where are you coming from?"

"We left Highcliff five days ago," Axel answered, though he couldn't think of how it was any of this boy's business. "Why don't you give that poor horse a rest? I've been sitting under that tree over there, and it's nice and cool. Join me."

The man ignored this and asked, "Were you in Highcliff when the boy killed the dragon? A boy named Axel. . .or something like that?"

Axel looked at Winthton. "Yes, we were there then." He was beginning to worry about his gold. *Now that I'm rich, there'll be people who'll want to take my money away from me or to take advantage of me. I must be careful of what I say to strangers.* "Why do you ask?"

With an air of much importance the man answered, "I have been sent to bring him to the king. Is he still in Highcliff?"

Axel smiled at the messenger. "No, he left five days ago."

The young horseman worked his horse over close to Axel, "What I ask you is not to be laughed at, boy. I am on serious business." He pulled a cloth from his sleeve and wiped his face. "The king has been searching for this Axel for a week or more. First, we heard he had killed a dragon in Tightly, now he's killed one in Highcliff. That's some dragonkiller. Two in the last few weeks. The king has us out looking for him." His horse reared, and when it settled down, he asked, "Did you hear which way he was headed?"

Before Axel could answer, the young rider dismounted and stood close. They were about the same size, but the messenger's sense of importance made him act as he were a good deal taller and older.

Axel spoke even slower. "I didn't tell anyone in Highcliff where I was headed."

The messenger slapped his riding crop against his leg and said sharply, "I didn't ask you where you were headed, boy. No one cares where you go. It's the dragonkiller everyone is hunting for. There have been two dragons that the king and I have been trying to get rid of since last fall. We—He would like to have this Axel teach his knights what he knows about dragons. Just this year, the dragon has killed or wounded six of his best men. Now, if you know anything about where this Axel went, it would be best for you to tell me where he can be found. And you be quick about it. I've got to get to Highcliff before dark."

Even though this man thinks too much of himself, I hate to see him abuse that horse any more today. "My name is Axel and this is Winthton."

With much impatience the man said, "Who cares what you call your friend. Now, I want—" He frowned and looked hard at Axel, "What did you say your name is?"

"Axel."

He stepped even closer, "Is this some kind of a joke? If it is, I'll have your hide for it."

Axel put his hand on Winthton's back, "And this is Winthton."

"I'm looking for a dragonkiller, not some kid with a sorry looking donkey for a friend." He mounted his excited horse and looked down at Axel. "When you get to Willardville, you better watch what you tell people. When King Willard's not happy, nobody's happy. They'll not take kindly to some kid playing jokes there now." He jerked his horse roughly back on the road and galloped on south toward Highcliff.

Axel stood for a long time watching the messenger and his horse rise out of one fold in the road and then dip down out of sight into the next one. The dust hung in the air in a fine tan cloud and took a long time to settle. He didn't want to continue until the air was clear again, so he sat back under the tree. Winthton grazed nearby. "That young man was in a hurry, Winthton. He sure had some place to go. And how important he felt getting there. Here we both are trying to get ahead by helping the king, so I guess we're going the same way, but he's kicking up an awful lot of dust doing it." Axel looked over to his friend, "It looks like we're famous, Winthton. If the king has heard about us and wants to meet us, that might be a good sign. We may be able to head back to Greenwater before much longer." Winthton ate grass.

When the dust had settled, he led Winthton out onto the road, and they continued on their way to Willardville. They had been traveling for hours through prosperous looking farmland. It was much different than it had been near Highcliff. These fields had been plowed and, in some, Axel could see short, light green growth. The houses had a well-kept look, their roofs repaired or newly thatched, the gardens weedless.

Axel first saw the castle just at dusk. They came over the rise of a small hill at a bend in the road, and there on a point of land above the sea, its windows shining golden as they reflected the setting sun, towered the king's home. The great square keep had at least eight rows of windows staggered up its sides. The crenelated walls between the towers that dominated each corner were made of massive stone blocks. Rising huge from the cliffs, the castle looked not so much as if it had been built, but that it had grown there.

To make the castle easily defendable, it had been

constructed on a high promontory that looked out over both the sea and countryside. There were sheer cliffs on three sides that fell to the rocks, hundreds of feet below. Even on this calm, summer day, the waves crashing against the base of the cliffs created clouds of spray and mist that hid the lower portions of the cliffs supporting the walls. On the one side that faced away from the water, on a curving spine of land, twisted a narrow road to the high gates in the wall. Both edges of the roadway dropped straight down for more than a hundred feet.

The approach to the castle was sharply uphill, then leveled off and ran along the crooked neck to the gate. Just this side of the gate was a drawbridge spanning a deep gorge cut into the rock. The castle had been in the king's family for many generations, and the design had proven to be a good one for the castle had never been taken, though many had tried. But, that had been long ago. King Willard, if not loved by all of his neighbors, was at least not hated.

In a narrow valley off to the left, Axel could see the town of Willardville. It had grown a great deal in the last few years. Originally, it had housed just the people who served the castle. Many who worked for the king, of course, lived in the castle itself, but there were services a great castle needed that couldn't be supplied by the people who lived with the king. There was a need for things other than foodstuffs. There had been a time when everything a king and his household might need could be supplied from within the walls, but this king's staff had grown so large that this was no longer possible. The town had grown with the king's needs, until the castle was dependent on the town, where originally it had been the other way around.

The road up to Amory Castle met the one Axel was on just short of the outer wall. There were many people who were leaving the tall gates. At this time of day, those who worked in the castle were headed toward town and their homes. Axel turned onto the narrow road that ran atop the thin spine of land that separated the castle from the coast. The people he met coming from the castle looked at him but none spoke. When Axel reached the gate there was a partially armored man with a pike standing on the edge of the lowered drawbridge who challenged him. "What business you got here, boy?"

Axel stopped just short of the arch and answered, looking up at the tall guard. "We have come to offer our services to the king."

The man looked beyond Axel, then frowned and asked, "Who's 'we'?"

"Axel and his donkey, Winthton."

The guard looked Winthton over and then did the same to Axel, "Which a you is the donkey?" he said, then laughed loudly. "Which is the donkey? That's good, and it's hard to tell." He was really laughing now and slapping his leg with his free hand, but he managed to gasp out, "What would King Willard need a you?"

Axel was embarrassed by the man and didn't know how he should behave. He had never talked to a king's guard before. "We're dragonfighters and have come to kill the dragons that have been causing trouble for the king."

Some of the people passing out of the gate had heard parts of this conversation and had stopped and were listening.

They were smiling now and glancing at each other. When Axel said that they were dragonfighters, some of the men laughed openly. The guard raised his voice and spoke to the people standing around. "Our troubles 'er over, now. We got a real dragon fighter here who's come to kill the dragons fer us."

Some of the people in the crowd joined in, "He looks the right size for a dragon's breakfast."

"Who rides and who walks?"

"I've a snake in the garden at home what needs killing, boy. Do you do heavy work like that?"

All in the group were laughing at Axel and Winthton, when a man in a uniform came riding out of the castle and stopped at the gate. The people quickly continued on toward town and the guard turned serious.

"On your way, boy. Ya can't block the gate this way."

The rider held his large, dark horse next to Winthton, who moved over closer to Axel. "What's the trouble here, guard?"

The guard was standing very stiffly and spoke in a formal way, "Sir, this boy says he's a dragon fighter, and he asked to see the king. He'll be out a here in a bit and on his way." He turned to Axel. "Take your donkey and leave, and I don't want to see ya here again."

The mounted man raised his voice, "Hold on there, guard." He turned to Axel and said, "Boy, what do you call yourself?"

"Axel, Sir."

"You say you're a dragon fighter?"

"Yes, Sir."

"You've killed a dragon?"

"Yes, Sir, two. One at Tightly and one at Highcliff."

"You the boy the king's been looking for?"

"I don't know, Sir— "

The guard interrupted, "See, Sir, he's just a boy full of no good," and he turned to Axel, "Get on with ya, boy, before ya get in trouble."

Axel looked up to the man on the horse and said, "Axel is my name and this is Winthton."

The man turned his horse around, nodded at the guard, and said to Axel, "Follow me, boy."

Axel could tell Winthton was nervous in the presence of the huge horse, so he took his lead and together they followed the man over the drawbridge and through the gate into the castle.

No one he had ever talked to had been in or even seen a castle before, so Axel had no idea what to expect. But, whatever happened, this was the most exciting day he was ever going to have. He was entering the castle of the king. What a thing to do.

He followed the man past the gate-house and was amazed at the size of the inner court. He had always imagined a castle was like a large walled house. But, from where he stood, it looked more like high walls with six or seven towers spaced around it. There was one square tower that was the tallest thing he had ever seen. It looked to him as tall as seven or eight houses piled on top of each other. The other towers were not so tall but each had a pole at its peak, and flags were flapping in the wind at their tops.

All of the windows on the outside walls were narrow slits and it was the same even here, on the towers, inside the wall.

On the left side of the courtyard, there were lower buildings built right into the walls. These must be where the people live, he thought. On the far side, across the center of the hard-packed dirt courtyard, there were workrooms. He could recognize the blacksmith shop by the anvil standing near the door.

Axel, leading Winthton, followed the horseman who rode past the living quarters to the far side of the courtyard and dismounted at the stables. He handed his horse over to a stable boy and motioned for Axel to do the same. They passed under an arched doorway and walked down a long hall to another large door. When he entered the great hall, Axel could hardly believe what he was seeing. He had not thought it was possible for a room to be so big.

At the far end there was a fireplace large enough for a man to stand in and hold his arms out and not touch the sides. Even though it was not a cold day, the air in the room was cool and the fire looked good to him. A man in black robes was sitting at a long table that took up much of the center of the room.

The guard motioned for Axel to stay where he was and then walked to the seated man. They talked in low voices for a short time.

Axel had a chance to look at the room. On most of the walls there were dark-colored drapes that hung almost to the floor. The ceiling was crossed with heavy, wooden beams and was impossibly high. A number of doorways lead off, he guessed, to other rooms.

The robed man came to where Axel was standing and stopped in front of him. His face was much heavier at the jaw line than at the top, a curious pyramid of a head. He looks like his cheeks are full of nuts, Axel thought. After pausing and studying Axel with his pale, watery eyes for a moment, the man walked on. Axel didn't know whether to follow him or not. When the man got to a door, he turned and looked back and waited until Axel rose to follow, then disappeared around the stone archway. Each time Axel turned a corner in the maze of halls, he saw the black robe disappearing around one ahead of him. When they climbed circular stairs, he could hear the shuffle of the man's shoes on the stone steps above him.

Near the top of what Axel thought must be one of the towers, he could look down a long, dark hall. The robed man had stopped at a door and was talking to a guard, then he turned the corner and Axel never saw him again.

When Axel arrived at the door, the guard opened it and motioned him in. It will be fun to tell Molly about this, he thought. It amazed him to think he was going to see the king in person. The room was much grander than any he had seen so far. The high ceiling was covered with pictures painted around a great hanging lamp holding what looked like hundreds of candles.

As Axel followed the guard across the red and black carpet to the far corner, he tried to follow the pictures around the lamp. He had to keep turning in circles to make out the paintings of people, babies and what looked like horses with horns. Axel had never seen a picture, but had heard people, who had talked to people who had seen some, talk about them. He thought that pictures were put on walls. Strange what people do when they have money.

The guard reached out and turned Axel around to face a

corner. Propped in a large chair which was lined with cushions sat a fat, sleeping man. Axel turned to ask the silent guard where the king was and was surprised to find the man was almost to the door. He watched him leave, then turned again to the man in the chair. The man wasn't fatty fat; rather he was very big. He did have rolls on his chin, and his stomach pushed against his heavy robe and was higher than his chest. His small feet, in pointy-toed slippers, were resting on a short stool.

Axel moved closer. He could hear soft snoring, and the man's lips fluttered when he let his breath out. Somewhere in the castle a large bell rang, the sound deadened by the heavy, dark drapes that hung on the walls. On one side of the room there was a huge hanging. It was woven of cloth and was bright with pictures of a seated man talking to two others in what looked to Axel like a very small castle. Next to these figures were two men on horses, and they were all standing on lions with their lances stuck in large pigs. When he heard the sleeping man cough, he turned and said, "You woke up. Good. I've been waiting to see the king. The guard let me in." He crossed the room to the chair. The man had the bluest eyes Axel had ever seen. His voice was deep and kind as he said, "We drop off now and then. Bad habit We have. What is your name, boy?"

"I'm Axel, the dragon fighter. I've come to help the king get rid of his dragons."

"You are Axel, eh? We would have thought you might be a bit bigger." He moved his feet off the stool and motioned toward it. "Sit down, Axel, and tell Us how We can kill these dragons."

Axel sat. "I've come to see the king. I'll have to kill the

dragons myself. I can't tell anyone else how to do it."

"You can tell me." The big man pointed toward his chest with one large hand. Axel saw that all of his fingers had rings on them. "We are the king."

Axel jumped up. He didn't know what to do now that he was standing or what to say. "I—You didn't say—The guard should have—"

The king laughed. "Sit back down, boy and tell Us what you can about killing these beasts so We can tell our knights."

"Oh, Sir—er, King. I don't know how to—what to call you. . .Sir."

The king smiled and said, "You may call Us Your Majesty. Now, what about telling Us how you kill these terrible beasts."

"I'd like to, but I promised Sidney I never would. It was part of the bargain we made when I carved his ess."

The king leaned forward in his chair. "What did you do?"

"His donkey ate his ess, and I had to make him a new one, and he made me promise I wouldn't tell anyone."

"But, you just have. You told Us," the king said, frowning at Axel. "And We don't understand what the donkey ate. Go over that again."

Axel sat down on the stool and leaned forward. "You don't understand." He jumped up, then didn't know what to do with his hands, so he put them behind him. They were wet. "I'm sorry, Sir—Your Majesty." He stepped back and bumped into the stool, started to fall and just caught himself.

"You may sit, Axel." The king had his eyes closed now.

This was a problem, because Axel didn't want to insult the king, but still, he couldn't break his promise to Sidney.

The only thing he could do would be to explain it in the best way he could and hope the king would understand.

He was well into the story of how he had met the wizard and the bargain they had made. He had just told King Willard about carving the ess because Winthton had eaten the first one, when he again heard the soft snoring.

Now what to do? Can an ordinary person wake up a king? Could I do that? If so, how is it done? Tap on the arm? The shoulder? That doesn't sound right at all. Should I wait? If so, how long? He turned and looked around the large room for some sign. There was none. The king snored on. Axel waited for what seemed like a very long time. In the presence of a king, any length of time would seem long. He waited first in front of the stool, then next to it, then he sat.

"The donkey liked wood, eh?"

Axel jumped up. "What?"

The king had spoken and continued, "You were saying something about the donkey eating the ess."

Had the king really been asleep? How is one to know? He had been snoring. He said to the king, "I promised Sidney that if he were to help me learn about dragons I would carve him a new letter, and that I would never tell anyone what I learned from him. That's why I can't tell you or your knights how I kill dragons. I'll have to kill them myself. I have to keep my promise." Axel was afraid that he had made a mistake saying no to the king. He now didn't know what to say or do. He looked at the king and said, "Even kings have to do that, don't they?"

King Willard stood. He was even bigger than Axel had thought. When he was standing, he didn't look nearly so fat. "Of course kings keep their promises," he said, looking down at Axel. "We wish we had a wizard who could make people keep their promises like your wizard can. Ours got sick and died last winter. Shame. He was a good one. We've been looking at some new ones but haven't found one We feel We can trust. What did you say this wizard you know is called?"

"Sidney."

"Yes. . .well. A promise is a promise. We have to respect that. But, what are We to do about these dragons?"

"I've come to kill them for you, Your Majesty."

The king put his heavy hand on Axel's shoulder. It felt good to Axel, and it was even heavier than his father's had been. "We cannot have that. Our knights would never stand for it. Jealous bunch they are. We will have to think of something." The king sighed and sat back down. "In the meantime, you are to stay here in the castle. We will look after you in good style. The guard at the door will show you where you are to stay. You have a horse?"

"No, Your Majesty, but I have Winthton with me."

"A friend is he?"

"In a way. He's my donkey."

The king laughed and said, "You call him Winthton?"

Axel nodded and answered, "Yes, Your Majesty."

The king pulled the stool back under his feet and leaned back against the cushions. "He will be taken care of too. Anything you need, you just ask for it. You better practice whatever you do to kill dragons. We might have to use you."

Axel didn't know how he was supposed to say goodbye to a king. He had seen his father shake a man's hand once, but is that right for a king? He said, "Thank you, Your Majesty," and started to back away. As he did so, he heard the king snoring softly.

The guard led Axel to a small room in a far corner of the castle. It had the largest bed he had ever seen, and next to it was a small table with a lamp. He thanked the guard and said that he was sure he would get lost if he tried to find his way about alone. The guard asked him if he was hungry. When he said that he hadn't eaten since noon, he was led to the kitchen where a heavy old woman with very dirty hands gave him some cold meat. It tasted like beef, but not like any he had eaten before. There was bread, cheese and a mug of ale. Axel asked if there was milk and the woman brought him a pitcher of it, then left him alone to eat.

The next morning, after he had discovered the kitchen again and eaten, he set out to find Winthton. It took him a long time to make his way there. He'd had to ask four men standing along the walls which way to go.

Winthton was glad to see him. Axel could tell because the first thing his friend did was lip his ear. Winthton had been well taken care of. He had had a clean place to spend the night, and there was feed left, so he must have had all he wanted.

His bow and target sack with the old rags in it were hanging on the wall. He felt through the rags and couldn't feel the small leather bag. Quickly he dug into the sack and was greatly relieved to find that the gold was still there. In his excitement at meeting the king, he had forgotten about the gold. He could have lost it all. He would have to be much more careful.

He put his things on Winthton's back and led him out of the stable and across the courtyard toward the gate. The people who had been leaving last night were just returning to work. Axel was surprised that this time they looked at him with a great deal of respect. There was no laughter or ridicule. Some of the serving girls smiled at him, and the men all nodded.

There were high clouds piled up over the hills to the west. They were dark and shaped like another mountain range, only higher and farther away. It looked like there might be a storm in the afternoon, but the sun was shining, and he had a few hours before there was a chance of rain.

When he got to the end of the narrow road that led to the castle, he turned back to look at where he had spent the night. He had never dreamed that he would ever be in such a grand place. And, he had even talked to the king. *What an adventure this is turning out to be. When I started out in the spring, I had no idea that it would come to this. I guess I owe it all to Sidney. If he hadn't taught me how to kill dragons, I'd be dead by now, or I'd have had to go back home a failure.* He could hear the men in Bobson's inn laughing at him when he would have had to walk back in with the jug. *"Ho, the great dragonslayer returns. Killed any dragons today?" But, even worse than that would be not being able to marry Molly, and her marrying Cedric. But, I can't think about that. That can never be. I already have more money than anyone in my village has ever had. Even if I get no more, I'll be rich enough to marry her and buy a small farm.*

Just before Axel turned off the road into a woods that was deeply shaded with huge trees cutting off most of the sun, he turned to look back the way he had come. Just where the road turned, a dark shape darted to the right and disappeared in the brush. Axel led Winthton off the road and between the trees. As soon as there was shade, the air was cool, and he could smell the damp ground which was covered with long bladed, dark green grass that was so heavy and dense there was no underbrush. The large and very old trees were widely spaced and had heavy, low-hanging limbs that made a ceiling in the forest no higher than the king's chamber. The morning sun slanting through the new leaves created leaning shafts of light that lit patches on the dark trunks and made patterns of lighter green on the grass.

Axel was able to jump and catch the end of a limb and pull it low enough to tie a piece of twine to it and hang his sack. *I haven't practiced my shooting since before I killed the dragon at Highcliff. I must keep at it for my life might depend on it. I'll never get more than one shot at a dragon, and if I miss. . .*He wrapped the ends of four arrows with rags as if he were going to dip them in oil. They had to be the same weight and have the same feel or his aim would be off when he needed it most.

He started the bag swinging. *Sometimes dragons swing their head from side to side, and I might have to shoot at a moving target.* After he had practiced for an hour, he found that he could hit the swinging bag if he aimed where it would be when the arrow got there. When he first practiced with the swinging target, he had tried to follow it with the bow, but when he did that, the arrows always passed behind the target. When he could hit the bag ten out of ten tries, he took the rags off the arrows, took down the target and put his equipment on Winthton's back.

As Axel was making his way out of the woods, he thought about what Sidney had told him about dragons talking to each other. *What if these new dragons that have been giving trouble to the king have heard about how I killed the one at Highcliff? What if the king's dragons won't open their mouths? I won't stand a chance if I have to fight them with my sword. Will I be able to run fast enough to get away? Some dragonslayer I am, thinking about how fast I can run. Still, it's worth thinking about. I sure don't want to get killed now that I'm a rich man.*

When they reached the road again, Axel saw, walking quickly toward the castle, what looked like the same darkly dressed man he had seen just before he had turned into the woods. He could think of no reason why anyone would want to watch what he was doing. He had told the king he would kill the dragons for him. He sure wasn't going to leave before he had done what he had said he would. It's just someone out for a walk, he decided.

After Axel gave Winthton a bit of hay and cleaned out his stall, he sat in the corner and watched out the doorway as dark clouds rolled over the high walls of the castle. There was thunder in the distance, and as he sat there, it grew louder, and soon he could hear the snap and crack of the lightning. On the close ones, Axel could feel the boards of the stall shake and could feel the sound through his body.

He thought about the wedding Molly and he would have. He would like to be able to invite his friends to come and help them celebrate. . .*if I had any friends. The only person I can consider a friend, other than Molly, is Sidney. He'd never come. Or would he? He'd have to travel to Greenwater, and he said he hates to travel. No, he wouldn't want to come. I'll have to have just my mother.*

He thought about his father. He would give anything if he could be with them for the wedding. And Axel was sure he would have liked to be there. This would be a big day for him—if he were alive. His son a rich man. Getting married.

Buying a farm. Being a father himself. Axel felt his throat tighten up, and there were tears in his eyes as he thought about how much he missed his father. He needed to talk to him again. He wanted to feel that large hand on his shoulder. He needed that special look they had shared.

Axel heard a horse approach the stable, and from where he sat, when he looked over the top of the stall, he could see the guard who had ridden the horse out to the gate when he had first come. He was talking to another man who must have been walking, because he couldn't see him.

"He took the donkey with him?"

"But, he didn't ride. They just walked along together. He don't look like he could kill a rat to me."

"Where'd he go?"

"To the woods just right a the road."

"And?"

"By the time I got to where I could see what was going on, he was shooting arrows at a bag. He'd tied it to a tree with a rope. He'd start it swinging and step back and shoot arrows into it. Dumbest thing I ever saw."

"Did he hit it?"

"Ya. He was pretty good."

"What else?"

"He had rags tied to the ends of the arrows."

The men now were too far into the stable for Axel to hear any more. I was followed. The man in the dark clothing. The king must want to know how I kill dragons. He can't believe I do it with my old sword. He must think Sidney gave me some magic. They'll figure out what the rags are for, then they'll try to kill a dragon by shooting at it with burning arrows. They're in for a big surprise. They won't know that they have to shoot the dragon at just the right time and hit it in the throat when it has its mouth open taking in air. And I can't tell them either. They try and they'll get killed and there's nothing I can do to stop them. If Sidney were here he might release me from my promise, but I can't do that on my own. The most I can do is warn the king that if his knights try to kill the dragon with burning arrows, they'll get killed. II ask him to, maybe he'll stop them.

13

Axel In For Knights

Axel left the stable and after asking for directions three different times, found his way to the hall where the king had his rooms. He had to see if he could save the lives of the knights. The same guard was standing outside the king's chambers. Axel didn't hesitate this time, but spoke right up, "I want to talk to the king."

"What about?"

"I have to try to save the knights from getting killed by a dragon."

The guard tilted his head back and said, "What's that got to do with seeing the king? I happen to know he's busy."

"It won't take long."

The guard thought for a moment then opened the door and slipped inside. Axel could see past the guard's shoulder to the corner where he had seen the king yesterday. King Willard was sleeping in the same chair. When the door opened again and the guard stepped out, he said, "The king's in a meeting now. I asked him to see ya this afternoon. Come back just before dinnertime. He might see ya for a moment."

There was nothing to be done about this. Axel waited most of the day, walking about the castle. It was a huge place. Late that afternoon when Axel heard the bell ringing in the tower, he went again to the king's chambers. This time, when the guard saw him walking along the dim corridor, he motioned him to hurry.

By the time Axel got to the doorway, the guard had the door open and was urging him to enter. King Willard was awake this time pacing back and forth in front of another man who was sitting on the stool.

This man was bandaged around the chest with a blood-soaked cloth. His face was badly cut and very dirty. One arm was in a sling suspended from around his neck. When the king saw Axel enter the room, he walked over to the door to greet him. "Axel, We have been thinking of you. Nice of you to come to see Us again. We would like you to talk to Sir Bruce. He and three other knights have had a terrible battle with one of the dragons." He led Axel to the seated man and continued, "Sir Bruce here is the only one to live. Terrible thing. Terrible." The king was wringing his hands together and standing over the wounded knight.

Sir Bruce looked carefully at Axel, and his eyes said that he didn't think much of what he saw. Axel looked carefully at Sir Bruce, and the knight didn't look nearly as large as the king had when sitting in the chair, but he did look solid and strong. He made Axel feel very young and inexperienced. This was a real fighter. There was the scar of an old wound on his face which ran past his left eye to the corner of his mouth. The back of his right hand, the one in the sling, was badly scarred from some previous battle. His voice was low and heavy. "You the dragon fighter we heard about?" His deep-set eyes were intent on Axel's face.

The king put his hand on Axel's arm. "This is Axel. It is said he killed the dragon at Tightly and the one at Highcliff. Quite a boy."

The knight had not taken his eyes off Axel. "How'd ya do it, boy? Some kind a magic?" His right lip came up a bit, almost as if he wanted to smile but no longer could with the old cut on his face. "How'd ya kill those dragons?"

Axel's voice sounded high-pitched and childlike to him, "I can't tell you that, Sir, I've promised Sidney I wouldn't ever tell. But, I did kill them, and I have said I will kill these two for the king if he wants me to."

The knight looked down at the floor for a moment, then up at the king. "I saw three good knights killed by this beast today, and ya say this boy can kill it? I say, let's ask him real hard how he plans on doing that." The knight reached out and grabbed Axel's arm. It hurt so much that Axel was dizzy for a moment and the room had spots all over it. "Tell us, boy. How ya gonna do it?" The king touched the knight on the shoulder, and when Sir Bruce looked up, the king shook his head slightly. The knight let go of Axel's arm and said, "All right, let him try. If he gets to be the dragon's lunch, that's good enough by me."

Axel tried not to rub his arm and turned to the king, "I tried to see you this morning to warn you not to let your knights try to kill the dragon with arrows, but you were busy."

The knight sat up. "How ya know we tried arrows?"

Axel didn't want to tell the knight in front of the king he knew he had been spied on. Maybe a small lie wouldn't be bad. "I just guessed. Tell me what happened?"

The knight's voice was hard, "Three good men died. That's what happened."

Axel said to the king, "If I knew what happened, maybe I could suggest something. You might even let me kill the dragon for you, now."

The king looked at Axel for a moment then turned to the knight, "Sir Bruce, tell Axel how our three good men died."

The knight looked off across the room. Axel could tell that he was again in the cave seeing the dragon killing his men. His voice was much softer than it had been. "We took bows with us. The arrows had rags tied around the tips, and we dipped em in oil and lit 'em before we shot.

"When we got to the cave the dragon wasn't there. We stood behind some bushes near the entrance and waited. It glided right into the opening. It's a big cave, see. Just before it set down, it turned and saw us." The man stopped talking for a moment, breathing hard, then went on, "A big fella, and as mean a one as I ever saw." His eyes shot to the king, then back to the floor. "As soon as he touched down, we lit the arrows and stepped out to shoot. He turned to face us at the entrance, and all four of us shot at once."

The knight sat silently for so long that Axel thought that he wasn't going to go on. The king stood still and waited. Axel looked from the king to the knight and back. The king shook his head slightly from side to side as he looked into Axel's eyes.

When the knight spoke again it was straight at Axel. It was almost, Axel thought, as if the knight were blaming him for what had happened. "The arrows just bounced off the scales. They were good hits. War bows, not hunting. Good hits with heavy arrows, and they bounced off. Those burning arrows didn't do a thing to that beast. He came at us pounding his feet on the floor and he stomped us. We had our swords out and tried to fend him off, but he just kept coming and stomping." He paused, then shouted, "He. . .stomped. . .my men."

The knight stood now. He was taller than Axel and very powerful looking, even with the bandages on his shoulder and arm. Axel could see tears running down the man's scarred face leaving clean tracks in the dirt. "Why didn't the arrows work?" He was shouting and clearly in a rage. "My men are still there. . .being. . .eaten!" The knight hung his head and sobbed.

Axel looked at the king just as the king stepped in front of the knight and said, "You need rest, good knight. Go now. We will talk again of what we must do. I know you did what you could for your men. You are a brave man. We value your service." He walked the knight to the door.

When the king came back to where Axel was waiting, he looked as if he had been beaten. He was much taller than Axel, but he seemed to Axel to have diminished in size somehow. When he spoke, even his voice was smaller. "Yesterday We told you We might have need of your services. Well, We do now. Will you kill this beast for Us?"

How could anyone refuse such a request? Axel was excited. He would have said yes even if he knew he'd be killed. There was no way to refuse this great man. He started to speak and couldn't. The words wouldn't come out of his throat. He nodded. King Willard understood. He put both his hands on Axel's shoulders and looked down into his eyes. "Thank you, Axel. We knew We could count on you."

The king turned Axel toward the door and spoke as he was walking him across the room. "We know you can't tell Us how you plan to do it, but is there anything you need? Do you want help? We have men who would go with you."

"Thank you, Your Majesty. I must go alone."

"When?"

"In the morning."

"Come to Us as soon as you get back. You are a brave young man. We will remember what you have done for Us." The king opened the door himself and held it for Axel to leave.

14

It's No Picnic On The Beach

Axel knew he had a problem. He had promised the king that he would kill the dragon for him, but how could he do it when it was possible that the dragon had heard about how he had killed the others with fire?

Sidney was right. Dragons are smart. And they do communicate with each other. The ones I've killed didn't have a chance to pass on any messages, but others must have been to the caves and have seen what happened. Dragons must know how they make fire and seeing the other dead dragons blown all over the caves must realize how they died.

Now that that won't work anymore, what can I do? I sure can't kill one with my sword. Sidney said something one day about knowing what to do when faced with a problem. Let's see. . . 'We have to see this as a problem.' What would he say if he were here now? I can see his old smooth face, and hear him lisping. If he were here he would help me. We'd have a conversation, and he'd help me think of a way to do what I have to do and not get killed doing it.

"Sidney, I've got this problem."

"What ith it, Axthel?"

"I have to kill a dragon, and it won't open its mouth to take in air to blow fire. It learned not to do that. What do I do?"

"We have to look at thith ath a problem."

"That's what I'm trying to do."

"Firtht, we have to know what the dragon doeth do."

"He killed three knights by stomping them to death. He didn't even try to burn them."

"Good. We know how the dragon killth. Now, we need to find out how to get it to try to burn you. If we can do that, you can blow it up like you did the othereth."

"Right. That's the problem, how do I do that?"

"Dragonth breathe fire when they're mad, don't they?"

"Sure, we know that."

"Tho, all you have to do ith get it mad. Eathy."

"I have to get the dragon mad? But the king's knights got it mad and it stomped them."

"You have to thtop it from thtomping you, and when it can't thtomp you it will get mad enough to try and burn you. The problem ith thimple. You work it out."

"Hey, wait, Sidney."

The imaginary conversation was over, and Axel was faced with his problem all by himself again. All he had to do was get the dragon mad at him, not let it stomp him to death and then shoot it when it tried to burn him. *If this wasn't so serious, it might be funny. Sidney sure wasn't a whole lot of help. I'll just have to do this one by myself.*

Let's see. . .a problem. We take this one step at a time. That's the way to do it. If I break it down into parts, it should be easier to solve the parts than the whole problem all at once.

Number one, make the dragon mad. Number two, don't

let it stomp me. Number three, shoot it with a burning arrow. Not bad. One is easy. Dragons are always mad. All you have to do is go anywhere near them and they get mad. Three I can do. I've done it twice already. Two is the problem. If I can solve number two, I can kill this dragon and survive.

Keep. . .the dragon. . .from. . .stomping me. Axel was pacing back and forth in his room. Five paces one way, turn, five the other way, turn. *How do dragons stomp? How does anything stomp? With its feet. Good. All I need to do is make it hard to stomp me. Like. . .give the dragon sore feet, or something.*

Axel looked down at his feet. He took off his boots and put them on the floor by the door, as if there were a person in them. He began to approach the boots like the dragon might, stomping his feet, but there wasn't enough space in his small room for him to get the feeling of an attacking dragon.

He took the boots into the hall and put them together, facing him. His room had a carpet, but the hall had large blocks of stone for flooring. Rough, with ragged joints. He backed up about fifteen paces and began to flap his arms as if he had just landed. He hissed. . . .He reared. . . .He bluffed. He began to stomp on the floor and roar.

He advanced on the boots, taking great strides by slamming his feet down on the stones. Stomp. . . Stomp. . . Stomp. . . His heel hit a sharp edge and he jumped and grabbed his foot with both hands. He was hopping on one foot and holding onto the other when it hit him.

Put something sharp on the cave floor and the dragon will do just what I did. It won't be able to stomp. It'll be so mad it hurt its feet, it'll try and burn me, and I'll have it. Thank you, Sidney.

When Axel picked up his boots and turned to go back into his room, he saw a figure dart out of sight at the far end of the hallway. *I wonder what that person thinks I'm doing. Here I am in the hall, attacking my boots by hissing, roaring, and stomping them to death. He must think I'm really mad at my boots to do that.*

The king's blacksmith shop was by the stable. Axel had seen it when he had first come to the castle. The blacksmith was just banking the fire when Axel got there. It didn't take him long to explain what he needed. Everyone in the castle had heard by now that he was someone special, that the king liked him and that he was a dragon killer who had killed two dragons. There were few men alive who had done that.

Axel told the large man by the door of the shop what he needed, but when the blacksmith asked what it was all about, Axel said he couldn't say. The blacksmith did, however, agree to make him what he said would work. The idea wasn't new, in fact, he had made something like them before. He would make twenty sharply pointed double stars. No matter which way they landed when he threw them, a point would be up. Axel thought that twenty should be enough. The blacksmith said that he could pick them up in the morning. It would take him most of the night, but he would leave them in a bag outside his shop before he went home. Axel thanked him and told him he thought the king would like what he was doing to help.

Axel checked on Winthton, making sure he had food and enough water. He explained to him that they would be going out early in the morning to kill another dragon. Winthton drooled on his shirt, so Axel figured he was pleased by the news. After checking that he still had enough oil in the flask he had been given by the cook for the arrow in the morning, he left Winthton and headed for the kitchen.

Axel rose long before daybreak. His room was cold. He headed toward the stable, and a draft in the hallways of the old castle caused the light from the oil lamps hung on the walls to waver and the shadows to move.

He knew how far he had to travel before daylight because he had visited the wounded knight in the evening to see how he was and to find out where the dragon lived. The knight hadn't been happy to see him. He didn't feel he had done anything to offend anyone, but the man was wounded, and maybe that was it.

When he had knocked on the knight's door, a gruff voice had loudly said, "What ya want?"

Axel entered. The wounded man was propped up in bed, and there was an empty bottle next to the lamp on a small table near him. "I came to see how you're feeling." The knight turned away from the doorway and said nothing. Crossing the small room to the bed, Axel stood and looked down at the wounded man. He didn't know what to say. He felt the knight didn't care if he had come or not. "I'm sorry about your friends." The knight turned far enough to flick his eyes at Axel's face then back to the far corner of the room.

The knight said something that made Axel think that he might have been keeping an eye on him. "I hear ya saw the blacksmith this afternoon."

"Yes, he's making me something."

"What ya gonna do with the stars?"

Axel didn't want to lie to the knight, but he couldn't explain what the stars were for. If he did, the knight would want to know why he wanted the dragon to be mad at him, and then he wouldn't be able to tell him because of his promise. He just shrugged and said, "I had an idea they might come in handy in the morning. I'm going to need any help I can find. How is your arm tonight?"

He turned and faced Axel and asked, "Ya gonna throw them at the beast?" He was smiling now.

"No, I thought I'd put them on the floor."

"Fat lot a good that'd do ya."

Axel shrugged. "It may work. I hope it does, though. How's your arm?"

The knight looked hard at Axel and said, "Think you're pretty smart, don'cha, boy?"

"The idea wasn't mine. It was Sidney's thinking that did it, not mine."

Axel could see that the knight had been drinking for a long time. He thought he probably needed it for the pain. Axel didn't know what to do. He stood quietly by the bed and waited for the knight to say something, but the wounded man continued to look away. He finally said, "Sidney is a wizard and he's very smart." The knight said nothing. "He helped me understand how to kill dragons."

The man turned and, squinting his eyes against the light of the lantern on the table by the bed, said, "Magic, was it?"

"No, just good ideas about how dragons work."

"Ya killed it with knowledge, eh?"

Axel realized that there wasn't anything he could say to the knight that would make him feel better. He asked for directions to the dragon's cave and quietly left the room.

* * *

Leading Winthton while following the knight's directions wasn't easy in the dark, but Axel did find the inlet where the dragon lived in the cave. He got there just before the sun came up. He left Winthton tied to a bush far enough from the beach so he wouldn't be seen if the dragon got away from him and took off. Axel didn't want Winthton to be its breakfast.

Axel lighted a lantern the cook had given him which helped greatly as he made his way along the water's edge by great boulders and old trees that had fallen from the cliff and had been washed onto the beach by the waves. When he was just below the cave, he could just see its dark mouth against the lighter color of the cliff. After studying what he could see of the climb, he blew out the lantern and left it on the beach. He had to be careful not to make noise, though. It wouldn't do to wake the beast until he was ready.

The sand was soft on the steep slope up to the cave, with large stones scattered on it. His feet sank deeply, and he had to pull himself up by grabbing onto the stones. He could just see them because they were a bit darker than the lighter colored sand. A cold, wet wind blew off the water, and Axel could smell the salt and dead-fish seaweed. But even with the wind at his back, just before he reached the cave, he could smell again that sweet, throat-tightening, rotting meat smell of dragon food. He had forgotten how bad it was. And the flies.

There was enough light now so that he could see where to put his feet, and he could begin to see the flies, where before he could only hear them. There wasn't much of a shelf in front of the cave, but this dragon didn't need one. The cave mouth was so big that it could fly right in. He remembered the knight saying that the dragon had glided in past them before they had seen it.

Axel softly lowered the bag of stars, then set down his bow. Holding his arm across his face to cut down on the smell, he took the bag and walked fifteen paces into the cave. At this point the sides sloped in and it quickly became narrow. It was so dark that he couldn't see the floor, and he placed his feet very slowly. Even so, he could hear slight sounds as his boots stepped on and pushed aside bones, not just the rattle they made when the small, dry ones rolled away, but the squish of flesh when he stepped on the ones that still had meat on them. The disturbed flies rose in black masses, and the buzzing was so loud it drowned out the sound of the waves on the beach.

He carefully placed the stars across the mouth of the cave, then as slowly as he had entered, backed out to wait. He dipped one arrow in oil because he felt he would get only one shot, and he checked that the rags were tightly wound around it.

The sky behind him changed from black to a lighter shade of gray, then began to glow with faint, pink lines along the horizon. The whole eastern sky turned a light blue just before the sun broke above the waves. As the sun's rays lit the shelf of the cave, he could see the stars in a line across the rough, stone floor. Soon he could make out some of the smaller bones, and the dark clouds of shiny green flies shone in the sun. Even when breathing through his mouth, the smell was so powerful it closed his throat.

Axel felt small, standing alone there on the shelf, his back to the ocean, half way to the cliff's top. There was nothing in front of the cave to hide behind this time. He would have to stand on the shelf and wait for the dragon to come to the mouth of the cave. *It will see me standing here with the light at my back as soon as it turns the corner back there in the darkness. If I light the oil too soon, it will know what I plan to do and it won't work. I won't be able to light the arrow until it hurts its feet and gets really mad.* He placed the fireboard by his feet and again dipped the end of the arrow into the flask of oil. He fit the arrow to the bowstring, and held the bow and arrow with his left hand and the flint with his right.

As soon as I shoot the arrow, I'll have to dive over the lip behind me to get away from the blast. He looked again behind him. The steep slope of sand and rocks ran down to the beach, about fifty feet below where he stood. *Even to roll down to the water's edge would be better than to be here when it blows up.*

He turned back quickly when he heard a bone roll on the floor, and there facing him was the dragon. It was huge, a very dark green fading to black in the dimness of the entrance. Its slitted eyes glowed in the dull light of the rising sun. The long, scale-covered tail was out of sight, still around the bend. *It must have seen me, but it isn't moving, just standing there looking. It's thinking. It's remembering what it learned about other dragons that have blown up, and it's remembering how it stomped the knights.* It was very hard to stand there and not run. It was all Axel could do, though. If he tried to run, the beast would be on him before he got even half way to the beach. He was committed now, and he had no choice. He had to wait until it stomped its feet.

The dragon moved a few more feet toward the light. Now Axel could see its tail thrashing back and forth and could hear it striking the walls of the cave on both sides. The dragon hissed, a high-pitched wet sound, its forked, black tongue slowly sliding out and back between dry lips. The light crept along the floor of the cave, and in a moment it would reach the stars. They would then be easy for the dragon to see. *It won't know what they are, but it will know that they weren't there yesterday.*

The points, as long as Axel's fingers, were touched by the sun, and they gleamed dully in the light. The dragon looked down and must have seen them for it reared back on its haunches, filled its lungs with air, tilted its head up and roared. The sound from its huge mouth filled the cave with enough force to hurt Axel's ears. It was some time before the echoes died away. The dragon never took its yellow-slitted eyes off Axel, and it was swaying back and forth, its tongue darting continuously. Axel could almost feel it thinking, wondering what the points of light were on the floor and why this man was standing there alone, facing it.

Dropping its front feet to the floor, it charged. Axel hadn't expected this, and it was a moment before he could get his legs to work. The dragon had covered almost half of the distance to him before he could move. When he did, he jumped backwards to the lip of the shelf, tripped, fell, and rolled. When he stopped he was lying on his side, the bow by his legs and his right arm twisted under him. He expected any second now to feel the dragon's teeth crunching into his back. He looked back over his shoulder just in time to see the charging dragon's right front foot mash down on one of the long, sharp points of a star. It quickly lifted its foot and Axel could see the star deeply imbedded in the pad. It howled in pain and rage and jumped to one side and landed firmly on another point. It screamed and thrashed its tail against the walls of the cave so hard that scales were torn off and thrown to the edge of the shelf. It stomped its front feet as it started another charge and drove a point five inches into a hind foot. Its red eyes shone with hate and frustration, and its thrashing head flung long strings of saliva onto the walls. It whirled on Axel, leaning its head forward and down.

This is just what Axel had been waiting for. Keeping his eyes on the enraged beast, he reached down and felt for the fireboard. . .It wasn't there. When the dragon first charged, he must have dropped it. He had the bow, the flint, the arrow, and the dragon was about to suck in air. He saw the fireboard five long paces from him. Axel was surprised to see the firestick still in the hole. Somehow it hadn't broken in the fall.

He could hear the rush of air being sucked in. Crouching, he glanced once up at the dragon and dove for the fireboard. He dropped the bow and grabbed at the fireboard with his left hand and, as he was rolling onto his back, struck the flint on the steel. The firestick flared, and he pushed it against the rag tied to the tip of the arrow that was next to the bow. It burst into flame.

Axel twisted over onto his knees and looked up. The dragon towered above him, but its head was still lowered. By the sound of the air being sucked in, he could tell it was almost full and was about to close its mouth. But, he was too close to shoot. The explosion would kill him. He had to get some distance away, and that meant that he had to turn his back on this monster. But, whatever he did, it would have to be in the next second or two.

Axel grabbed his bow, nocked the arrow and ran toward the lip of the shelf. Just before he reached the edge, he whirled and faced the dragon. In one motion he brought the bow around as he pulled the bowstring back. He didn't have time to aim. The beast was closing its mouth. He shot.

Axel was diving over the lip toward the water when he felt the force of the blast slam into his back. The rough jolt when he first hit the sand knocked the air from his lungs. He couldn't breathe as he bounced and rolled between the large stones toward the water. His body stopped rolling when he hit the hard sand at the water line. Stunned, he lay there, his upper body being washed by the waves of the incoming tide.

And that's the way they found him—face down in the sand, his hair and shirt burned, his body cut and bleeding, the waves lapping against him.

15

Green Eggs And Axel

Axel woke in his room, in bed. A girl, about his age, was washing his arm when he opened his eyes. "Who are you?" he asked, and his head exploded with pain.

The girl looked startled when he spoke. She turned and looked behind her. Following her look, Axel saw that on the other side of the room stood the king. She said, with her head turned away from the bed, "He's awake, Your Highness."

King Willard walked over to the bed and looked down at the new hero. From where Axel lay, the king looked very tall. The room was dark, the only light coming from a lamp on a table at the side of the bed. Reaching out, the king placed a hand gently on Axel's shoulder. "You have done a great thing, Axel. We all are proud of you. How do you feel?"

"Light-headed, Your Majesty." Just talking hurt.

"You rest and let Marie here tend you." Axel could see the girl's cheeks redden. Her black hair fell to her shoulders, and when she bent forward to dry his arm, it hid her face. One eye looked at him through the dark veil. The yellow light from the lamp shone off her hair and made her skin glow golden and fine.

Axel looked past her at the king, "Thank you, Your Majesty. Is the dragon dead?"

Leaning back, the king held his arms out to the side and shouted, "Ho, ho. Is the dragon dead? My boy, that dragon is all over the inside of that cave. We have never seen anything like it. You really chopped it up. It looked just like the dragon might have exploded. You must be a lot stronger than you look." The noise the king made really hurt Axel's head, and he didn't know what to say. The king continued in the same very loud voice. "When Our men brought you back and told Us what you had done, We just had to see for Ourselves. What a job you did on that beast."

"But, stink. How could you stand it? We took camphor and soaked cloths to breathe through, but still—You were lucky to escape. We found bits of dragon on the ceiling, walls and all over the floor of the cave. There was even some outside on the sand, and We found one bit down by the water. When you feel like it, We want to hear everything. Every detail. The knights want to hear it too."

"But, Your Majesty—"

"They're eager to try the same things on the other beast we have. They want all the details."

Now I've got a real problem. The king has asked me for help, and I can't give it to him. All I can do is tell him I can't help. Axel tried to sit, then fell back. Marie put her hand on his shoulder to hold him down. "I'm sorry, Your Majesty. I can't do that. Do you remember when I told you about my promise to Sidney?" The king frowned and then nodded. "I still have to honor that promise. I'll do anything you ask me to, but I can't break my promise."

The king smiled and said, "Of course. Sorry, We forgot." He reached out and put his hand over Axel's. "You rest. The knights know enough now to kill the last beast without you breaking your promise."

The king slapped his thigh. "The idea of the stars was a good one. We collected what we could find of yours, and the blacksmith is making more. We brought all of your things back, too. Now Sir Bruce wants to be in on the kill. He will be leading the knights. They will kill our other dragon the day after tomorrow."

Axel again struggled to sit up. This time the king pushed him back down. Surprising himself for speaking this way to the king, Axel said, "Your Majesty, don't let them do it. The dragon will kill them. They don't know how to use the stars and have them help. There's more to it than that."

The king patted Axel on the arm, "There, there, now. You rest. Let Us worry about what the knights can and cannot do. We have brave and good knights. They will be able to take care of themselves and that beast."

Forcing himself to a sitting position, Axel cried out, "Please, Your Majesty—"

The king spoke sharply, "Axel, We order you to lie back down and rest."

Axel relaxed. What else could he do? The king had ordered it.

The king and Marie turned to go, leaving the lamp lit. As Marie was opening the door for the king, Axel saw her turn and look at him and smile. She is a very kind person, he thought. The shadows wavered on the walls and drapes, and in them Axel saw again the dragon's yellow eyes glow and the black tongue slide out and back between its hard, thin lips. He wondered how he could kill the last dragon now that it might have seen the stars and understood why they were in the cave. *What else do I know about dragons that I can use?* This time he didn't need to imagine Sidney talking to him. Axel saw the dragon just before it charged him. It was near the mouth of the cave and it was thrashing its tail from side to side. Thinking of it as a problem, Axel slept.

Later that day, Axel woke thinking of Winthton. When he swung his legs over the side of the bed, he found his shoulder and both legs were stiff, and it hurt to move. He had to steady himself against the wall when he put on the new clothes someone had left for him. He had never imagined wearing such fine cloth.

After Axel had found the stable and had taken care of Winthton, he stopped at the blacksmith's shop. The big man was finishing up the knights' order for stars. The blacksmith recognized Axel and greeted him with, "Well, the stars I made ya must a worked, eh?"

Axel nodded, "They were perfect. Thanks for making them for me." The man smiled. "I see you're at work on more."

"The knights asked me for some. I guess they're gonna use em on the other dragon. Good riddance, I say."

Axel asked, "Do you have any time to make me something today?"

"Sure. I'd make ya anything. The whole castle heard what ya done yesterday. I guess anything ya want, ya got. What ya need?"

"Look here." Axel took a piece of charcoal and drew a design on the wooden wall of the shop. "It'll need a short piece of chain here. These hooks should be three-in-one, like this." He put the backs of his hands together, and using his fingers, demonstrated what he meant. "Then, on the other end, it needs a wedge I can drive into a crack." He looked up at the heavily muscled man. "Can you do that?"

"I can make anything ya can draw a picture of. When ya want it?"

"I'll need about six. Can you make them by tomorrow morning, early?"

"I can have 'em by late this afternoon, if ya need 'em. That do?"

"Would you put them in a bag like you did the stars and leave them by the door again so I can get them real early?"

"Sure can. What else ya need?"

"If you have a short hammer, I'd like to use it. Oh, one other thing. Do you know where the other dragon lives that the knights are going to kill?"

"Everybody knows. We have ta so we can stay clear. That whole part of the country is empty now. That dragon has killed everything for miles around." He took the charcoal and began to draw on the same wall. "Look here. This is the castle, here." He drew an x. "Here is the road up from the south," and he drew a line up to the x. "This here is the sea," and he drew another line. "Ya keep going north about three hours. Off to the right ya see some hills, turn toward 'em. There's this one tall rock. Like a chimney, see. This dragon lives down the chimney."

"Down inside the rock chimney?"

"Ya, and there's no way to get at it."

"Then what do the knights want the stars for?"

"That's what I ask em. They said there had to be another entrance. See, nobody's ever been there and come back. But the knights figure with the flaming arrows you use and the stars to hurt the dragon's feet, they find the other entrance, they can kill it." The blacksmith wiped his face on his arm.

"What do ya do with the stars? What's that got to do with killing the dragon? I always thought that dragons would be tough enough without ya hurting their feet. It didn't sound like the knights knew for sure what they was for either. And why the hooks? What ya do with it all?"

"I'm sorry, I can't tell you. I promised I wouldn't tell anyone."

The large man looked closely Axel for a moment, but he didn't say he didn't believe him. "I guess ya know what you're about. I sure don't understand it." The blacksmith shook his head and turned away. He stopped moving for a moment, turned back and said, "Say, why ya want to know where the dragon lives, anyway?"

Turning to go, Axel said. "I'm worried about the knights. I sure don't want anyone to get hurt."

The blacksmith was pumping hard on the bellows. "I'll. . .have. . .the. . .hooks. . .tonight."

"Thank you, blacksmith."

Axel took a long nap that afternoon and woke in time to have the cook fix him some supper. When he checked his equipment he found the string on his bow had been darkened by the blast, but it looked strong. He still had six arrows, but there wasn't enough oil in the flask. When he went to check on Winthton, he filled it from the lamp hanging on the wall of the stable.

Just as he had promised, the blacksmith had left a bag outside his shop. Axel took it back to the stable and dumped it out. The six chained hooks looked just like his drawings. They were all the same. On each one there was a wedge on one end of a short chain. On the other end were three very sharp, barbed hooks, much like fish hooks, that were fastened to one shaft. The whole thing was as long as both of his arms stretched out.

Axel had worked on the assumption that this last of the king's dragons had seen one or more of the stars. *It'd be dumb not to think this. The king's men didn't find them all. It might have figured out what they were used for.*

Since the first of the king's dragons had learned enough to be afraid to try and burn me, I have to expect this second could learn as well. It might not fall for the star trick.

The king's men will all be killed if they rely on the stars and flaming arrows to kill the second dragon. The first one had stomped to death three men. How many would die this time? I have to do what I can to help the king's men even if they didn't want me to. If the dragon learned not to breathe fire, or to stomp its enemies, how would it choose to fight? Axel had figured out what he had to do the night before, just as he was drifting off to sleep. He lay there thinking that if he were the dragon, what he would have to do to kill the knights if he couldn't burn or stomp them. *What weapons do dragons have? They can bite, slash with claws, stomp, burn, and bash with their tails. In the confines of a cave, there isn't much room to move about. The dragon isn't going to chase me. It could break a wing too easily. If it couldn't chase and it couldn't bite or slash, then it would have to use its tail.*

How would it do that? Dragons have long ones, and they can control them easily. It would turn sideways and lash out with its tail. So. . .if I were to fix a hook to the wall behind me, and then stand there until the dragon tried to bash me with its tail. . .and duck at just the right moment, the tail might get caught on a hook. If that happened, it sure ought to make the dragon mad enough to lose its temper. If it got mad enough, it might try its fire. And, if I'm quick enough. . .and lucky. . .I might get a shot with an arrow. Risky, but that's all

I can think of.

Axel and Winthton were on the road early the next morning. Of course, he hadn't told anyone that he was leaving or what he had in mind. He was sure the knights would have tried to stop him if they had known what he was up to. The king would have told him not to go. It must have been that the guard at the gate hadn't been given orders not to let him out, so that wasn't a problem.

The torches burning on each side of the doorway when Axel reached it reflected off the iron bars of the first gate. The guard standing by the large wheel that worked the drawbridge saw Axel and challenged him. When he asked to be let out, the man grunted, but did turn and let off the lock and lean on the long spokes. The wheel squeaked and the chains rattled when the bridge was lowered, the sounds loud in the dark and empty courtyard. Axel was afraid that someone might come to find out why it was being lowered so early, but no one did.

The sun had burned off most of the overcast so that the countryside was gray instead of black. Axel saw, off to the right, the hills the blacksmith had told him about. The low spots in the road were still covered in dense fog, a white mist that hid them from the early sun. They turned toward the hills. On the upslopes their heads would surface first, and it looked like their heads were floating in a lake of milk. At the top of one hill Axel saw the chimney rock on the far side of a heavy woods. The bottom of the narrow tower was still in fog, and he couldn't tell how high it was or what the ground was like leading up to it. He was too late to catch the dragon asleep in the chimney cave. He would have to wait until it left its lair before he placed the wedges in the rock.

Axel and Winthton rested under a tree just inside the

woods, and Axel kept his eyes on the tall rock. The chimney was about two bow shots away, so he could see clearly when the dragon lifted its head out and looked around. Axel whispered, "There it is, Winthton. The last dragon we'll ever have to kill. This will be the end of it for us." From this distance, it didn't look to be a very big one.

It stayed in the chimney for a while with just its head showing, then lifted its body to the rim. It sat there like some scaled bird looking over the hills. The fog pulsed and shifted against the chimney much as water might against a lighthouse. With a piercing cry, the dragon launched itself. At first it sank into the top layer of fog as it glided on its outstretched leathery wings, then began to pound them against the air. It lifted itself over the low, misty hills and disappeared into the gray morning. The disturbed fog whirled and shifted, then settled down again into smooth waves.

Axel tied Winthton to a small tree, and taking his bow, quiver, sack of chained hooks, a coil of rope which he placed over one shoulder, short hammer, oil flask and fireboard, he ran downhill through the white fog toward the chimney. When his head sank below the surface of the mist, he had to slow down, but he felt he should be as quick getting into the rock as he could. There was no way to know when the beast might return, and he couldn't be caught in the open. *It's too late now, but it would have been good if I had come other mornings to watch what it does, but there wasn't time. I have to kill it before the king's knights get here tomorrow.*

When the ground began to slant upward, Axel thought that he must be close to the chimney. He had to be careful walking now, because the ground was littered with stones and small boulders. The fog still was higher than his head, and it was only slightly lighter when he looked upward. Holding his hand out in front of him so that he wouldn't run into the chimney, he stumbled around for some time before he felt the rough, stone wall of the dragon's entrance. He could see the stone only when his eyes were just inches away. Axel ran his hands over the ridged wall of the chimney and thought that it would be easy to climb. The weathering, that had washed all the surrounding land away from this harder stone, had cut ridges around it for its full height. Like climbing a ladder in the dark, he thought. It wasn't nearly as tall as he had thought when he had first seen it. The climb was easy and soon he pushed his head above the fog and could turn and look about. No sign of the dragon, and he couldn't hear beating wings, so he continued climbing, and shortly he was standing on the rim. He stood where the dragon had been when it launched itself.

There was a moaning of fast moving air coming from the black center hole, bringing with it the familiar stench of rotting meat and dragon guano. After carefully looking for the returning dragon, Axel pounded a wedge into a crack in the stone rim, tied the rope to one of the hooks, and easing carefully around the sharp points, lowered himself into the darkness. The stench was overpowering, the updraft driving it into his face.

The inside of the chimney was dry, and the descent was not difficult. The circle of light above him got smaller the further down he dropped. The inside of the shaft must go below ground level, he thought. He was almost at the end of the rope when he felt stone beneath his feet. Making sure he had a good footing, Axel let go. *The strong wind means that I won't be able to light a fire down here. I won't be able to see where I'm going, and I don't want to wander around in a dragon's lair in the dark, maybe to get lost. I wish I'd thought to bring a lantern. Too late now to spend time thinking about what I should have done. This might be the one I can't kill.* Axel realized that he would have to climb back out and try to find another entrance. Some place where he would stand a chance of surviving.

He had moved away from the rope, and when he turned to find it again, he tripped on a stone and staggered further into the cave where he fell into a pile of brush. *What would brush be doing down here?* Feeling in the darkness, he discovered that the sticks were woven and made a rough circle almost like a nest. . . . *A nest. The dragon's a female. She built a nest down here. This means she'll come back any minute. There might be a mate coming to tend the nest. There could even be a young dragon down here with me.* The darkness pressed in as Axel quickly felt his way across the pile of brush toward the small spot of light directly below the shaft.

He was still on his hands and knees, feeling his way across the nest, when his hand hit a slightly warm ball. It was the size of a small man's head and had a leathery feel. When he pushed on it with his finger, there was a bit of give. It was round like. . .an egg. *The rarest thing in all the world. I've found a dragon's egg.*

He quickly dumped out the chained hooks and lifted the egg into the bag. He had just reached the rope and was looking up at the circle of light at the top of the shaft when the light was cut off. The beast had returned and had settled over the hole. He was trapped down there in the dark.

Axel was stunned. What a perfect trap this was. Of the choices there were, he could think of nothing that might help. Still his mind whirled with the possibilities. *I have no way of knowing the size of the underground cave. . .If I were to wander around down here in this blackness, I could become lost and never again see light. . .I would starve or die of thirst stumbling against the walls. . .If I disturb the dragon, she will come down to defend her egg. . .Even though there would be a bit more light once she leaves the top of the tower, she would discover me and could easily kill me in this dim, confined space. . .When she leaves, the draft will start again, and I won't be able to light an arrow. . .The knights won't be here until morning, and the beast'll come down to her nest before then, so there'll be no help from them.*

Moving carefully and quietly, Axel sat down in the rough branches of the nest, the egg in his lap. He put his hand on its leathery shell and could feel slight movements. He absently stroked it as he thought.

The thing I have to do is figure this out as Sidney would. It was hard for him to concentrate in the total darkness. He soon began to see spots of light and even movements in the blackness. *I have to make a list of all the things I know and then use the list to examine the choices open to me and then pick the one action that seems to offer the most hope and do it. If I just wait here, it will come down and kill me.*

I know there must be another opening in the cave somewhere because of the draft up the chimney. There wouldn't be air movement if there weren't some place for it to come in. I could get lost down here if I wander around. I might fall in a pit or break a leg. Even if there's another opening, it might not be big enough for me to get out.

I'm below ground level, so I can't break my way out with the hammer. I can light a fire on an arrow tip now that she's shut off the air flow, but if she comes down, she won't try to kill me with fire because she knows that I could blow her up. If I start to pound in the wedges down here, she'll hear me and come down right away.

If I try and hide down here, she might smell me. She sure can see better in the dark than I can. She would find me. If I shoot an arrow up the chimney at her, it won't do any damage. Her scales are too tough. If I light her nest on fire, she'll leave the top of the chimney, but then she'll come down when the fire's out and kill me. If I climb up to her in the dark. . .What good would that do? I wouldn't be able to do her any damage.

What if I had the egg in my hands when I climbed up? She would see me and the egg and not want to take a chance of hurting the egg. What would she do? The only thing she wouldn't do is the only thing I want her to do, fight with her fire. She would stand on the rim and wait for me to come out and kill me, or she would come down to me. If I make a noise down here to attract her attention. . .put her egg in a far corner. . .she'll go to it. . .I climb fast. . .That's dumb. Axel was now seeing colored images in the darkness.

None of these things sounded as though they might save his life. He began to think of the weapons he had, what equipment he could use. *I have five hooks, the bow, arrows, oil, and a hammer. Wait. . .I have six hooks. One is still fastened to the rim.* In his mind he could see it now, hanging down inside the chimney. He had driven the wedge into the rock of the rim and tied the rope to one of the three hooks. *That could be something. How can I use that? If the beast starts to come down the shaft, she'll get hooked. Then she won't be able to come down any further. I won't be able to go up, but she won't be able to come down and get me either. The knights will be here in the morning. They'll hear her in the chimney and kill her. They ought to be able to do that if she's trapped.*

After they kill her, how will they know I'm down here? With the beast stuck in the shaft, dead, they might not be able to hear me shout. The dragon will be dead but so will I. . . That's not the best solution possible. Even if the beast weren't stuck in the shaft, I couldn't be heard down here. This nest is too far down.

What I have to do is figure a way to kill her and then not have her body plug the hole so I can climb out. The only way I can kill a dragon is by shooting it when it's mad enough to forget about the danger in trying to use its flame. That's why I brought the hooks. That was to make it mad so it would try and burn me. That's it. If she tries to come down the shaft, she'll get caught on the hook I tied the rope on. She won't be able to come down to get me, and she might not be able to back out. She'll be stuck there. She might be able to see me if I stand directly under her. Some light's bound to come around her body and down to the bottom of the chimney. The only thing she'll be able to fight with will be her flame. She'll be mad enough to do that with me down here with her egg. When she starts to draw air into her meth stomach, I shoot an arrow and jump aside. She blows up, the pieces fall down and I climb out. Simple.

Axel thought that this was the only thing he could do, but there were great dangers. If the dragon didn't try to burn him, he would be stuck down there with no way out and no way to signal the knights when they came. Not a perfect solution, but it might be the only chance he might have. At least he would be doing something. He felt he had been in the dark for hours, and anything might be better than just waiting for the beast to come down and look at her egg, or turn it over, or whatever she did to it.

Axel groped for the flask and dipped two rag-wrapped

arrows in the oil. There might be a chance to get two shots. He worked his way toward where he thought the shaft was. There was no way to be sure, but when his head hit the rope, he knew he was directly under the dragon.

He fitted an arrow to his bow and placed the flint between his teeth and the fireboard with its firestick in the hole on the stone floor between his feet. Everything was in place and he was ready. Still, he hesitated. To start his plan meant that he could be that much closer to his death. He had to do it, but it was hard. He thought of Molly and it gave him the strength to begin. He tapped gently on the wall of the shaft with the hammer tap. . .tap. . .tap. The beast shifted. A crack of light showed. Tap. . .tap.

The dragon lifted her body and Axel was flooded with light. It seemed very bright after the blackness. He could see the silhouette of the beast's head as she turned and looked down the shaft. Her green-black head remained in the center of the circle of light for what felt to Axel like a very long time, then most of the light was cut off as the dragon's body filled the flue. Her claws scraped against the stone as she started down.

Axel could tell by the sounds she made when she embedded herself on the sharp points of the hooks. The barbs caught, and she began to struggle against the chain. He could hear her wings pound the walls and her feet dig and scratch. When she realized she was caught in the shaft, she tried to back out. Axel could see the slight bands of light shift from side to side as she thrashed her body about. Her struggles became frantic.

It was then that he began to yell and pound loudly against the wall of the chimney with the hammer. When he stopped for a moment, the beast was still. *She's trying to understand what's down here.* He pounded on the wall again. . .then listened. The dragon beat against the sides of the shaft in frustration and rage. She screamed. The sound, magnified by the tube of the chimney, pounded against Axel like blows from something solid. She dug at the flue with her claws and teeth, and stone dust and bits of broken claw rained down.

When she became quiet, Axel went back to work. Tap. . .tap. . .tap. She was silent, listening. There was only a thin slice of light that came to the bottom of the chimney, but Axel had to hope there was enough for the beast to see him. He shouted up against the darkness and the smell, "I have your egg down here. Come and get it," and he pounded hard with the hammer against the wall.

When Axel stopped to listen, he could hear the dragon listening. He moved to give the dragon the best chance of seeing him. Then he heard the long, wet sucking of air. This was it. He couldn't be sure just where the beast's head was, but he had no choice. He would have to aim by sound.

He took the flint from between his teeth. Reaching down to the fireboard, he struck the flint against the steel. The firestick caught. He pulled it from its hole and pushed it onto the oiled rags tied to one of the arrows. The inside of the chimney jumped out at him in the light of the burning oil. He aimed up the shaft. The dragon's head was directly above him. The slitted eyes reflected the yellow flame. Her mouth was opened wide, and he could see into her long, slimy throat, and he aimed at the back of it, over her writhing, black tongue. He fired, then jumped away from the shaft.

White, red waves—crashing black smoke—stone dust—red teeth—grit and pain.

A tremendous explosion. It hurled him against a rough wall he hadn't known was there. Debris clattered and plopped down the shaft. Scales, teeth, flesh, and bits of rock fell for a long time. There were clouds of dust. When most of it had cleared away, Axel went to the bottom of the shaft and looked up. He had to step on mounds of bloody flesh to do it. There was much more light. He had done it. The rope was hanging there waiting for him, and he pulled on it to test it. It pulled down. When Axel looked up, he saw and heard the rim of the chimney coming down with it. He jumped out of the way as large chunks of stone fell at his feet. Then the rope curled down into a pile at the bottom of the shaft. The hook and chain fell next with a great deal of dust.

I've killed the dragon, the chimney's clear, but I'm trapped down here. There's no way out until the knights come, if then. I'll just have to wait. In the meantime I have to figure out a way to signal them that I'm here. Unless they climb down the chimney, they won't hear me if I yell. I'll have to wait till morning and see if I can hear them. If I know they're out there, I can shoot a burning arrow out of the top of the shaft. They should be able to see that.

That sounded to Axel like a good plan. But first, he had to move most of the stone and dead dragon from the bottom of the shaft to find the firestick and oil flask. He was covered in bits of flesh, blood and dust by the time they were found. But, the flint was gone; it had disappeared in the debris. After moving most of the flesh and bones, and almost all of the broken pieces of the chimney, Axel felt carefully among the smaller pieces of stone and dust for the flint. By now it was evening and too dark to see what he was doing, and he wasn't sure if it was even still at the bottom of the shaft. He gave up and slept in the nest, curled around the egg.

The knights found Winthton still tied to the tree and knew that Axel was somewhere near. When they didn't see the dragon, they began to call. Axel heard them as he was examining the egg in the early morning light that was flooding down the enlarged opening. He was surprised to see that it was dark green, with faint black and yellow lines in it, like blood vessels. He had ripped long strips from his shirt and tied them to an arrow. When the knight's shouts seemed close to the shaft, he shot the arrow up the chimney.

The rest was simple. When the knights saw the arrow with its long tail fly from the chimney, they lowered their rope. Axel climbed out with the egg in the sack, and after many questions and some answers, and in great spirits, they headed back to the castle.

16

Party Time

As Axel and the knights came over the hill and turned the bend, they could see flags flying from poles raised on all the walls of the castle. Brightly colored tents had been pitched in the fields on both sides of the road leading to the outer gate, and each of these had a flag fluttering in the afternoon breeze. It looked like the entire population of both the castle and Willardville were along the sides of the roadway waiting for them.

There was music and singing, and the sea breeze brought smells of roasting ox and pig. There were lines of people traveling to the area from town. Axel was surprised to see so much activity, and he thought, I have come back in the middle of a fair. "We've never seen anything like this, have we Winthton." The donkey lipped his ear.

Someone in the near crowd spotted the group as they crested the hill, and a high-pitched cry went up. People ran down the road toward the small band of returning warriors. Axel noticed the knights now rode straighter in their saddles and made their horses prance. Even Winthton walked with his ears stiff and pointed upward. The crowd surged around them dancing and passing up bottles to the knights.

Marie was there wearing a bright blue and white dress. Two or three times she reached out and touched Winthton's side as she walked beside Axel, but she didn't say anything to him. He glanced at her from time to time on the way toward the tent area, but he couldn't catch her looking at him.

When they reached the first tents, Axel asked, "What's the fair all about, Marie?"

The beautiful girl pushed the hair away from her face and laughed. The sound was clearer to Axel than the music and singing of the nearing tents. He liked the sound of her laughter but didn't understand it. "Was that a funny thing I asked?"

Marie reached out, took Axel's hand and looked up into his face. "You're a hero. It's all in honor of what you have done for us."

Axel turned and looked all about him. The crowd now had reached the area of the fair. Smoke rose from the pits where cooks were roasting whole pigs and even oxen on huge spits. Musicians were playing for groups of people. Children ran through the area chasing each other. Near the road was the largest and most colorful tent, and when they got close they could see King Willard sitting on a chair, surrounded by his court.

"All this for me?" Axel asked, turning to look at Marie.

Marie looked up at him and said, "As soon as Sir Bruce's messenger got here with the news that you and the knights had the dragon trapped and were killing it, King Willard ordered this fair. The people really hurried to get everything set up for your return." She laughed again and gave a little skip. "Isn't it grand?"

A young girl with a handful of yellow and blue flowers held them out to Axel. By the time he saw her, Winthton had reached over and taken them gently with his lips and was eating them. Axel could see tears start in the child's eyes. Reaching down, he lifted her to Winthton's back. The donkey stopped walking, and Axel remembered what Sidney had said about him lying down if anyone mounted him. Winthton looked at Axel, gave his ears a reproachful twitch. . .and walked on. Axel reached over and rubbed Winthton's ears. The donkey didn't notice. The crowd around them cheered. Holding the lead, Axel walked Winthton to a nearby rail. Marie pointed to the rail in front of the king's tent. She smiled up at him and motioned for him to follow. He did, and as he tied the donkey next to the large horses, thought, such a grand place for Winthton to spend the afternoon. He helped the girl down, and she ran off to tell others of her ride on the dragon-slayer's mount.

Marie led Axel to the table set outside of the king's tent. She stood and looked up at him and smiled. Axel didn't know what to say, so he glanced back to see how Winthton was getting on with the king's horses. He was surprised to see that his donkey was not paying any attention to any of them. Now *he* feels superior, he thought. He turned back and said to Marie, "My friend feels good about where we put him."

Marie said softly, her hand touching his arm, "We all are very proud of what you have done, Axel. Especially me."

"Why is that? I mean why especially you?"

"Because I think you're wonderful, Axel."

Axel was embarrassed by this praise and didn't know how to respond, so he remained silent.

When they came near the king's table, King Willard

rose. All the other nobles there rose with him. The king called out, "Axel, my boy. Welcome back. You're the guest of honor here, or did Marie tell you already?"

"Yes, Your Majesty. What a surprise."

"Come and sit with Us." The king motioned to an empty chair next to him. "We have a ceremony planned shortly." He smiled at Axel. "You will be the honored one then, too. The man who rid the world of the curse of dragons." He put his hands on Axel's shoulders and looked into his eyes as he said, "We are sure they will write ballads about what you have done. Do you realize what this means? You have killed the last dragon ever."

The air left Axel's lungs. He couldn't breathe. He had not realized that that was what it meant—his killing of the small female dragon—until the king said that. He looked at King Willard and asked, "The last one?"

"Yes, my boy. There are no more and there never will be any more. What a wonderful thing you have accomplished," and he patted Axel on the back.

Axel's face had lost its expression. "That was. . .the last one. . .in all the kingdom? And I. . .killed it?" Axel stood.

The king also stood, and now looked down at him. "You do not seem excited, Axel. What is the problem? Are you still surprised that you could do it?"

Axel turned and looked in the direction he had traveled to kill the dragon. "Couldn't there be more somewhere else? Isn't it possible?"

The king laughed and shook his head. "No, no, my boy. That was positively the last one. We looked into this very carefully before you got here." He pushed Axel down in the chair and sat next to him. "The ones at Tightly and Highcliff and the two that We had here were the very last ones. We sent messengers to all corners of the kingdom to ask for help in getting rid of them. They all told Us that they hadn't had dragons for many years, and they didn't know how to help Us. Those beasts were nothing but trouble, and now they're all dead. We owe you a great deal."

Axel heard again the anguished cries of the female when she knew he was in the cave with the last dragon's egg there would ever be. His eyes stung when he thought of her trapped and in panic, digging and chewing at the inside of the stone chimney. She had been trying to save her child. She must have known what was down in her nest with the last egg she ever would lay. *I wanted to kill dragons, and I have. I have killed them all. There never will be another one. . .ever. . .for all time. Unless. . .* He looked to where Winthton was tied. He had to lean out to see around Marie, who was standing there smiling up at him. The king looked where he thought Axel was looking and said, "Marie, get Axel a drink, would you?"

She started off, then asked, "What would you like, Axel?"

". . .What?"

She came back and touched him on the arm. "What would you like to drink?"

"Would there be milk?"

The king laughed, "Anything you want today, you can have, Axel."

"Then milk would be fine, Marie." Axel watched her walk away. He was thinking of Molly. Marie was a beautiful girl, but he was in love with Molly and thought of Marie as a friend. When he turned back, he saw that the king had fallen asleep. Axel watched the activity around him and thought of a world with no dragons.

Marie returned with a large pitcher of cool milk which

she placed in front of Axel on the table, then sat near him. They were in the shade with a breeze cooling them, and they watched the steady procession of entertainers who came to the king's tent to perform: acrobats, jugglers, musicians and clowns. The king slept.

The knights, who had come back from the dragon kill with Axel, came and sat in a row behind the king. They had been drinking wine and ale and were full of jokes and were excited because of the killing.

Axel was watching two men who were performing a mime, when the king called over one of the guards. "Have the knights gather here." The guard hurried off. He turned to Axel and asked, "Are you enjoying yourself, Axel?" and he slapped him on the back.

"Oh, yes, Your Majesty. This is a fine fair. I have never been to one like it."

King Willard smiled and asked, "Where are you from? Your home?"

"Greenwater, Your Majesty."

"Is that where you are headed when you leave Us, or would you like to stay here? We could use you if you would like to live with Us."

This was indeed an honor. Axel was excited at being asked. He glanced at Marie and noticed she was smiling at him. "I'm honored, Your Majesty, but I plan on marrying a girl who lives in Greenwater. I must return to her." Marie gave a short squeak, jumped up and ran from the table.

The king watched her go then turned to Axel. "There is no helping some things."

"What is that, Your Majesty?"

The king started to smile, then his expression turned serious again. "Where does this wizard friend of yours live?"

Axel thought for a moment. He had never thought of Sidney's house as being in a place with a name. How to tell the king where he lived? "He doesn't live in a place, Your Majesty. He has a small house in a valley about five day's walk from Greenwater."

King Willard was looking at Axel closely now. "Tell Us about him. You say his name is Sidney? How old is he? What is he like?"

Axel didn't understand for a moment what the king wanted, then he remembered that the king had been looking for a wizard. *Maybe he would like to have Sidney for his own. Would that be good for Sidney? What the king decides to do might well depend on what I tell him this afternoon.*

Sidney had talked about the life of a wizard being hard. He doesn't have much money. His house is very small and the barn is a mess. But, the valley where he lives is one of the most beautiful places I've ever seen. Even so, Sidney might like the idea of living in the king's castle and working for King Willard. And, it would be a good thing for the king, too. I like the king. He's a kind man, and I'm sure he'd be good to Sidney. I think Sidney would like to live here.

Axel looked about him at all the happy people. The countryside was rich and beautiful, the king had no problems with neighbors that he had heard of, and he needed a wizard and was impressed with how Sidney had helped him. It could be a good thing for them both. He said to the king, "He's a good and kind man who knows a very great deal. It's hard to tell how old he is, but there are no lines in his face, so I don't think he's very, very old."

Nodding his head slowly, the king asked, "Do you think he would like to live here and work for Us?"

"I don't know, Your Majesty. I could ask him when I go

past on the way home."

The king smiled and said, "Would you do that for Us, Axel?"

"I can't promise what he'll say. He has a home there, and he seemed happy enough where he was."

The king held his hand against his chest and said, "You could ask him to come and talk to Us about it, couldn't you?"

"I will try, Your Majesty."

King Willard nodded, shut his eyes for a moment, then he smiled and looked at Axel again. "Thank you, Axel."

The knights had been arriving while the king and Axel had been talking, and now there was a large group of them standing about the tent and table. The king stood. All the others seated at the table and in rows behind it also stood. The king said to one of the knights, "Give Us your sword, Sir Roger." The knight slipped his sword out and handed it hilt first to the king.

Axel tried to speak, but the sound he made was a squeak. The king looked down at him and raised his eyebrows. Axel tried again, "I'll try really hard, Your Highness."

The king laughed and turned to one of the guards standing by the table and commanded, "Bring Charger to Us."

The king turned back to Axel and said, "Axel, kneel before Us." Axel knelt on the ground in front of the king. *He's about to cut off my head!* The king laid the blade on Axel's left shoulder then on his right. "You are a brave man, Axel. You have done a great service for Us and Our kingdom. You have not asked for pay or a reward, but gold could not pay for your service to Us. It was too great. We will give you the highest honor We can. You are now a knight in Our kingdom. Rise, Sir Axel."

Axel was stunned. A knight. While he rose to his feet, the group around them cheered. He looked up at his king. "I don't know how to be a knight, Your Majesty. What do I do?"

King Willard smiled down at him. "As a knight in Our kingdom, you can do anything you wish. . .if it is done with honor and goodness in your heart. You can serve Us here or anywhere you want to live. You will always be a knight and will always serve Us. What do you want to do?"

Axel felt foolish talking about his plans with the king in front of all the knights. When he spoke, his voice was so soft he could hardly hear himself, "I. . .We talked about buying. . .there's a farm—"Axel stopped trying to talk and thought about what had happened to him. *I'm now a knight. The king has just made me one, and I'll act like one.* Axel straightened his back and looked his king in the eyes. His voice was clear and loud enough for all those near the king's tent to understand, "I will be a farmer. Molly and I will be married, and we will farm as much land as I can afford to buy."

The knights were shocked. A knight farming like a serf? Unheard of. This Axel was brave, he had shown that, and the king had just made him a knight. . .but really. A farmer? They looked at each other and smiled. This new knight was going to walk behind a plow horse.

The king's laugh rolled out over the fairgrounds. The knights laughed with him. Axel felt as if he had been kicked in the chest. He could hardly breathe and looked at his feet. Tears pushed behind his eyes and his throat closed tightly. Then he felt the king's heavy hand on his shoulder. It felt much like he remembered his father's hand feeling, firm, heavy and warm. He looked up, his eyes wet.

The king had stopped laughing now; he looked serious. "Wonderful, Sir Axel. Wonderful." Those kind, blue eyes were smiling at him. The king raised his voice to speak to the crowd around them. "Sir Axel will be the first knight in Our kingdom to farm. We think that is an excellent idea. We wish We had thought of it." He raised his voice. "We command you, Sir Axel, go to Greenwater. Marry your Molly. Buy a farm and farm it. That is an order from your king."

The tears were now running down Axel's face. He tried to thank King Willard, but the words wouldn't come out of his tightened throat. He could hear, as if from a long way off, the voices of the other knights.

"Good idea."

"I've been thinking of doing it myself."

"About time one of us did that."

"Cheers for Axel."

And they yelled in unison, "Hurray for Sir Axel. . . Hurray for Sir Axel. . .Hurray for Sir Axel!"

As the knights were crowding around congratulating Axel, the guard who had been sent for Charger, returned. The king motioned him over and took the reins of a large, white warhorse.

"Sir, Axel," said the king in a loud voice, "Charger is the best horse in the kingdom. He is Ours. We want you to have him. He is yours, Sir knight," and he handed the reins to Axel.

The horse was taller than Axel. He was taller than even the king. He was wide and heavy, bred to stand the shock of a full charge in battle. A very valuable animal indeed. On his back was a war saddle with its high back and heavy pommel. Axel ran his hand along the huge horse's neck and the muscles of his chest. He turned back to the king and said, "Thank you, Your Majesty. I will take good care of Charger on my farm."

The king laughed, then yawned. "We are not sure you can teach him to pull a plow, but if anyone can, you are the man for it." The king sat down and fell immediately asleep.

The knights crowded around Axel and congratulated him. Sir Bruce pushed his way through the crush of men and stood in front of Axel and said, "I misjudged you, Sir Axel. I want to make up for it. I want you to have my sword." He held out his heavy battle sword, hilt first, to Axel.

Axel started to say that he couldn't accept, but the intense look on Sir Bruce's face stopped him. He said, "I take this as a special honor, Sir Bruce. Thank you," and he took the rust encrusted sword Sidney had given out and replaced it with the new one. When he looked for a place to put the old one, Sir Bruce reached for it and slid it into his scabbard. "I'll be proud to wear yours, Sir Axel." The knights cheered again until Axel was embarrassed by it all.

Axel looked over to where Winthton was tied. He caught his friend looking at him, but as soon as their eyes met, Winthton looked away. He tied Charger next to Winthton so they too could become friends. When he ran his hand down Winthton's neck the same way he had done with Charger, Winthton turned and looked at him, then at Charger and yawned. Axel walked back to the king's tent to have another glass of milk.

In the morning, he thought, I'll head for Greenwater. I'll have to stop and see Sidney first. It was then that he remembered the priest in Tightly. I should stop and see the priest for a bit, too. I owe him a visit.

17

Return Match

Axel remembered the glade at the side of the river where he had met the warrior on his first trip to Tightly. He had been on the path as it rose toward the high hill that overlooked the town for two or three hours now.

When he reached the branch in the road that led to the place where he had rested and met the wounded man, he led Charger and Winthton down the slope to the water to drink, then sat under the same tree and had his lunch. Winthton and Charger had become good friends and chewed companionably together on the lush summer grasses.

Axel must have fallen asleep in the warm shade, for the first that he knew that he had company was when Winthton drooled on his face. He looked up, and standing looking at him was a good looking young man about his own age. He was holding the reins to a beautiful horse. Axel smiled and said, "Hello, I didn't hear you approach."

The stranger was dressed in fine clothes, and lashed to his horse behind the saddle was expensive armor. The young man inclined his head slightly. "My name is Jeffrey. I am a dragon fighter, or I will be when I find a dragon to kill.

What is your name and where are you headed?"

Jeffrey had spoken as if he were used to having his questions answered. He has the bearing and speech of one who has wealth and education, Axel thought. But what a waste for him to search for dragons. There must be many things he could do that would be much better for him than that. He said, "My name is Axel. I'm on the way to Tightly. Sit down and share what food I have."

Jeffrey looked up the path toward the top of the hill. "Do you know of any dragons in this region?"

Axel stood. "I know there are none. I know that to be a fact."

"Then I have no time to waste with you. I am anxious to kill my first one. I will bid you good day."

"You haven't killed a dragon yet?"

"No, but you can see that I am well prepared to do so. I have the finest armor my father could buy for me."

"I can see that. And a beautiful horse, too."

Jeffrey mounted easily and sat tall on his horse. "Can you direct me to a town that might have had dragon trouble lately?"

"I can give you some good advice if you want it."

"On how to kill dragons?" He laughed. "I don't think I need that. I have been thoroughly trained in the use of modern weapons." Jeffrey's right hand moved to his sword.

Axel wanted to tell this man about his experience with dragons. There was no point in him continuing to search, and he could help him understand that. "Even if there were dragons, you wouldn't be able to succeed with your sword or even a lance. You would need—" he paused and tried to think of a way to say what this man needed to hear, "to see a man like Sidney. He can help you. He can teach you lots

216

about. . .what you're searching for. It might save you. . ." Axel couldn't think of a word that expressed what it might save the young man from. He lifted his shoulders, then let them drop.

"Sidney? I have heard of a wizard by that name, though I doubt he could teach me much I don't already know."

Axel realized that there was no way the young man would listen to and benefit from his experiences, so he said, "Do as you like. I know there's no dragon in Tightly, and that's the last town this side of the mountains. Sidney lives in a valley four days to the west." Axel walked down the bank and led Charger up to where the man was. "You should see him before you go any further."

"Can he tell me where there is a dragon I can kill?"

Axel mounted Charger and led Winthton to the path. "He might be able to direct you in some way. He sure helped me." He turned in the saddle and looked back at Jeffrey. "It would be best if you traveled straight to Sidney's valley before you searched any further."

The young man adjusted his sword belt and said, "I may not take the advice, but thank you just the same." He rode back down the trail the way he had come.

Axel watched the man ride off to his uncertain future, then he turned the other way and looked at the mountain. Even though he was familiar with it, it was an imposing place. Its flat, vertical sides were as uninviting now as they had been the first time he had seen them. The big difference, he thought, is that this time I know what's up there. This time I'm ready.

The entrance into Tightly was much different this time than it had been the first time Axel had walked in. He rode in looking every bit the knight.

Sitting tall in the rich saddle, he nodded to people from high on the beautiful Charger as he passed them on the street. Even Winthton had a look of dignity as he trotted along behind. Children ran alongside them, and the men of the town paced them on the edges of the street. There were a number of young women who looked at him boldly and smiled when he noticed them.

Axel tied Charger to the rail in front of the temple, then turned to the small crowd which had gathered around him. "Is the priest here?"

A fat man pushed his way to the front of the crowd. "He lives in a small house behind the temple, Sir. I'll tell him you wish to see him," he said, and hurried off around the side of the building.

While Axel waited, he talked to the townspeople. "Has Tightly been bothered by a dragon this summer?"

One of the women spoke up, "Our priest arranged for a dragonkiller to rid us of the dragon last spring."

"You must have had a reward for the killing."

"Oh, yes," she cried. Axel could see some of the men nod at this. "We was sorely bedeviled by the dragon, Sir. The whole town gave gold to the priest to hold as a reward."

"It must have been a great deal of money."

One of the men said, "We all gave what we could. The way we was losing livestock couldn't go on. We had to do something."

The rest of the people nodded and one spoke up, "I lost fifteen sheep in just one year."

Others now added, "I lost two cows last winter."

"My John saw it carry off his prize bull. Late in the spring it was."

"Little Jamie just disappeared. We think that's what

happened to him."

Axel agreed that dragons were terrible things. He said loudly, "I came through here last spring and talked to your priest. He seemed to be an honorable man and one you could trust with your gold." The people around him said nothing but one or two nodded their heads.

The priest, followed by the fat man, came out of the open door of the temple and stood on the steps above the crowd. Axel dismounted and walked up to where they stood and said, "Good afternoon, Priest. You may not remember me, but I stopped here last spring."

The old man leaned close and looked at Axel with his cloudy, pale eyes, "You look familiar to me, Sir. What is your name?"

"Axel."

"I remember that name, and your face looks like I might have seen it before. Did you wish to give to the temple?"

"I might already have done so." Axel put his hand on the leather bag of coins hanging on his belt.

The priest saw the gesture, smiled and said, "Learn the joy of giving. Learn not to hide from duty. Give as much as you can. Tell me what we talked about."

"Killing the dragon."

Axel could see that now the old man remembered. The priest moved back a step. His eyes shifted to Axel's horse, then to his new clothes. He straightened some and said, "The temple is always ready to help in any way it can." His eyes shifted nervously to the townspeople and back to Axel. "The temple serves the people. The temple and the people are one. I do work for the people and the temple. Tell me what you need."

"Do you remember what you said about the payment for

killing the dragon?"

The priest gestured behind him and said much more softly, "Sir, why don't we go into the temple and get out of this hot sun. . .somewhere we can talk privately?" He turned to go back inside.

Axel spoke sharply, "That won't be necessary, Priest." He could feel the people lean closer. "Do you remember what you said about the selection of the egg for the killing of a second dragon?"

Now the priest's eyes darted quickly from Axel's face to the intently listening crowd and back. "Of course, I remember. These good people entrusted their gold to me to be paid for the dragon's death."

Axel's voice was even and low when he asked, "What about the amount?"

Some of the men looked at each other, then moved even closer. The priest pulled out the wooden figure and began to rub it between his fingers. "The good people of this town agreed upon the reward. The weight in gold equal to the weight of one egg." He looked to the crowd for confirmation. The people nodded yes, it was so. The old man pulled his hood up and over his head. "The people of this town made an agreement and it was kept. Now, what else do you require?"

Axel looked back at the much larger group now. "I can see that these are honorable people, and that they trust you. . .as they should be able to." The priest leaned closer now. His hands had stopped their movement, and a slight smile appeared on his wet lips. The crowd waited. Axel looked at the people standing in front of him near the entrance to the temple and asked the priest, "Do you remember what you told me about the selection of the second egg for a second dragon?"

Looking closely at the back of Axel's head for a long moment, the priest nodded his head slightly and said, "We have no second dragon."

Axel turned and faced the priest and said, "True, last spring you had only one. But if there had been two?" Axel could tell that the priest was relieved to be off the topic of the payment for the first dragon. *He must have collected much gold and kept the difference between what he paid me and what the town expected him to pay. The people in town didn't know he had balanced the gold against a songbird's egg. They must think he used a chicken's egg, which would be much heavier. He not only cheated me, but he cheated the towns-people, too.*

The priest spoke in a much louder voice now, "Of course, I remember what I said. If there was a second dragon you could select the egg." He laughed softly, "But there is no need for us to go into all of this. There is no second dragon. And even if there were one, the money is gone and the people have no more gold."

Axel took a step closer and looked into the priest's eyes and said, "The money is all gone?"

"Of course it is."

"All of it?"

". . .Yes."

"The people have no more gold?"

"No," The old man turned, looked at the crowd and said, "They gave their gold to me to keep for the reward."

"And you did that?" The men and women crowded even closer now. Axel could hear murmurs. He and the priest were surrounded by a very interested group.

"Of course I. . .What else would. . .I kept the gold

in. . .Why do you question me, Sir?"

Axel took the wooden figure out of the priest's hands and pulled him closer by pulling on the thong around his neck and spoke directly into the old man's face, loudly enough for the others to hear. "If there were a second dragon, where would the reward come from if the people don't have more gold?"

The priest shot his eyes from Axel's face to the people who were now leaning forward. He was silent for a moment, then said softly, "I. . .Well there is. . ." The priest pushed the hood off his head and looked at the people crowding around him and said much more loudly, "I would pay the reward."

"With the temple's money?"

The priest hesitated, then said, "Well. . .no, I have saved a little."

"A little?"

The priest pulled the figure from Axel's hand, stepped back and faced the crowd. "If there is evidence of the killing of a second dragon, I will pay the reward myself. With my own gold."

"And I would be able to select the egg used to balance the gold?"

Axel could tell the priest was suspicious now, but he had to continue; he was trapped. The old man nodded and said, "You could select the egg."

Axel could see the priest working it out in his mind. He must be thinking that this couldn't be too costly, because: first, there is no second dragon and second, even if there were one, and he had to pay a chicken egg's weight in gold for its death, he wouldn't be out any more gold than he would be if he had used a chicken's egg for the first reward. Not too bad a deal.

Axel leaned very close to the old man's face and

whispered, "Thank you, Priest." Then he turned to the crowd and said loudly, "The priest is trustworthy and will do what he has said he will do. I know when I get to the dragon's cave there could be another dragon there." The people were shocked. There were cries of, "No," and, "Please help us."

Axel held up his hand. "If there is evidence of a dragon there, I will bring back proof that it is no longer a danger to you. I was the one who killed the first dragon." He turned to the priest for confirmation. The priest nodded his head.

Axel could see the people look at him with new respect. "When I bring back proof that you do not have a living second dragon, the priest has agreed to pay the reward with his own money." He glanced at the priest who he saw was smiling at the crowd. "Your priest has made the same reward that he made the first time, the weight of an egg in gold. His own gold. But this time he has agreed to let me select the egg." Axel smiled at the people. They laughed, for they thought it couldn't make much difference who picked the egg, all chickens are about the same size and lay eggs of about the same weight. "I must get ready now for my climb up to the dragon's cave in the morning. You should thank your priest for his generosity."

As Axel walked Charger and Winthton toward the stable, he turned and looked back at the temple and saw the people crowded around the priest, shaking his hand and patting him on the back.

Once again, well before dawn, Axel left the town where he had spent the night to start the climb up the mountain. This time there was no fear, only a certain gladness that now he was able to take care of himself and not be taken advantage of. He would be able to do a good turn for the people in Tightly, too. The old priest would have to think twice now before he tried to cheat the townspeople again.

The only things Axel carried up the mountain cliffs with him were his water bottle and the dragon's egg. He had made a sling and carried the egg, which he had wrapped in old clothes, slung from one shoulder.

It seemed a much shorter climb but it was still very hard this time, and when he got to the ledge where the dragon had lived he set the egg down and rested. He looked out over the countryside. The river sparkled brightly in the sunlight as it wound past Tightly. The forests, now dark green, stretched in rolling waves to the west where he knew Molly was waiting for him. In just a few more days he would be home. What a surprise the people in his village would have when he arrived. He would marry Molly, and they would buy that small farm he had dreamed about. And have children. And he would teach his son to plow. And way over there. . .the place got further and further away each time he thought of it — there would be the small house for his mother.

Axel unwrapped the egg. It was cool to his touch. He didn't know if it should stay cool, or if it would hatch if it got warm. Cool might be better because it had not changed since he had found it. The cave was certainly cool, and he didn't need to go very far into its darkness. After setting the egg down on the rough floor, he stepped back outside.

He climbed down to the first ledge below the one the cave faced. After waiting a moment, he started the climb back up. He had to be able to tell the people in town the truth about climbing onto the ledge and finding the egg in the cave. A knight couldn't lie.

When he again reached the top, he put his hand on a projecting piece of stone to lever himself over the edge. The stone crumbled away, his hand was now full of small pieces of soft stone and air, and he fell backwards. He frantically grabbed at a small bush growing from a crack in the dark stone of the cliff. He hadn't used it on his first climb because it hadn't looked strong enough to hold him, but now he had no choice. When he swung over to catch hold of it, he had to let go with his right hand to do it, and if the bush wouldn't hold him, he knew he would fall to the next ledge, at least a hundred feet below. He grabbed the bush at its thickest part, near the stone, and put his weight almost fully on it. The bush held.

He was able to swing one foot to the edge of the ledge and walk himself up feet first. Just as he had most of his weight on the ledge, the bush came lose, the roots pulling out of the dirt embedded in the cracked stone. Axel flipped over on his stomach and pushed with his hands as hard as he could on the face of the cliff below the ledge.

He was facing down toward the valley far below, straining with every bit of strength he had to keep from pitching over the ledge headfirst. Charger and Winthton were feeding, and they seemed small enough to be two of his carvings. He spread his legs wide to get as much traction as he could on the smooth, stone surface of the ledge. His arms were hanging down in front of him and his hands were flat against the rough stone face of the cliff. By pushing very hard with his fingers on the surface of the rough stone, he was able to move his right hand an inch or two and then his left. The cliff was faced with small, sharp projections, and he could feel them cutting into the flesh of his palms, but that couldn't matter now. He was making progress. His center of gravity was shifting to the ledge. With a last great heave with both hands, he pushed his body onto the flat surface.

Axel turned over on his back and tried to relax. He was

shaking all over, but he was safe now. With both hands, he pushed the hair out of his eyes. It was then that he saw how badly he had cut his palms on the rough stone of the cliff's face. He wiped his hands on his shirt to examine the cuts, then stood on shaking legs.

When Axel entered the cave, he saw one of the dragon's teeth he hadn't seen the first time he had been here. After he picked it up, he had to wipe his blood from it to examine it. He put in his pocket then reached for the egg, and nearly dropped it because the blood on his hands made it slippery. He had to roll the egg into the sling. On the way down, Axel had to wipe his hands frequently on his clothes so he could get good grips on the cliff's face.

Charger and Winthton were where he had left them. He strapped the egg onto Winthton's back and headed for Tightly. This time the trip to and from the mountain went much more quickly because he had Charger to ride. He was back in town long before the sun set.

The town's people were waiting for him. There was a small crowd where the path met the road into town. They saw the blood on Axel's face and clothes and knew he had been in a battle. He said nothing as he rode into town, and the people were so impressed with his appearance and silence that they didn't dare to ask any questions. Axel felt they must think he had killed a dragon and were too impressed to talk to him until he gave a sign that he wanted them to.

A very old woman, dressed in rags, stood near the edge of the road. She was leaning on a rough crutch and she had walked a long way to greet him. Axel couldn't ignore her. He stopped Charger and motioned to the woman to come to him. It took some urging from the crowd before she limped over to stand next to Charger. Axel smiled down at her and reached into his pocket and handed her the bloody tooth. As he rode on, he heard her tell the group of people around her trying to get a look at the tooth that the blood was still wet. One man said, "He must have ripped it right out of the mouth of the dead dragon."

The crowd grew when he entered town, and they all followed him to the front of the temple. The fat man again went to fetch the priest, who must have been waiting, for soon they both appeared at the front door. The crowd began chanting, "Axel killed the dragon. . .Axel killed the dragon."

Axel dismounted and walked up the steps to face the priest, who said, "I see you have returned from the mountain."

One man called out, "Yes, and he's been giving away dragon's teeth all the way into town."

The priest looked at Axel's bloody clothing and face. "Is this true? Have you given a dragon's tooth away?" Axel nodded. "Did you get it in the cave at the top of the mountain?" Axel nodded again. "Did it have fresh blood on it?" Axel nodded. "So, you have come for the reward?"

"We will need a large scale," Axel said, smiling at the priest.

The priest told one of the women standing next to him, "Fetch us an egg, woman."

Axel said, "Wait. I have the choice of the egg this time. Do you remember that?"

The priest was silent for a moment, and Axel saw him blink hard. He opened his eyes and said, "Of course. Pardon me, Sir."

Axel raised his voice so that the people standing around them could hear him clearly, "And you are going to pay the reward from your own gold?"

The priest's voice was impatient. "That's what I agreed to, yes."

"And the gold is to equal the weight of the egg I choose?"

The priest hesitated. There were shouts from the crowd. "That right," and, "We heard the priest promise it."

The priest hesitated again, then said, "All right, that's what I said. You can pick the egg. I don't see what the fuss is all about; all eggs are about the same," and he smiled.

Axel stepped down to where Winthton was and took the sling from his back. He placed it on the first step of the temple and looked up at the priest. "Send someone for a large scale."

A man with a blood-splattered, leather apron called out, "I've got one in my shop that's the biggest in town," and ran across the street. He returned in a moment and placed a heavy balance scale on the steps.

Axel unwrapped the dragon's egg and put it on one side of the butcher's scale. That side of the balance arm dropped hard to the stone of the step, and Axel looked at the priest.

The townspeople crowded close.

"What is it?"

"Move, let me see."

"It's a giant egg."

"A dragon's egg?"

The old priest's face had turned white. He yelled, "That's not a chicken egg. You can't use that!"

Axel said in a low voice, "Was it a chicken's egg you used the first time you paid me?"

"Of course it. . .Now, wait I. . .You can't expect me to—"

The cries of the crowd drowned him out, "Pay Axel," and

"Pay, Priest, pay."

The priest's hands were flying over his wooden figure now. The crowd was getting louder, "Pay. . .Pay. . .Pay."

Axel stood close to the old man and said quietly, "The gold?"

The priest nodded his head and hurried around the temple to his house. He returned very shortly carrying a bag with both hands.

He knelt next to the scale and began taking coins from the bag and putting them in the empty dish on the balance arm. The pile grew. Axel could hear the people in the crowd begin to ask each other where the priest had gotten so much gold. The pile grew. Some coins fell off the dish, and the priest scrambled after them. Finally the egg moved slightly. The next few coins caused the egg to lift enough so that its dish was no longer touching the ground. The priest looked up at Axel. Axel slowly shook his head. The priest added one more coin. The people held their breath. And one more coin. The needle quivered. One more and the egg lifted again. Axel was rubbing Winthton's ears, paying no attention now to the pain the priest was in.

It took nine more coins before the needle settled on the center mark. The priest stood, the bag hanging limply from his fingers. He tried to speak. He opened his mouth, and the crowd waited. No sound came out. The people could see him strain. When he fluttered his hands, he dropped the bag and a high squeak came from his tightly held lips.

Axel stepped up to the scale and took a handful of the coins and put them in the bag at his waist. There were still a great many left on the scale. He looked out over the crowd that had filled the street in front of the temple. Standing behind the others was the old woman he had met on the road to Highcliff. Next to her was the small boy, still sucking his finger. Axel took three of the coins from the bag at his waist and stepped down to the path, and the people parted in front of him. They turned and followed him to the old woman. Axel took her hand and placed the three coins in it and closed her fingers over them. He turned and said in a loud and clear voice so all could hear, "There are poor people in your town. Use the rest of the gold on the scale to feed them. Give it to someone you can trust. Have him save it for when one of you needs help. Then spend it."

Axel carried his egg to where Winthton and Charger waited. When he was close enough to put his hand on his saddle, he reached into his shirt and rubbed lightly the piece of lace Molly had given him. Smiling to himself, he put the egg back in his pack, mounted Charger, and taking Winthton's lead, turned south out of town, toward home.

18

The Program

When Axel got to the rim of Sidney's valley, things didn't look to him the way they had before. It could be that he had come the first time in the spring when the trees were just starting to bud. It could be that he was higher now; he had walked into the valley the first time, and this time he was riding Charger and was seeing the valley from a more lofty perch. Or, it could be that when he first met Sidney, he was a frightened boy with no skills, setting out on an adventure, and he was now returning a respected knight. That would give him a changed view of most things. Whatever changes there were, the valley was still the most beautiful place he had ever seen. Axel was excited to be back in such a place and about to meet his friend again.

While still a long way off, he could see Sidney sitting on the ground, leaning against the front of the small house with Sylvia perched on his shoulder. Sidney's letting the sun warm his hands, he thought. The old man must have been asleep and dreaming, for when Axel rode close, he could see Sidney's hands, which were resting on his knees, twitch and gesture. Sidney looked up as Axel led Winthton to the wagon wheel.

"Hello, Sidney."

Sidney squinted in the bright sunlight but said nothing.

"It's me, Axel. I've come home." He swung off Charger and walked up to the seated man. "Are you all right?"

"Axel? Is this the boy I told about dragons?" Sidney jumped up. "On such a fine horse." He walked around Axel. "Good clothes. I'm surprised you're even alive." He put his hands on Axel's shoulders and looked him in the face. "I thought you would be dead." He brushed tears away from his face with the back of a twisted hand.

"Well, I'm not. The things you taught me about dragons saved my life. Let's both sit here in the sun and I'll tell you all about it." Axel sat near where Sidney had been sitting.

Sidney sat next to him and said, "Tell me about your summer."

The two friends spent the rest of the afternoon talking about Axel's adventures. Sidney wanted to know all the details about everything, and Axel told it all, except about his last conversation with the king. He explained about killing the dragons. He spent a lot of time talking about Willardville and what a fine man the king was. He told Sidney about the castle and the sea. When he was done, Sidney was silent and looked off across the valley for a long time.

"What are you thinking, Sidney?"

". . .What did you say, Axel?"

"What were you thinking about?"

"Nothing important."

"Something."

"I was thinking that it would be good to be young again. . .to have adventures. To live when there were lots of dragons. . .To meet kings and live in castles." He gestured with his crooked fingers and said, "You know, the usual stuff."

Now it was Axel's turn to study the valley. The two men sat and watched the shadows lengthen and turn blue on the meadow between the rounded tops of the old mountains. There were brief wind-patterns on the surface of the small lake, and three geese glided in to land on the smooth surface, their honking clear and distant. They had different images in their minds, but they were both thinking about dragons. When the cries of the small female receded into the distance in his memory, Axel said, "Would you like to stay in a castle instead of living here?"

It took him a long time answering, but finally Sidney turned and looked toward his front doorway. "No, my boy. If I wanted to live in a castle, I would. I only stay here because. . ."

Axel was surprised to see the tears running down his friend's face. He turned away and looked at the trees on the hills for a bit. . .long enough for Sidney to wipe his cheeks.

When enough time had passed, Axel said, "Sidney, I've been sent by the king to marry Molly. He said it was an order. After we get married we have to buy a farm. He said that, too. I have to do these things. This is the most beautiful valley I've ever seen. I have a trade for you. Are you interested?"

Sidney looked up sharply. "A trade, you say?"

"That's right."

"Last time it worked out. What's this one?"

"I need a farm. You should live in a place where you'll be needed. I have an answer for us both."

"You want me to live with you and Molly? I don't think so. I don't get along with people. Mostly they don't like me much."

Axel laughed, then spoke quickly, "No. The king asked me to see if you'd like to live in his castle with him. He needs a. . .wizard. I told him all about you, and he thinks you'd be perfect for the job. He really needs you, Sidney. You'd be doing him a real favor. Molly and I would like to live in this valley and farm it. Could we trade?" He looked into Sidney's eyes. "I'd give you as much gold as you want for the land. It wouldn't be as if you'd be going to the king without any money. You could be quite rich. I've a lot of gold."

Sidney stood and Sylvia fluttered to the ground. "Hold on now, boy. Let me get this straight. You pay me for this valley, I go and live with the king and I'd be his wizard. Would he pay me, too?"

Axel also stood now. "Sure he would. The king's a very generous man. He gave me Charger." He gestured toward the horse. "There's just one thing, though."

Sidney threw his hands in the air and said, "I knew it. There is always just one thing." The old man walked in a small circle, muttering under his breath. Axel noticed that Sidney kept glancing at him as he circled. Sidney stopped, flapped his arms once and slapped them against his legs in resignation. "What is it this time?"

"You'd have to come to my wedding."

Sidney turned and shouted, "What?"

"I want you to come and see me get married. You're the only friend I've got and I want you there."

Sidney began to dance in the dusty path to the house, a crazy one-man jig. "I wanna go. You couldn't keep me away. When do we leave?. . .When's the wedding?. . .I don't have a good cloak." He grabbed Axel's hands and swung him around. "I'll have to have someone make me one. Let's get started. I'll just get a book or two and we'll be off."

Axel laughed and said, "Let's start in the morning. I've been on the road for days. It takes four or five days to get there if we walk, and if we started now, riding Charger, we could do it in one day, but it'd be night by the time we got there. Better we start very early in the morning."

Stroking Sylvia's back, the old man said, "Fine. Give me a chance to do something I've wanted to do for a long time."

"What's that?"

"How would you like chicken for dinner?"

Axel was shocked, "But she trusts you, Sidney."

The old man petted his chicken and said, "Just a joke, my boy. Just a joke."

Sidney wanted Axel to spend the last night in the bed, but Axel insisted that he sleep in his old corner. He felt better that way. They started for Greenwater as soon as it was light. Sidney had tied his things on Winthton's back, and they both rode on Charger. Sylvia rode on her usual perch, Sidney's shoulder. This evening Axel would see Molly again.

19

The Perfect Match

Charger easily carried the two men to Greenwater. Even with the extra load, Axel pushed the warhorse very hard, for he was anxious to see Molly.

It was just coming on dusk when they turned away from the river and entered the village. Axel felt he had been gone for a long time. Greenwater looked small to him. After all, he had stayed in the king's castle for a short time. He was more traveled than most of the people who had ever lived here. He was a rich and famous man. A dragonslayer.

The door to the King's Road Inn was open. Bobson was sitting on the bench which ran along the front of the building, his back resting on the rough board siding. His hands were lying on his paunch. He was asleep.

Axel and Sidney dismounted and tied Charger and Winthton to the rail. Sidney put Sylvia on the saddle. A number of people had gathered to wonder at the size and beauty of the great warhorse. Never in their lives had they seen such an animal.

Bobson woke and standing, said loudly, "Welcome, strangers. The inn is open for business. Dinner will be ready soon. Come into the tavern and have a drink." He smiled and waved toward the door. "You must be thirsty after the long trip. Where are you traveling from?"

Sidney stopped at the door and waited while Bobson hurried inside. Axel followed. By the time they got to the bar, Bobson was behind it rubbing his hands together. "First, what will you drink? Then, I want to hear the news."

Sidney said, "We'll both have ale."

Bobson, for the first time, looked closely at Axel. He squinted in the dim light and said, "You look familiar. Do I know you?" The light in the bar was not dim enough for the lamps to be lighted, but it was too dark for Bobson to make out Axel's features.

Axel said, "Yes." Bobson smiled, and Axel was sure he hadn't heard his answer.

"Now, what would you like to drink? We have both ale and stronger. Would you be staying in the inn?"

Sidney yelled, "Give us ale." Axel held up his hands, indicating that he didn't want any, so Bobson turned and put one of the mugs away and filled the other one. "You be staying with us in the inn?"

Sidney nodded, and Axel said very loudly, "I'll stay with my mother."

Bobson's mouth fell open as he turned to put the ale on the bar. "Are you Axel?" He leaned closer. "Yes, you are. We thought you left for good." Bobson turned toward Sidney and said, "That's some horse out there. Never saw one like it in this village. Where'd you get it?"

"It's not mine," Sidney said.

"I imagine you had to pay a good price for it. Mind if I ask what it cost?"

"It's not mine," Sidney yelled.

"Don't have to yell. Who does it belong to?"

Two of the regulars of the tavern came shouting through the door. "Hey, Bobson, whose horse?"

"What a beast."

"A beauty."

They rushed up to the bar and looked closely at Axel and Sidney. They were farmers and were still covered with pieces of dried grass from bringing in hay. The taller of the two said, "Is this Axel? In such fine clothes?"

Bobson put two new mugs of ale on the bar and said, "That horse belongs to this stranger here." He looked at Sidney. "What's your name?"

"Sidney. And the horse belongs to Axel."

The three men turned and looked at Axel. Bobson started to speak when Molly came into the room from the back of the bar. She cried out, "Axel, I knew you'd come back." She ran to him and threw her arms around his neck and hung on tightly.

Bobson yelled, "Here now, we'll have none of that. Molly. . .stop it."

Axel and Molly saw nothing and heard nothing but each other. Both were talking. Both were listening. Staring into each other's eyes. In love. Together.

"I thought you'd never come back."

"Now we can buy that—"

"Everybody said you'd run—"

". . .four dragons, and I couldn't wait to—"

"When can we—"

"Let's talk to your father."

Still holding each other they returned to the bar.

Bobson was frowning. "That's no way to carry on in

here, Molly. What if Cedric walks in? Think about what that would mean to me and the inn. And, what would the good folks in the village say?"

Sidney had been nodding his head, smiling, and half dancing there at the bar. He looked from Molly to Axel and said "I can see what you were talking about, Axel. Fine looking girl. Fine."

Axel turned Molly toward his friend and said, "Sidney, this is Molly." He couldn't let go of her.

"Molly, Sidney taught me what I needed to know to stay alive. He probably saved my life."

The two farmers forced their heads into the tight group of excited people. "How did you almost die?"

"What happened?"

"Where were you?"

"How'd you get that horse?"

Bobson yelled, "What'd he say? . . .What?. . .What?"

Axel had to explain his trip. The two farmers and Bobson wouldn't be put off. He was anxious to be alone with Molly, but Bobson said she couldn't leave the bar until he had told them all about the dragons. He wasn't anxious to talk about that part of it, but they insisted. That brought up the king. And then he had to tell about what the king had given him. Bobson's attitude changed toward Axel as soon as he heard about him being knighted. Now there was no charge for the drinks, not even for the milk Axel had asked for. It looked like the start of a party.

When Axel turned to look for Sidney he bumped into Cedric and said, "Sorry I bumped into you, Cedric, it's pretty crowded in here." Cedric grabbed the front of Axel's shirt and pushed him against the bar. Axel looked into Cedric's eyes and said, "This is no way for grown men to behave, is it?" Cedric's growl started deep in his throat. Bobson saw the movement and reached over the bar and grabbed Cedric by his collar and dragged him to the back of the room telling him to quit bothering his important customers. Bobson followed him out the back door, and Axel didn't see him again.

Other men had come in, and they had to be told all about Axel's adventures. They told others, and with each telling the story got grander. Sidney thoroughly enjoyed himself. He really liked parties and fit in perfectly with the men in Greenwater.

Axel and Molly were able to slip away. They made plans and kissed. They held hands and kissed. They walked, looked at the mid-summer moon and kissed. Axel told Molly about Sidney's valley. She kissed him. Molly told Axel how lonely she had been, and he kissed her. They would be married as soon as he could bring the priest to Greenwater from the next town. What about Cedric and Bobson's agreement with his father? Molly said that she could take care of Cedric and that he wouldn't be a problem.

What would Bobson do without Molly's help with the inn?. . .We could build a small house for Axel's mother at the edge of the valley. She could live there. . .Would she like that?. . .No, she would miss her friends and her ale. Would Molly's father have to hire someone to help at the bar and inn?. . .Yes. . .Would Axel's mother rather stay in the village. . .Yes. . .What to do?

They would be married. Their parents might not like it, but they had their own lives to live. Together. These problems could be solved later.

Suddenly Molly pushed Axel away and, after waiting a long moment, said in a very serious voice, "I hate to leave my father alone. He doesn't hear much anymore, and there's a lot of work to do here, and I do most of it, and when I'm not here anymore—"

Axel drew Molly back to him. They had walked to the edge of the village. It was full dark now, and the trees cast soft moon-shadows across the roadway.

Axel wasn't sure he understood exactly what Molly had on her mind, but he continued with the same idea and in the same serious voice. "If there was just some way we could work it so my mother and your father didn't have to be alone, we could get married and not have a thing to worry about. But, I can't think of anyone who could stand my mother. She talks all the time and is so crabby she would drive almost anyone crazy." Axel had a small twitch of a smile on his lips that Molly noticed.

Molly began to grin and came back quickly with, "My father has problems, too. He was so mean to you when you asked him if you could marry me, I'll never forgive him. And besides, he's getting old, and his hearing is getting so bad, most of what's said to him he just doesn't hear at all." She smiled up at Axel. "I have to shout right at him now for him to hear me."

Axel looked at Molly.

Molly looked at Axel.

They both laughed. Of course. Perfect. They turned back toward the town, their arms around each other. They laughed and kissed all the way back to the inn.

After Axel had fed and watered Winthton and Charger at the stable, he walked them to his home. His mother was where he had left her and looked the same to him. Although he didn't want to spend the rest of his life with her, he did feel sorry for anyone who was as lonely as she had been.

"Mother, wake up. I'm home," he said, as he touched her shoulder.

Her hair was in long strings of dirt, and when she looked up at him from the table top, where her head had been, he could see that her eyes were bloodshot. Her voice was cross. "Axel, where have you been? You've been gone most of the summer, and you left me here all alone to do all the work. If that's not just like you. I suppose you had a high old time off running around. Well, let me tell you something, young man, you're not going to come back and eat and lie around here and not help out. I've had to do it all. I even had to cut firewood." She leaned back in the chair. "Well, say something."

"Hello, Mother."

"Is that all you can say to your mother after all I've done for you? Where have you been? It's even been lonely here without you. But, it's been cheaper not having to feed you. So, talk, boy."

Axel sat at the table across from his mother. It felt to him as if he had never left at all. "I can't live here any more, Mother. Molly and I are going to get married and move to a valley about five days from here. You can't stay here by yourself."

"What are you talking about? You can't get married; you're just a kid."

"We plan on having the wedding the day after tomorrow."

"How are you going to support her? You can't bring her here. This isn't your farm yet. Not until I'm dead, it's not."

"We don't plan on living here. We're going to farm a valley and have it all to ourselves. You can come to live on the farm near us if you want to."

His mother was wide awake now. "What farm? Axel, what are you talking about? Make sense."

"I don't know any other way to say it, Mother. Molly and I are moving, and you can come with us."

Axel's mother was frowning deeply now, "Come with you where?"

"To a really nice valley about five days east of here. There isn't a town anywhere near it. It's in the mountains. You'd really like it. There wouldn't be anybody else around to bother you. No town or bar or nosy neighbors at all. Molly and I have talked about it, and we decided you would like to have a little place all your own." Axel gestured with his hands as he said, "We could build you one at one end of the valley and we could live at the other end."

"What?"

"Doesn't that sound nice, Mother?"

She stood up from the table. Her long dress caught under one of the legs of her chair and she ripped it loose. "Do you mean to tell me that you expect me to live way up in the mountains and never see anyone? Not on your life you don't. I'll stay right here. I did fine all summer without you and I can do all right from now on. But, what will I do for money? You can't expect me to go without, can you?"

"No, I guess not. I hadn't thought of that. We'll just have to think of something else."

Her voice rose. "You can't just leave me here all alone." She was pacing back and forth in front of her son now, wringing her hands.

Axel looked closely at his mother as he said, "Bobson was saying almost the same thing this evening about when Molly leaves. He'll be very lonely, too." He looked at his mother's face. Nothing happened to it for a short time, then he could tell that she was getting an idea.

She lifted her hands and pushed her hair back from the front of her head. "He is a fine man, but I don't have too much to—"She squinted in the dim light and said, "What will he do for help when Molly leaves?"

"That's what was worrying him. He'll have that inn all to himself. He takes in a lot of money with the bar business alone. He's going to need someone right there with him. I feel sorry for him, all alone like that." Axel sat at the table and looked at his hands.

Axel's mother sat across from him. "I always say a person's got to take care of himself. I used to say that to your father, and I still say it. I'm not young anymore." She looked at the backs of her hands and rubbed at the dried skin a bit. "But, I'm not that old either."

Axel looked up at his mother and said, "Maybe Bobson was saying that just this afternoon. He must think about you a lot. He must have told Molly that lots of times. You're a fine looking woman."

His mother ran her hands down the sides of her dress. "I used to be and I could be again. I guess I could fix myself up if I had a mind to."

"Mother, I know you could. Tell you what. Why don't you do that in the morning, and we'll go and have a drink with Bobson. Even if it's in the morning, it'll be okay because we'll be celebrating the wedding."

"Now, that'd be real nice. I'd like that, but I don't need to drink anymore. I haven't had any ale for most of the summer." She paused then and looked at him with her head tilted over on one side. "What'll you do for money? You can't come in here and expect to drink in the morning on what little I have. You've been gone long enough to have earned enough to get married on, you can give a little to your mother."

"I was able to save quite a bit. I might even be able to give some to you to help Bobson fix up the inn, if things work out the way he wants them to. You know what I mean?" He smiled at her.

She lifted her chin and pushed back her shoulders, and said, "I might not move to that valley with you and Molly. I always said I never would be a burden on my child, and I never will be. I can plan my own future. I don't really need you now, and I won't need you then. How much did you have in mind to give me to fix up the inn?"

Standing, Axel said, "It's been a long day, Mother. Let's go to sleep now, and I'll have a talk with Bobson in the morning when we go there. You need your sleep, too."

Before blowing out the lamp, Axel brought his pack into the house. Putting it carefully on his bed, he took out the egg, sat with it in his lap and examined it closely. It felt slightly warm to him when he ran his hands over its dry, leathery surface. He thought again of its mother's cries and how hard she had tried to get to it after being hooked in the chimney.

As he was putting it back in his pack, he was sure he felt the surface move. A slight pressure on the palm of his hand. He held it firmly in both hands and waited to feel it again, but he felt nothing and returned it to its bed in his pack.

Axel went to his bed that night thinking things might work out well for everyone. He wondered how Molly had done in her talk with her father.

20

Post-summer Wrap Up

The news of the coming wedding—always a big event in such a small village—Axel's return as a hero for having killed the dragons, and the beautiful warhorse, Charger, all contributed to the excitement the next morning in the village of Greenwater. How does such news spread so fast?

By the time Axel and his mother got to the edge of the village the tavern was already full with villagers and farmers who had started early to drink and discuss. The women and children were expected to join them later in the day.

When the men, who had to stand outside near the road because of the crowd already in the tavern, saw Axel and his mother turn the bend and head into the village, they let out a loud cheer. This brought out the people from inside the tavern. They all surged out to meet the new hero and his mother.

Axel was relieved to see the crowd, for he had had a trying morning. His mother had been straightening his things for him when she had come across the bag of rags with the gold in it. The house was still fairly dark when he had heard, "Axel, get up." She pushed his shoulder with her hand and said, "Axel, wake up and talk to me. After all, I'm your mother and this is my house, and I have a right to know what's going on here."

Axel opened his eyes and looked up into the dim light of the house and his mother's eyes. The lamp was still burning, for the sun hadn't been up for very long.

His mother had risen early, either because of the excitement of her son's coming wedding or because of the expected morning trip to the tavern to talk with Bobson. Her hair was still wet and hanging in limp strands around her head. Her good dress had been washed and was hanging on a piece of twine stretched across the room in front of the fireplace.

"It's very early, Mother."

"I don't care about that. I wanna know what you've been doing."

"I've been sleeping. Can we talk later?"

She pulled the blanket off the bed, grabbed Axel by the hair and pulled him to a sitting position. "You get up."

"Yow. That hurts," he cried, holding his head. "What's this all about?"

She had been holding the bag of gold behind her back. She now held it before him. "This is what this all about. I want to know where this came from." She shook it. "Where?"

Axel reached for the bag, but she pulled it away. "Is this what you're gonna give Bobson to fix the inn? Well, it's too much. You don't have to buy that girl. Just a little of this would be plenty." She dumped the bag out on the table. The gold coins gleamed in the yellow light from the lamp. Stirring them with her hand, she said "There's a fortune here. How much is mine?"

After pushing the coins into a pile, Axel reached for the bag. She held it away from him and said, "Not till you tell me where it came from and what you're gonna do with it."

"I owe the gold to Sidney. It's his for the valley, Mother."

"Who is this Sidney, anyway? How do I know that's the truth? Why do you owe it to him? You've got to tell me what this is all about. I'm still your mother, after all. You owe some of this to me, not to some Sidney. Who raised you, anyway? All these years I've had to work to keep you in food and clothes, and the first time you have anything you want to give it away." She glared at him. "Now talk, Axel."

Axel had to tell the story again. He started with meeting Sidney and the studies they had done on dragons. When he got to the first dragon killing, she stopped him by holding up her hands. "Stop right there. You're not going to tell me you killed a dragon. There aren't any more, and if there was, you're just a kid. You couldn't kill one if you had to. Now, I want the truth."

"All right, Mother, I won't tell you I killed a dragon. But, the gold doesn't belong just to me. Sidney's a wizard, and if I don't take care of his gold, he might feel bad."

She held her hands to her face and cried, "A wizard? Oh. . .oh. . ." She began wailing and pushing the coins into the bag as fast as she could. Some rolled off the table and she hurried after them. "Help me, Axel. We've got to get this gold to that wizard before he does something awful to me."

Axel was holding the bag for her. "He's not like that, Mother. Sidney is a—" Axel stopped and looked at his mother, then started again, "Good idea, Mother. We should get this to him before he gets mad at all of us. After all, he and I do have an agreement about the valley. I did promise him I'd give him gold for it. There even may be a little left to give to Bobson. We'll have to see." They soon had the gold put away and the bag tied up again.

Axel's mother held Axel by the front of his shirt and said, "Now, Axel, you've got to take it right out of here and give it to him."

"We'll meet him at the inn this morning. Why don't you dry your hair and we can leave?"

Axel thought his mother looked the best he had seen her look in years. Her hair was clean and combed, her good dress was clean, and the one tear in the arm had been mended. She had only the one pair of boots, but she had tried to wipe them clean. She had scrubbed her round face until it shone. She doesn't look bad, Axel thought. Bobson will like having her working in the tavern and doing the cooking. She should like it, too.

Axel's mother turned and looked behind her when the crowd cheered as they entered the square. "Axel? What's going on?"

He smiled at his mother, "Maybe they like the way you look?"

She patted her hair. "It can't be that," she said, smiling as she looked around. "It looks like everyone I ever saw is here." The crowd surged around Axel. There were new questions from some of the men who had been thinking about his adventures. There were lots of questions from some who hadn't been there last night.

When two women took Axel's mother to one side to congratulate her on her son's success, Axel looked for Molly, but she must have been working in the tavern.

He pulled his mother to the inn, and they were followed inside by as many men as could crowd into the small room.

Bobson was behind the bar drawing ale, and Molly was carrying food and drinks to the tables. There was a great deal of shouting and general noise in the tavern. Almost a party.

Sidney was standing near the bar talking to a small group of men. He looked up when Axel and his mother entered, and called out, "Axel, over here." He pushed by one of the men and led Axel and his mother to the bar.

Axel said, "Sidney, this is my mother." He turned to his mother and said, "Sidney is the man I owe the gold to, Mother." She backed up a step as he handed the bag to Sidney.

Sidney hefted the bag and looked up at Axel with an obvious question on his face.

"It's for the valley, Sidney."

"Oh, of course. The valley," and he put the bag under his cloak.

Axel said, "Sorry I didn't give it to you last night. There was some misunderstanding about it this morning. I feel better now that you have it."

"Yes, so do I." Sidney held up the bag. "This is for the valley I sold to Axel. He'll like living there," Sidney said, as he started to turn toward Axel's mother. "Are you going to stay with him and Molly?"

She had a mug of ale in her hand and was talking to Bobson. ". . .so I thought of all the boys I've ever met and Axel is the best one I ever knew. I used to say that to his father. Axel is a good boy. That's the way I raised him and that's the way he turned out. I'm sure glad he and Molly are going to get married. She's such a nice girl. I've been telling him for years that he should take an interest in her. She comes from such a good family. It's important for the better families to stick together. Don't you think so?" Bobson was smiling at her with a blank look on his face. She said, "Don't you agree with me?"

"Oh, yes," Bobson said, "It looks like it'll be a fine day."

She spoke loudly, "Did you talk to Axel yet about fixing up the inn?"

Bobson smiled and nodded, "You're right. I never had so much trade at this time of day before."

She continued, "We should talk about it. I always say that most things can be worked out. It isn't as if he doesn't have the money to help you out. After all, if he's going to marry Molly, it'll still be in the same family." She turned and looked for Axel. "Don't you think so?"

Bobson was filling a mug, "What?"

"I asked you if you didn't think so."

"Oh, yes indeed. Fine boy. Make Molly a good husband. Wants to farm I hear."

She went behind the bar. "Let me help you. I'm a good worker. You'll see." She tied an apron over her dress and started to fill mugs from the barrel.

Axel and Sidney had gone out to the front porch and were standing near the door. Sidney was squinting and holding his hand over his eyes. "This light is very bright, Axel. For some reason I don't feel so good today."

Axel laughed. "It might be something you drank last night, Sidney."

Sidney took his hand down and said, "Why did you give me all that gold? The valley isn't worth but a small part of it."

"Later I may ask you for part of it back. You can keep it for me till I do. I may want to give some to Bobson to help him fix up the inn. Molly and I sure won't need it all on the farm. I'll have to buy some things, but there's a lot of money there."

Sidney was looking at the far end of the square where there was a man in a dark brown robe walking toward them. "Is that a priest, Axel?"

"It looks like it. It sure would be lucky for us if it is. I wonder if he'd marry us. It'd save me a long ride. Let's ask him."

The priest agreed to do this, and the wedding took place just after Molly and Axel's mother had put out large plates of food for the guests. Everyone in the village was a guest, so a lot of food had to be prepared. Axel's mother had worked very hard, and Bobson was pleased to have the help. Axel saw him looking at her a number of times.

She talked to him constantly, and he nodded his head occasionally. It looked like a good arrangement for everyone.

Molly said she wasn't ready that day to get married. She had clothes to prepare, but the people in the village talked her into it. After all, the guests were all here and the priest was ready and Axel was anxious.

The ceremony was held in front of the inn. The sun shone brightly on the young people, and the crowd drank and ate and enjoyed the short service. Bobson and Axel's mother stood side by side and looked very proud. Sidney had cured his headache and had a great time. Winthton had been brought to the inn and tied to the rail. He lipped Axel's ear during most of the ceremony. Axel didn't mind. They were still good friends.

Later that afternoon, when Sidney was talking about heading back to his valley, Axel gave him the egg. "Sidney, this is the last dragon's egg there will ever be, and last night I think I felt movement."

Sidney looked into Axel's eyes for a long time, then took

the egg and pressed it to his ear. He stood that way for a bit, then said, "If so, we should be able to hear or feel. . . . Yes. I think so." He turned it over and over, pressing his hands gently on it, then held it to his other ear. He shut his eyes, then squinted them together as he pressed the egg hard against the side of his head. He opened his eyes and looked at it with wonder and said very softly, "And I think one on this side; there may be two." He was looking at it carefully and running his hand over its smooth surface, feeling of it with great tenderness. "We'll just have to wait and see."

Axel leaned toward the egg, touched the green and gray surface and said, "Two what?"

Sidney jerked away and said, "Never mind, Axel. I'll take good care of them. . .er, it."

Axel frowned, then said, "Sidney, I want you to take Charger. He won't do me any good on the farm and you need a horse. He's a good one. It's a way I can thank you for helping me."

Sidney was pleased. He smiled hugely and ran his hand down Charger's neck and said, "Thank you, my boy. If you ever need him, you can find us at the castle."

When Axel turned toward the inn, he almost bumped into a tall, slender boy who had edged up to him and had been standing there quietly. He waited for the boy to speak, and when he didn't, Axel said, "What is it, boy?"

It must have taken courage for the boy to talk to this knight, but he looked up and pushing his hair away from his face, said "Sir Axel, are there any dragons left alive? My father said you killed the last one. Is that true?"

Axel looked at Sidney who still had the egg in his hands but was putting it into the bag of rags. Turning back to the boy, he asked, "Why do you want to know about dragons?"

The boy looked down at his feet for a moment, then back into Axel's face. "Someday I want to be just like you. If there aren't any dragons left, how can I do that?"

Axel motioned toward his friend who was tying the bag with the egg in it onto Charger's saddle and said, "Ask a man like that one. One who knows a great deal about what you need. . .and other things. One who will help you when your time comes."

Axel walked over to the rail where Sidney was standing on a box getting ready to mount Charger, and Sylvia was shifting her weight from side to side on the saddle getting ready to mount Sidney. He looked up at the old man and said, "If you ever want to live in the valley again, Sidney, you'll always be welcome. Just come."

Sidney's smooth face smiled down at his friend. "I'll be there if you ever need me, my boy." Sylvia fluttered to Sidney's shoulder, and with some effort, the old man clambered upon the saddle, took the reins in his twisted hands and looked down again and slowly nodded. Axel looked up at his friend and, squinting against the brightness, grinned and nodded back. The old man turned the great warhorse toward the fork in the road and headed for their valley.

Axel walked to where the boy was waiting. He placed his hand on the boy's shoulder and could feel the bones and new muscles, and squeezing gently, he smiled into the boy's face. They turned together and watched Sidney ride slowly into the late afternoon.

As the road neared the river it turned downward so that first the horse's legs and then the horse passed from sight.

Soon, all that could be seen were Sidney's bald, egg-shaped head and Sylvia as they bobbed gently above the dust and shadows.